I0725394

BREATHINGS OF THE MOON

BYRD NASH

ROOK AND CASTLE PRESS
SAINT CHARLES, ILLINOIS

Publisher's Cataloging-in-Publication Data
provided by Five Rainbows Cataloging Services

Names: Nash, Byrd, author.
Title: Breathings of the moon / Byrd Nash.
Description: Saint Charles, IL : Rook and Castle Press, 2025.
Identifiers: ISBN 978-1-954811-33-1 (Amazon paperback) | ISBN 978-1-954811-34-8 (IngramSpark paperback) | ISBN 978-1-954811-31-7 (Kindle ebook) | ISBN 978-1-954811-32-4 (EPUB)
Subjects: LCSH: Magic--Fiction. | Memory--Fiction. | Women--Fiction. | Magic realist fiction. | Fantasy fiction. | Paranormal romance stories. | BISAC: FICTION / Fantasy / Contemporary. | FICTION / Magical Realism. | FICTION / Romance / Paranormal / General. | FICTION / Women. | GSAFD: Fantasy fiction. | Occult fiction. | Love stories.
Classification: LCC PS3614.A724 B74 2025 (print) | LCC PS3614.A724 (ebook) | DDC 813/.6--dc23.

The life of the dead
is placed in the memory of the living.
Marcus Tullius Cicero

"At every rising and every setting of the moon the sea violently covers
the coast far and wide, sending forth its surge — It is as though it is
unwittingly drawn up by some breathings of the moon—"

Opera de Temporibus, Section XXIX, the Venerable Bede, 703 AD

Dedications
When I go,
I shall remember you best.

Abraham Underhill
great-great-grandfather
Sarah Underhill
great-great-grandmother
Twin girls
Died Scarlet Fever
Levi
Died WWI w.o issue
Seaborn
great-grandfather
Matthew
Married w children
John
Died WWII w.o issue
Nolan
grandfather
Catherine
grandmother
Annabelle
aunt
Marion
wife
Robert Bancroft
ex-Spouse
Brynn
mother
Unknown
Ryan
son
Zoe
daughter

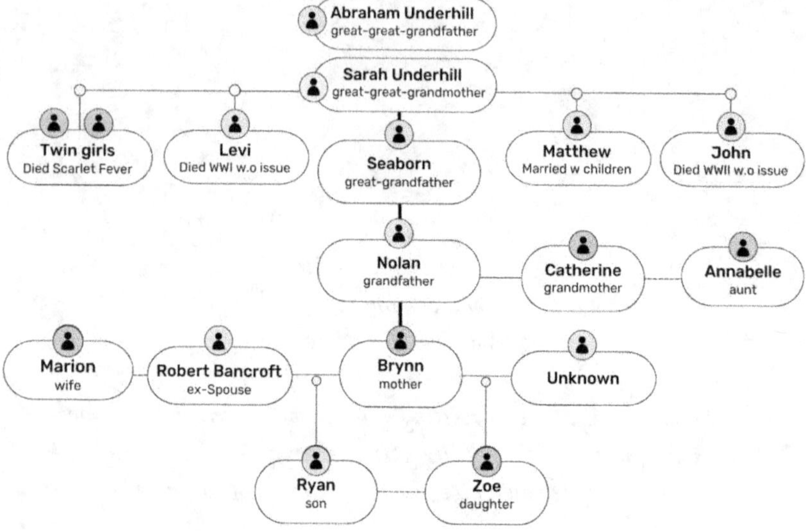

FAMILY TREE

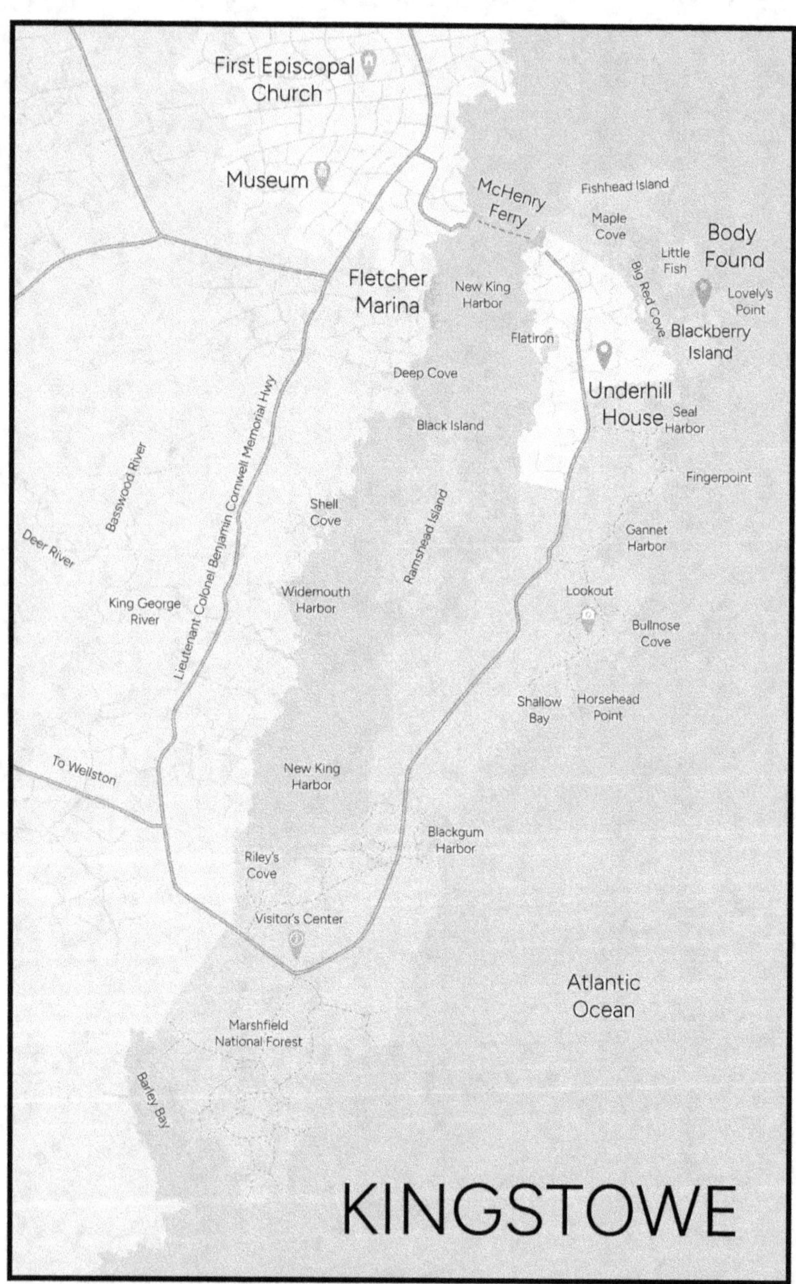

First Episcopal Church
Museum
McHenry Ferry
Fishhead Island
Maple Cove
Body Found
Little Fish
Fletcher Marina
New King Harbor
Lovely's Point
Big Red Cove
Blackberry Island
Flatiron
Deep Cove
Underhill House
Seal Harbor
Black Island
Fingerpoint
Basswood River
Shell Cove
Ramshead Island
Gannet Harbor
Lieutenant Colonel Benjamin Cornwell Memorial Hwy
Deer River
Lookout
Bullnose Cove
King George River
Widemouth Harbor
Shallow Bay
Horsehead Point
To Wellston
New King Harbor
Blackgum Harbor
Riley's Cove
Atlantic Ocean
Visitor's Center
Marshfield National Forest
Barley Bay
KINGSTOWE

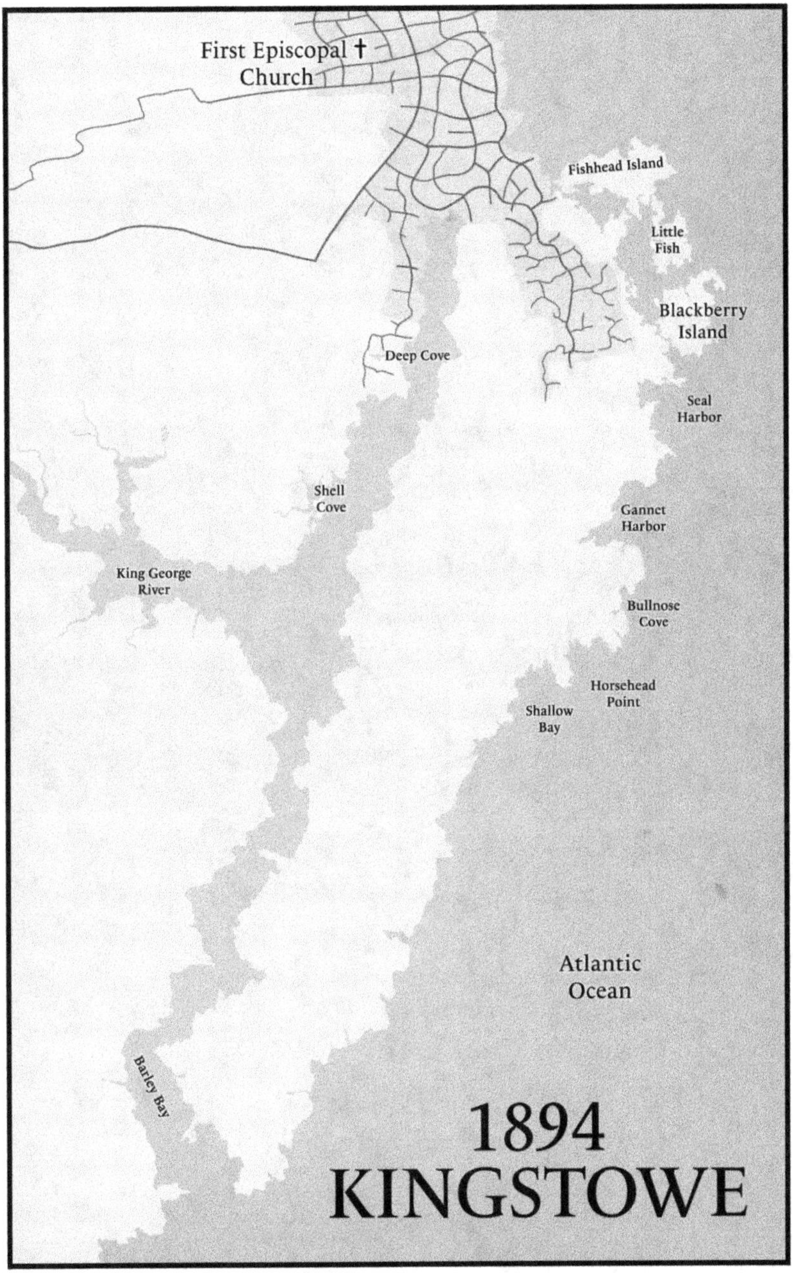

First Episcopal Church
Fishhead Island
Little Fish
Blackberry Island
Deep Cove
Seal Harbor
Shell Cove
Gannet Harbor
King George River
Bullnose Cove
Horsehead Point
Shallow Bay
Atlantic Ocean
Barley Bay
1894
KINGSTOWE

One

My brother arrives. This time, it has taken him two years to find me.

I rise from my desk to greet him and the woman standing at his side. Still living in the memory of Ashley Maxwell, I do not recognize them. They have nothing to do with Ashley's life as a beloved elementary school teacher, so my mind can't place them.

"Are you David's parents?" It is parent-teacher conference night, and I have met with everyone except this child's parents who never show, so I am surprised to see this couple arrive.

"Zoe, I have some bad news."

The name doesn't register. I have been Ashley Maxwell for some time, living off the memories that I devoured from her family and friends at her funeral service, where they mourned a life cut short by a drunk driver. I bring my papers over to the round table where I have been discussing the grades and performance reports of children. Tapping the edge of my stack of papers on the table to straighten them, I gesture for them to take a seat. They don't.

"David really is a bright child and with the proper encouragement—"

"They've found her."

With these words, he rattles my self-composure, and cracks in my mind start to form. I desperately try to re-seal them. *Ashley Maxwell, who always wanted to work with kids. Who hoped to have her own children one day when she met the right guy. She loves to eat cherries that stain her fingers and sing off-tune in the shower.*

My mouth is dry. I lick my lips, feeling their parchment texture.

He says again, a little louder, as if I am deaf, "They've found her."

My oldest stolen memory surfaces: *Quack-quack-quack goes the duck. I raise it high and make it dive into the water. My baby girl laughs.* Once again, I can feel the slippery smoothness of the water in the bubble bath, the thick rubber of the duck, and the smell of baby shampoo on my fingers as my memories meld with those of my mother's.

I'm glad to be sitting down, for I'm light-headed. The two of them seem at once far, far away, and suffocatingly close. Before I can stop it from happening, my primary self surfaces, emerges from the ashes of my borrowed personality.

"Where?" I ask.

"Down an old well. Out in the National, in some falling down shack."

As he tells me this, the woman beside him touches his arm, but the man is not interested in being soothed. He shakes her off and comes closer, bending down so his eyes meet mine, a hand-span away. They are magnetic; I cannot look away. Is he Charming me?

"Time to wake up, Zoe. We've got to go home."

Hairline cracks become yawning crevices.

"Is everything alright, Ms. Maxwell?" This is from the doorway, where the principal of Ashley's school is now standing. She picks up on Ryan's threatening posture and it disturbs her. One hand holds her cell phone, ready to summon help if need be.

"It's fine. This is my brother, Ryan." Some of her tension

releases, and she enters the classroom cautiously. We have plenty of experience dealing with irate adults during parent-teacher conferences, so her concern is natural.

But it only takes a moment before Ryan has her in the palm of his hand. Like all the men in my family, he is handsome, with a movie star jawline, square brow, thick dark brown tousled hair, and a fit masculine figure that women want to touch. Only my eyes see the flaw: the distracted underlying impatience that implies "I need to be elsewhere, so can we hurry this along?" His gift of being able to seduce you wars with his need to be doing and moving, accomplishing real things.

Your brother doesn't have time to deal with your foibles today, Zoe. Be normal for once.

His voice melts my superior, and she smiles back. Her hand comes up to smooth her hair, and she stands taller. At least she doesn't proposition him immediately, something I've seen happen before.

"I didn't realize Ashley had any family."

"We just got in from out-of-town. I'm afraid the situation is urgent. A family matter, you understand. I'm afraid my sister will need to take some compassionate leave."

Ryan's hand comes down on my shoulder, patting me, and it feels like the closing of a jail cell door. My time being Ashley is over.

Her brow furrows with concern, and she spares a glance at me to see my expression. I wonder what it tells her. Do I look upset enough to convince her I need to leave? Does she see the shock in my eyes his news gives me? My mother. Found after twenty years.

"I'm sorry to hear that."

Oh, how smoothly he guides her back to the door as they continue talking. He needs her gone so he can talk to Zoe, not the Ashley personality I've stolen.

My sister-in-law suggests, "Why don't we pack up your things?"

Because, of course, I no longer have a choice. I have been found. Collected like a lost child. The truant forced to return.

No goodbye to the class of impressionable nine-year-olds who will wonder why Miss Maxwell left. Yesterday will be their last memory of me. I wish I had made it more special for them, bringing cupcakes or gifting each student a pad of colorful sticky notes. They love writing on sticky notes at that age.

With the principal gone, Ryan shuts the door and locks it. I am sitting at my desk, sorting through drawers. I will leave most of it to whoever replaces me. Besides, I travel light; anything important, I keep in my head.

"About three months ago, the police told us they discovered a body in the backwoods at an old house that kids were using to meet up. Rotten boards were concealing the top of a well and they almost fell in. Scared the shit out of them, but at least they had sense enough to call in their parents, who notified the police. They weren't sure it was Mom until they matched the DNA."

"Dead," I whisper, hanging my head. Sure, it's been twenty years since I last saw her, but you always hope, don't you? That she got amnesia or had a mental break causing her to wander off. You believed she was living incognito somewhere. Like me, she was probably lost in a memory that swept her out to sea.

You look at faces you see at the grocery store and wonder if one of them is hers. You have a fantasy that you'd recognize her, and after you stopped her, she'd remember who she was. You would hug and cry about the lost years, but she'd come home. She'd come home.

My brother's voice is brittle with sharp edges from the anger he nurses. "I knew she would never leave us for some mystery lover. I told you that, didn't I? Someone took her, and our family did nothing to discover the truth."

"Alibaba tried." I regret saying that.

"Tried? Grandfather did nothing! He just let her disappear

without a fight. You were too young, but I remember." He grabs my wrist like a vise. "You remember now?"

His face is inches from mine as he forces me to take his memory.

"When's Mommy coming home?" asks Ryan. He is hanging over the back of the sofa, looking through the window to the driveway. The boy has done it every day since his mother left. Watching. Afraid he might miss seeing her return.

His grandfather grabs Ryan's upper arm and shakes him. The boy has always seen his grandfather as a giant and his mouth grows dry, not understanding what he did to make him angry. He's told, "She'll be back when she learns her lesson."

Perhaps it is the look on my face, but when Ryan pulls away from me, he is breathing hard. It is not often that we can share memories anymore like we did as children. Perhaps he forgets how disturbing it can be to remember everything in such rich detail as if you are living it again?

We stare at each other: his eyes are that pale caramel color inherited from Grandfather, and for the first time I notice the faint trace of crow's feet. Ryan whispers, "*You* can do something about it. You can *force* the truth from them."

I shake my head. "No. No. It doesn't work like that."

He seems not to hear me. "You can crack open their minds like a walnut, sort out the meat, and throw the rest away. You owe it to Mother."

Despite my denials, naturally, I am going back and will do what he says. Our relationship is this: I run, he catches me, I return. In my heart, I weep for losing Ashley Maxwell. She is dead now twice-over.

His wife, Jennifer, stands at the opposite side of the room, examining a wall decorated with bumblebees and spring tulips that describe cloud shapes.

I ask, "What did Grandfather think about them finding her?"

"After I got the news, we didn't have a long discussion."

The last time I returned was for my twenty-first birthday party when I exposed one of the founding family's married-in relatives as a pedophile. Despite knowing I had done the right thing, it hadn't gone down well, and the ranks among the town closed. But I was used to being shunned as the Underhill weirdo and the day I left, I mailed an anonymous letter to the police with details about what they could find on the flash drive he had hidden away.

"You're the Memory Keeper. We need to find out what happened to her. You owe it to Mom." Ryan sees the effect that mentioning her has upon me. There are other ways than Charm to get what you want. "If I could do it, I would. But it's why you need to return. Find out what Grandfather and the others were doing when Mother went missing. Get us the facts."

"That's what you never have understood, Ryan. Memories aren't facts. They have emotions attached to them. The older the memory, the harder it is for people to even think about what happened. Anything I learn will be colored by time, by nostalgia. It's been twenty years, for goodness' sake! Grandfather and Aunt Belle are *ancient*!"

He didn't hear me. Ryan never heard anything that went contrary to his own agenda. "Aunt Belle is insisting on a memorial service, and I'm not letting her or Grandfather decide what happens to our mother. We aren't kids to be ordered around anymore. We make the decisions about her now."

"Cremation?"

"I can't agree with that. What if her body might yield more evidence when they discover new techniques?"

The reality of all of this is starting to settle in and Ashley Maxwell has been swept away, leaving only Zoe Underhill. I say wearily, "How will this work?"

"I've got a plan."

"Of course you do," I murmured.

"The memorial will give us a reason to invite plenty of people who knew her. People you could read for clues."

Reluctantly, I admit it isn't a bad idea. When our mother vanished, we were kids; Ryan, nine, me, six. Our memories are practically useless in solving what happened. We need knowledge from adults around at the time of her disappearance. "And what about *your* job?"

"Compassionate leave. They all feel sorry for me while being greedy to hear all the salacious details." Ryan never discusses his private life with strangers, and for him, anyone outside of the family were strangers.

Sometimes, I wondered how much his wife, Jennifer, even knows about him. Across the room, she seems to be reading the poems the kids had written about the different types of clouds.

"So, you will help?" Ryan presses.

"Yes. But you may find out things you hadn't bargained for. Truth isn't comfortable, and little of it can be found in memories."

Two

olan's fury is flowing faster than water out the sluice gates after the spring rains. He is hurting, but worse, seething. His daughter will bend to his will. He raised her; Nurtured her. He owned her.

My grandfather grabs the banister rail of the second floor of our house and shouts down to the girl exiting the front door, "My home, my rules, missy!"

My mother is ripe as a summer peach; her mind as weightless as a late summer dandelion. She will fly free and make her own mistakes.

Brynn gives a dismissive laugh and a toss of her head like a colt does before he throws his rider. "You won't stop me, old man!"

Somewhere in the house, a child is crying, and a woman tries to hush her.

My brother and his wife are in the front seat of the car talking. They think I am sleeping, sprawled on the back seat. It's a ploy I've used often throughout my childhood - for memories only speak of the past, and if you want to know about current events, you must snoop. Especially when the discussion concerns yourself.

"How did she end up in New Mexico, of all places?!"

Ryan's reply is inaudible. Perhaps he suspects I am not napping, or he can't forget I'm an Underhill, who should always be handled with care. "Land-locked, Jen. She won't pick a state that touches the sea."

"But why did they believe she was Ashley-what's-her-name?"

He doesn't explain how I steal memories, using them to become someone from the inside out. Walking in someone else's stolen shoes, preferably far away from their original abode. Ashley Maxwell had died in Akron, Ohio; Ryan had found me in Las Cruces, New Mexico, where a private school didn't look too closely at a teacher's certification.

I don't dislike Jennifer, even though she's treating me like a tired parent dealing with a child not their own. She casts a glance over her shoulder and leans over saying to Ryan in a hushed voice. "You don't think she should be—? Under care?"

My body freezes as an unbidden memory rises in my mind of Aunt Belle talking to a man in a white coat, me sitting in the chair at her side.

"Zoe imagines she is other people. I'm sure there are some drugs or something you could use to make her more tractable, doctor. She's wild, you see."

Ryan says sharply, "Don't worry about her."

"But what about your grandfather? What will he make of her?"

Ryan is tired. We first took a plane, and now we are on the last leg of the trip, and he's been driving for over three hours.

"Who cares about Nolan? I don't."

"You don't mean that, honey."

Intense emotions can power memories. One of Ryan's comes flooding to the surface and I feel it even though we are not touching.

A jerk on my waist and I'm shoved back into the saddle after my fall by Grandfather. "Underhills don't quit. You need to get back on the horse that threw you, or you'll never ride again."

The horse moves, and Ryan can't stop it. The horse is not like a bicycle, and it won't obey him. For a boy who is meticulous about the clothes he wears, the food he eats, and the friends he makes, this lack of control — of power over another — frightens him.

"Think about the money—" Jennifer begins, and I feel embarrassed for her. Being raised with money, Ryan cares little about wealth, but it is not my place to correct his wife.

I know she dislikes me, as she thinks I am the reason for her husband's secretive behavior. But it is the family that has taught him to shield himself. He does not give all, fearing he will lose all.

Jennifer feels his admonishment and turns to look out the car window. Her contoured make-up enhances her cheekbones but from this angle, it transforms into flat planes like a paint-by-number canvas. Her eyeliner is perfect, and she is wearing false eyelashes.

This must be her daily beauty routine, her armor against the world, for she would never do this to impress me. She's been married to Ryan for five years, and he's seen under the hood, so it isn't for him either.

Feeling the tension between them, I fold myself away like a piece of origami paper into a smaller and smaller piece. Avoiding notice is something I know how to do. In a few minutes, it is almost as if I have disappeared for they begin to talk about issues back home, a real estate deal Ryan is working on, and problems at the bank where Jennifer works.

Free from their awareness, I close my eyes and think of Mother.

I enter my mother's room, my high school graduation cap in my hand. There are fresh flowers in the vase. Kneeling beside her bed, I rub my face into her bedspread, smelling fabric softener.

Tears start to fall. She's gone. Really gone. My graduation cap tumbles to the floor.

Where are you, mom?

Why did you leave?

Why didn't you take me with you?

By tomorrow, we will be back home; a place I've worked hard to avoid, back with the three residents who tried to fit me into a mold until I broke it and fled.

Grandfather. Nolan Underhill. Alibaba. Hard and stern to everyone but me, the granddaughter whose birth blew everyone's life to hell. Mom hadn't bothered to hide the fact that the dates she separated from her husband didn't work with her second pregnancy.

Owen Underhill. Nolan's brother. Paying his wife's medical bills from the pancreatic cancer that killed her had demolished his Underhill inheritance. He was forced to move back home a few years before my mother's disappearance.

Aunt Belle Mallory. My grandmother's sister. When Catherine married Nolan, her younger sister arrived with the wedding trousseau. After our mother disappeared, Grandfather informed us that Belle would nurture us, although nurturing wasn't what I received.

At the hotel, we get rooms with a connecting door. Jennifer is in the shower, and I am on the bed, gazing at the ceiling when Ryan tosses a book onto my stomach.

"What's this for?"

"It's a dream journal. I thought you could use it to take notes."

"A journal that anyone could pick up and read at any time. That might not be wise in a crowded house."

"Write it down in code."

I laugh. "Really? We aren't kids playing spies."

"Then hide it," he says, irritated.

Opening up the dream journal, I flip through and stroke the pages. The paper is soft under the rough calluses of my fingers, and each page has a little crescent moon in gold on the corner with three tiny stars. In the odd way that siblings know and not know each other, Ryan has picked a design that appeals to me. "You really think someone knows something?"

"Of course they do. Nolan, Owen, Aunt Belle, and Robert." He never calls his father dad, even though he spent all his summers after Mom left living with him. "They saw something, heard something, did something."

"Maybe Grandfather didn't want us to know things that would hurt us? What if she had a lover?"

Ryan rolls his eyes. "Sure, Zoe, knowing Mom had a sex life with a stranger will hurt me more than the police telling me they found our mother's body!"

"I only meant—"

He crosses his arms, trying to control his impatience. He is on edge, though he won't admit it, for the closer we get to home, the more we both feel it. The pull in our bones and the singing in our blood. It is disconcerting. Is this what birds feel when they are forced by their instinct to fly hundreds of miles to a place where they were born?

Ryan continues. "Listen, I've already heard it all before. I was old enough to remember the DNA test they did to prove you weren't Robert's daughter. Don't think I can't handle whatever any of them say about Mom; I've been handling it for some time."

I pick up the pen that came with the book and click it. "Obviously we need to talk with Grandfather and Aunt Belle. What was Cook's name? I just called her Happy. She made chocolate chip cookies to die for."

"Millie Farmer. She lives in Kingstowe, and now her niece Sally is in charge of the housekeeping and kitchen. Sally isn't at the house every day. She's married with twin kids and has a life. School. Gymnastics. Soccer. Whatever kids have."

Pushing the pen's button a few times, to enjoy its satisfying clicks. I ask, "Didn't Grandfather have some gardeners working about the place?"

"Mack Matthews and his son Rolf. Old Mack is in a nursing home. Dementia. I've visited him a couple of times, but his memory is pretty dodgy, but maybe you can pull something out of him."

I write down the names and Ryan's information about them. "I was trying to remember if that was the year the house was being painted."

He throws up his hands in frustration, shaking his head. "Jesus, Zoe, can't you remember that was the next summer? Snap out of your Ashley Maxwell daydream! Why the hell were you playing school teacher?"

"Because it was a nice uncomplicated life!" And it had love. Plenty of it. Kids were like dogs and would give you buckets of love if you acted like a decent human being. Sometimes even if you weren't.

"How can I count on you if you don't have the dates straight?"

"As I've told you many times, memory reading isn't like watching a movie or reading a history book. The puzzle bits have to be fitted together to make an entire picture. Dates get fuzzy. I bet you remember going to the dentist, but do you remember what day it was?"

"Okay," Ryan mutters. He looks away, still not happy he can't do this investigation himself. He'd rather be the knight in shining armor, avenging Mother all by himself, and not relying upon his sister and her odd gift that he never understood.

"I'll try to find some clues. Scout's honor," I say. "Who else should I meet?"

"Mom had a girlfriend back then. She's remarried now and

doesn't live in Kingstowe anymore, but I fully expect her to show up at the memorial."

The shower has stopped, and the doorknob is turning, so Ryan says quickly, "Jen doesn't know about what you can do. Let's keep it that way."

And I bet she doesn't know you can Charm the fishes from the sea, does she?

His wife exits the bathroom, dressed in jeans. She is wearing heels, not sneakers. Who does that?

Ryan gives her a quick kiss and says, "Hey babe, let's go get something for dinner and bring something back to Zoe. She wants some time to shower and grab some rest."

I can tell Jennifer definitely wants some private time with her husband. Best let her have some before we get back home, and things implode.

THREE

The mood in the car becomes brooding as we enter the city limits of Kingstowe. Familiar landmarks fly by. The corner store where I bought gum and candy after school. On this hill, I once crashed my bike and got a nasty gash on my knee requiring a dozen stitches. The ice cream shack has a new name.

This land is no dry desert with bright sunshine, studded with one-story houses designed to defend against the heat. No. This is the moody northeast, with square wooden houses with dormers, windows trimmed in white, that are framed with shutters. Porches with colonial posts.

It is the beginning of fall, the second summer, when families will host their clam bakes, with lobster and corn on the cob, all to be finished with a side of strawberry shortcake. It's when tourists start making the trek to see the foliage, from the yellows and reds I've seen so far, the invasion should be here soon.

No doubt, the locals are speculating at the local hardware store on what type of winter we will have.

I started tasting salt on my tongue as soon as we left the airport in the rental car. The sound of the surf is only increasing in my ears, as the clouds became gray, threatening rain the closer we got to Kingstowe. With our kinship to the sea, I'm sure Ryan is feeling the same headache which is trying to drill a hole in my forehead.

"I want to fill the car," says my brother. From the back seat, I see the gauge is half full. *A delaying tactic?* Despite his urgency to bring me back, he must feel the dread of arriving as much as I do.

We pull into a local gas station, *Danny's*, and after parking next to the pump, he opens his wallet and leans over the front seat to face me. He extends a hand filled with folded bills to me. "Get yourself something."

"Yes, *Dad*." I grab the money and tumble out of the car. Walking to the front door, I see the reflection of Ryan and Jennifer behind me. He is talking urgently to her, his hand waving.

There is a bored teen girl at the counter's cash register. She is resting her rear end against the back cabinet and stands up straight when I come in, trying to look alert and helpful. We exchange smiles.

I avoid the aisle where a man is stocking the shelves from boxes and go to the drink machine. Something cold sounds good so I grab a small cup and open the spout from a soda-slushie machine.

The door chimes again. Ryan enters and approaches the counter. "The card reader at the pump isn't working."

The girl's hand comes up to take his card but the man stops stocking the shelves, and orders her to leave. "Go to the back, Evelyn."

She looks between her manager and Ryan, confused. Her boss repeats himself, louder. "Go to the storeroom. I'll take care of Mr. Underhill."

Hearing our family name the girl abandons her post, and knocks over a mop standing in the hall to escape. She doesn't seem to hear my comment as she rushes by. "We aren't monsters."

The resemblance to Grandfather is only increased by Ryan's posture: shoulders back, head slightly back, chin up, and the flaring nostrils. You might as well be looking at a younger Nolan Underhill.

Blinking, I try to shake the ghostly feeling away. He's Ryan, my brother, not Grandfather. I take after Brynn, and it is probably why no one spooked at my entrance.

Ryan's voice, though pleasant, is flat in effect; it is a warning to anyone who knows him. "I imagine my money is still good here, despite being an Underhill."

The man takes the card and swipes it quickly. Too quickly. He has to run it again and his face is pale as he grinds out, "Money is fine. But I won't have you witching the girl."

"I'm not my grandfather." Ryan is as chilly as my drink.

"You're an Underhill, that's all I know."

Never do a deal with an Underhill.

The old schoolyard taunt springs back into my mind. *Quite the welcome home, huh?*

By this time, my drink is full, and I put a cap on it, grabbing a straw. I come up to the counter to stand beside him. We are siblings first, and loyal to each other in our way. I slide a five-dollar bill over the counter, showing the man my drink. "Keep the change for your trouble."

Slipping my free hand around Ryan's elbow I pivot him and we exit side by side.

"Grandfather and his paramours," he mutters between clenched teeth.

"Ignore them," is my advice. Something I had made a career of doing in high school.

Back in the day, Grandfather freely used his gift of Charm to seduce the women of Kingstowe. There are still angry fathers and husbands who see him as a Nosferatu, the horrifying vampire, rather than a Romeo. But none of those dalliances resulted in children; I am the only Underhill born on the wrong side of the blanket.

· · ·

In Kingstowe's main square is the monument commemorating the town's survival after the Great Gale of 1898. There is a statue of our ancestor, my great-great-grandfather, Abraham Underhill. He holds a bible in one hand, and his other clutches his hat that a gale-force wind is trying to remove.

At his feet, crouches his wife, Sarah, cradling a baby against her bosom. Her face hides in the crook of her elbow, as she shelters from the wind. As a child, I always imagined if I stared long enough, she would look up and see me, but the bronze is unyielding.

From downtown, we take the road to the McHenry ferry and Ryan pulls the car into line to cross the New King Harbor. This is the shortest route to the tip of the peninsula and to our ancestral home.

Ryan refused my suggestion to take the longer land route, the memorial highway that goes up through the National and thus avoid a water crossing. Most Underhills love the spray of salt against their face, the pitching of the tide as they stand on the deck of a boat, but I am wary of the sea.

The clang, clang is the noise the car produces as it rolls over the metal ramp; it is like a hammer against my nerves. A great force presses down on my chest, and the car interior suddenly feels claustrophobic. Finding it hard to catch my breath, I fumble for the car door handle, and as Ryan puts the car into park, I scramble out. Jennifer shoots me a questioning look, but my tongue feels thick and swollen, so I don't answer. Instead, I hear Ryan give her an excuse for my departure.

To the right is New King Harbor, formed after the Great Gale of 1898, broke through the beachhead and flooded the low areas to form Ramshead Island. To the left is the open sea. There is movement among the waves, the rising back of a whale, and I shiver.

With the feeling of being hunted, I rush through the alley of the parked cars, making my way to the other end of the boat that faces the peninsula where home is.

The tip is high ground, and it is why it survived 1898 even when the connection to the mainland was swept away by water and wind. There is a mix of evergreen pine among the yellowing fall leaves.

From wanting to avoid going home, now I just want to reach the land. My hands ache from gripping the railing too hard.

"Nothing is free, you know."

Turning my head, I see an old lady wearing a pair of well-worn overalls and wellies. Her shirt is plaid, and the sleeves are rolled up, revealing muscular arms darkened by age and weather. A mud-brown knit hat is pulled down over her wispy white hair.

I don't know her.

"I'm sorry? What did you say?"

She gives a lop-sided grin with a mouth that shows a gap between her top two teeth. "Under hill, over sea, is how the fairies go. All journeys have a cost."

Surely, Ryan had paid for the ferry trip? I dig into my pocket, bringing out the rest of the money he gave me earlier. "How much do you need?"

"What is a safe passage worth to you?" Her gaze leers at what I hold: a couple of twenties, a ten, and two fives.

I'm about to hand over a twenty when a man plucks the bill from my hand. He gives me an assessing scan up and down; a test I feel I fail.

The stranger is probably a little older than I, about Ryan's age. His face is unsmiling and the misty spray from the sea has fogged the lenses of his glasses, masking their expression. He explains as if to a child, "You don't pay for the crossing before you get to the other side." Ripping the bill in half, he hands one portion to the woman and tells her, "You'll get the second part when we reach the shore safely."

The old fisher-wife gives a hoot of laughter as she snatches the paper and tucks it down the front of her shirt. She pats her bosom, securing the money. "Are you her protector then, young man?"

"I intervened because I would also like to reach the shore safely."

She gives that raspy old lady laugh again. "Never fear, no danger today. But I make no guarantees for later." She walks away, her shoulders still shaking at some private joke.

He pushes the glasses up his nose and examines me. "You aren't like I expected. Far more human."

"Who are you?"

Before he can answer, I hear Ryan shouting at me. He is standing at the rail about ten yards away. "Come on! The ferry is pulling in."

Throwing him one more glance, I rush back to the car. When I get there Ryan is already sliding back into the driver's seat. Jennifer is scrolling through her phone, and doesn't look up when she says, "All good?"

My brother nods. "No problem."

FOUR

We exit the ferry, and from the back seat, I see his knuckles gripping the steering wheel tightly. Ryan is not as unmoved about our imminent arrival as he has pretended.

While the land had been scoured by the 1898 Gale, the scars were mostly gone now. Now this end of the peninsula is a community of homes with acreage for the wealthy of Kingstowe. The mansions are angled to enjoy a view of either the sea or the harbor.

Many are built in the same style as the smaller Cape Cod style homes, but bigger. Most of them were enlarged or rebuilt entirely in the 1950s and 60s to a strict code of needing to blend into what already existed, but I am surprised to see at least two newer mansions in a modern style. *Why ever did Grandfather allow those?*

Ryan slows the car before turning to enter through the open gates, and we start down the long driveway to the Big House.

After 1898, along with the gifts given to Abraham and his children, my Underhill ancestors bought as much land as they could. With money from the lumber trade and a new cannery, added with their newly gained Charm, they saw their wealth grow like Jack's beanstalk.

Our bible-holding ancestor left his church for the holy halls of commerce. The house is a testament to his success. It was designed by Rockefeller's favorite architects, William Adams Delano and Chester Holmes Aldrich, and was built in 1915 in a neo-Georgian style.

Before the house is a vast carpet of emerald-green grass and in the center is the beloved jewel of the county: Kingstowe's oldest white oak, the Majestic. I catch my breath; the tree's roots are clutching my heart, and I'm planted here whether I like it. She is a symbol of home more than the house ever was.

While all the other trees on the peninsula were bent or broken under the force of the great gale, the Majestic had stood firm. She was a symbol of that New England stubborn pride, but also a promise of tenacity and strength.

There is a friendly rivalry with the town of Granby, who believes their Dewey Oak in Connecticut is older. No one in Kingstowe believes that.

As we pass it, there seems to be a haze around the tree, and I sit up, looking harder. It shifts, and a shadow moves back, using the tree to conceal itself. Probably some sightseer who doesn't want Grandfather to shoot him for trespassing. Neither Ryan nor Jennifer notice it, for they are staring straight ahead at the house, which is filling our view as we advance.

The car crunches on the gravel as we pull to a stop in front. There are two other cars parked here already, both of some expensive make, with polished coats like gleaming thoroughbreds.

None of us says anything, not even Jennifer. Ryan releases the steering wheel and flexes his fingers as if he is trying to work out cramping.

I say in a very tiny voice, "No one has come out yet. We could turn around. Run away."

But it is already too late for the ogre found us.

"Your Aunt Belle," Jennifer murmurs.

Annabelle Mallory, my grandmother's sister, exits the front door of the house. She is wearing a tweed skirt and knit cardigan, thick hose, and strong shoes to better stomp on anyone's dreams. Aunt Belle waddles like a duck, the ends of her cardigan swinging out from her pear-shaped body.

Her advance brings up many memories that sting like rubbing alcohol on a scrape.

Annabelle was a surprise baby and when my great-grandmother Mallory was told by the doctor she was with child, she exclaimed, "I don't have time for that! There are chores to be done." When Annabelle was two, Great Grandmother Mallory staggered up from her sickbed to hang laundry on the line outside. The next day, the inflammation in her lungs killed her. We were told it was pneumonia, but I've always believed it was from stubbornness.

My grandmother, Catherine "Kitty," was Annabelle's older sister by twelve years. She always felt protective of her little sister and gave Annabelle a home after their father died. Sentiment saddled us with her, and it survived even after Grandmother Kitty's stroke, for Grandfather had asked her to stay on.

She has always been here in my memory, looming, watching, and criticizing. I can't think of one pleasant thought I have of the woman.

I am sitting at the kitchen table while Belle dishes out strawberry ice cream. It is the last of the homemade batch made over the Fourth of July weekend. The scoop she gives Ryan is twice as big as the one she puts before me. I am a child and have not learned yet to hide my feelings, so I start to wail over the unfairness of it. It earns me a slap on my wrist with a wooden spoon.

"He's a boy, Zoe. You get what you get, so don't throw a fit."

Her lessons taught me to disappear.

I shrink back in the seat, even as Ryan gets out to greet her. As Belle embraces him, her head barely comes to his shoulder. Jennifer stops a few feet from them, only witnessing, not joining, the reunion.

Exiting the car using the door on the opposite side of where they stand, I readjust my cheap sunglasses, which are totally unneeded with these cloudy skies, but they act as a good shield.

When Belle notices me, she makes no comment. Instead, with her arm around my brother's waist, she exclaims, "What a surprise! We weren't expecting you until tomorrow!"

With Ryan and Belle arm-in-arm, Jennifer drops back alongside me. Her face is neutral, which makes me wonder what thoughts she guards so carefully. *What did she feel about Belle's smothering love for her husband?*

Big House is not a clever name, but it does describe the place accurately enough. We enter through the double doors, which have been used to bring in the massive Christmas trees Grandfather always insisted on having. My memories supply the smell of pine, the chill of the air, the sound of carols playing in the background on the record player.

No. That isn't right. The second-story trees only happened after Mother's disappearance. Along with the Santa whom Grandfather hired in an attempt to make the holiday special for two half-orphans. But we had too much pain for a man in a fat suit to soothe so he was asked every year to bring our mother back. He lasted three holidays.

If you wore socks, you could run from the dining room and hit the marble tile in the foyer on a slide, skating across at least ten feet. Ryan and I sometimes raced to see who could go the farthest. Once, not realizing the floor had just been waxed, I slammed into the corner of the opposite wall. How many stitches was it that time?

I am barely aware of the people around us and follow them like a programmed robot into Grandfather's trophy room. It is large, and serves as the main entertainment room of the house. The built-in bookcase displays all of his trophies from sailing races over the decades. On the opposite side is a floor-to-ceiling row of windows, which gives a stunning view of the ocean and the light shimmering over the waves. I swallow hard.

"Zoe, my dear child." Grandfather beckons me.

Going over, I give him the expected obeisance: a kiss on his parchment cheek. But I am not quick enough, and he pulls me close. His vise-like fingers are around my wrist and as he drags me down to sit beside him on the sofa.

Grandfather Nolan. The smell of pipe tobacco on his clothes; and the deep clove spice smell of his aftershave, brings back a mix of feelings. The sweetness of orange pulp with a taste of the peel.

"Where have you been? You look thin as a bone."

"Oh, traveling a bit." I haven't seen him since I left on my twenty-first birthday, though I dropped him cards sometimes in order to keep the wolf from my door. Instead, I've been working alongside ordinary people who went to work every day, packed their lunch in a paper sack, and who wondered if they could afford a vacation. No trust fund. No gifts from some power I never understood. Everything is blissfully ordinary.

He turns away from me, his gaze already examining his grandson, reminding me again that all that matters is I'm back home again, under his eye. Ready to be displayed like the trophy on the walls.

I sit between Grandfather and his younger brother, my Uncle Owen. Although there is a difference of two years in their age, they both have the same old-man-muscled wiry build, the square chin, and the Cary Grant dimpled chin. A copy of Ryan but matured.

But all the same features on Owen seem faded and worn; a poor copy of his vibrant brother. Grandfather has the caramel brown eyes of a falcon; and while the same color, Owen's are those of a rabbit.

Owen bumps my shoulder with his own. "How are you holding up, kiddo?"

Before I can answer him, Grandfather says loudly, "Our girl is back home, Belle."

From across the room, my aunt gives an absent-minded nod. She is too busy talking with Ryan, asking his advice about how best to rent out the summer vacation cottage. It is in a town smaller than Kingstowe up north on the coast. Like Ryan's experience with renting out skyscrapers has anything in common with a beach cabin. But it makes Belle a part of Ryan's life and knits tight that kinship she craves. She wasn't an Underhill with gifts of Charm and Memory, but she knew how to work ordinary snares.

Blood and bone. Bind and Hold.

"I wouldn't rent it out at all, except we get a huge tax break on it if we do," Aunt Belle explains. Age is catching up with her, as her voice sounds high, almost breathless, and the back of her hands show defined veining and age spots. *High blood pressure?* Her bobbed hair is the color of dark steel, the gray having taken over the brown like crabgrass does an unattended lawn.

I know from family photos that she was once young and vivacious with a sparkle in her eyes. When she came back from finishing school to live with her sister, the two had been beauties, but it is hard to connect that girl with this woman.

Do you love me? It is said in a hushed whisper for she fears being discovered. I consider that stray memory gained from my aunt long ago. Loved and lost was my guess on what changed her excitement about life from a shiny penny to a tarnished silver piece.

Grandfather Nolan keeps up his jocular shouting. He is putting on a show and wants everyone to notice him. "What she means, Ryan, is that I'm an old skinflint. But that's how you make the real money, my boy. Trust me. Watch the expenses and run a tight ship."

His words are a double-edged chastisement. One to Ryan, infantilizing him with advice, but also as a slap to my uncle Owen. My uncle's inheritance was lost, drained to pay for his wife's pancreatic cancer treatments, which, in the end, still did not save her.

"Real estate makes a good tax break, especially if you use the savings to reinvest in the property," Ryan's words are mild as he fences with Grandfather. The two command the room's attention like strutting peacocks.

Jennifer is sitting by herself in a hardback chair, perched on the edge as if ready for flight. She once made the mistake of addressing Nolan as Grandfather, and he quickly corrected her. There isn't a truce between them; Jennifer had waved the white flag and folded.

It wasn't Ryan who told me this. It was a memory I had borrowed from Jennifer when we were driving here.

A woman enters with a tray of glasses and a pitcher of tea.

"Thank you, Sally," says Aunt Belle.

This is our new housekeeper, niece of the woman who I knew as Happy. I didn't think housekeepers still wore dresses, but she does. It is an unfussy, gray-flannel one-piece that hits decorously below the knee. Light brown hair, blue eyes, and a pleasant face, not at all the high-tempered type, which was probably why she still had a job here. The only one allowed a temper at the Big House is Grandfather.

"Will it be seven for dinner, then?"

To Ryan, Belle says, "We were thinking you wouldn't be here until tomorrow. So yes, Sally, seven for dinner. That won't be a problem?"

"As long as none of them are vegetarian."

"I don't think they are?"

For a moment, I thought about claiming to be vegan with a glucose intolerance and a nut allergy, but Ryan said Sally had boys, so she probably was used to dealing with unruly children.

"Sally Farmer took over from her aunt Millie since your last visit, Zoe," said Grandfather, not realizing I didn't need an explanation.

She gives me a sunny smile that reminds me of her aunt. "I'm

Sally Farmer Brixton, now. Married, with two boys. We've met before Zoe, back when we were all children. Though I was about five years younger than you. Do you remember?"

The smell of warm sugar as cookies are baking. The warmth of the room from the oven. Happy with her hands over a child's, as they rolled out the dough together. Using the green and red plastic cookie cutters to make the shapes of stars and bells. Red and green sugar in little shakers.

I hazard a guess. "Making cookies with your aunt?"

She laughs. "I'm sure we did! My aunt is always baking."

"I hope she's doing well?"

"She's fine. After my uncle died last year, she decided to retire, but she's still busy with her clubs."

"While I'm here, I'd like to visit with her."

"Sure. I'll get her phone number for you." To all of us, she says, "Your rooms are ready. Sheets straight out of the dryer, fluffed pillows, and fresh flowers."

Jennifer stands up, setting her glass down without drinking from it. "I think I'll go up and lie down for a bit. It was a long drive. I'll see you all at dinner." Both of the women walk out together and I hear them chatting about flowers; Jennifer is far more comfortable talking with the help than the Underhills. I can't blame her.

For the first time, Aunt Belle glances at Grandfather, and when he nods at her, she asks my brother, "I want to show you what we've been doing with the new stone patio."

Ryan finishes his drink and sets it aside on the tray. "Sure."

Owen rises. He moves heavily, his shoulders sagging. "I guess I'll go work on my bonsai collection. Maybe you can stop by, Zoe, and visit with me later?"

"Sure," I say.

He goes out the way Jennifer did. Throughout these exchanges, Grandfather's grip on my wrist has not slackened.

When we are alone, he says with satisfaction, "Now let's have a real talk."

FIVE

"Do you remember?" Using words from our childhood game, Grandfather starts the difficult conversation he wants to have with me. A few years after Mother's disappearance, when I was about nine, he discovered my memory talent, and immediately started to use it for his needs.

"I remember everything," I reply, using the proper counter-phrase to that game.

Grandfather's mind is carefully blank even while we are touching. I can only harvest memories when people are actively thinking of them, as he knows. He is wily, and I will need to catch him off guard if I am to learn anything.

"Good. Good." He gives me a grin, flashing white veneers against a tan face, and drops his hold on my wrist.

He is a man who could film commercials as an old cowboy or sailor. Unlike Aunt Belle, there remains much of his younger self in his face, and it is easy to understand why he could seduce so many women. Add Charm and the women of Kingstowe never stood a chance.

Despite being eighty-two, he remains lean in build. While

some men gain fat as they age, the years have stripped Nolan and Owen of the excess, revealing stone.

He wears a light blue polo shirt with the name of his sailing club embroidered on the front and chinos. Seeing him on the golf course, you'd know he has money. Looks, money, and Charm? A killer combination.

"Ryan told you what is going on? Why you need to be here?"

"Yes, Alibaba."

He gives a watery chuckle. "That old name! I haven't heard that in a while."

"Doesn't Ryan use it?"

"No. His father taught him to address his elders as if they were his peers, so he calls me Nolan."

I say nothing. Ryan's father is Robert Bancroft, whom my mother cuckolded with a bastard. I am the cuckoo's child; we just don't know who the cuckoo was. All of this we learned when Robert's parents insisted on a DNA test shortly after my birth.

When my mother, Brynn, vanished, my brother spent summers with his father and his new wife traveling the globe: Paris, London, the Bahamas, while I stayed home with Grandfather. Did I resent that? No, because Ryan had hated every one of those summers.

We stare at each other, and I realize he wants something and thinks his Charm will get it, so I brace myself for something unpleasant.

"Brynn never told you who your daddy was?"

"No."

That sucker punches me. Now *that* I am defensive about.

Noticing he leveled me, he releases my wrist, patting the red ring his fingers have left behind. "Now, pumpkin, we have to find out who killed Brynn. The identity of your daddy might be an important clue to that."

Swallowing hard, I say, "Maybe it was an accident? She could have fallen." Was that any better? Some slow death where no one heard her screams for help as she lay dying?

"The police don't seem to know much. Or care much." Grandfather is disgruntled. Some cop must have ignored him. "They say it's a cold case and they have crimes they need to worry about today, so it will probably take months before they can get around to doing anything about it."

Grandfather shows me the first non-calculated emotion since I walked into the room, as he is no actor and his eyes glisten. "I loved her so much."

"I know you did."

That's what drove her away. It's what drives me and Ryan away. Your love suffocates us, for it demands we be a mirror to reflect only you.

"You know I've kept her room as it was when she left?" Yes, how could I forget the shrine right next to my bedroom? The one I walked past every day to go to school. "I gave the police a brush from her room that still had her hair in it for the DNA."

The last time Mother's brush touched her hair, it took the strands that would identify her dead body.

Enough of this.

"It was a long drive. I think I'll go stretch my legs."

Outside on the front porch, I zip up my jacket and stuff my hands in my pockets. The need to move, to escape, grows stronger. Walking around to the back of the house, I hear voices: Ryan and Aunt Belle. *Nope.*

I do a 180, and in my spin, collide with my Great-Uncle Owen. We apologize at the same time. His face looks older than Grandfather's though he is younger by two years.

"I am glad you are home, though I just wish it was under better circumstances." His voice is very much like Grandfather's, but a little softer and more hesitant. It is as if Grandfather has gone through the Looking Glass and came out as a distorted reverse shadow of himself.

"Yeah." A teaching memory surfaces and my heart contracts from the loss of Ashley Maxwell.

The faint voices of children in the playground as I take my turn watching them during recess. One runs up and grabs my legs in a bear hug. She looks up and gives me a mischievous smile. "I caught you!"

"What's new with the historical society?" This and his Bonsai are reliable topics, and Owen's dead eyes catch fire with excitement.

"We finally got our grant! After decades of trying, we scored a pretty good one from the Smithsonian. It's funding a new exhibit about the Gale."

The Gale happened over a hundred years ago, but in this house, it was like yesterday. Great-great-grandfather Abraham and his amazing win over the storm, saving the town through his prayer. It was only months later that Abraham understood he had not only emerged as a hero but also as one with a gift to Charm. Good fortune smiled upon him in everything he did. A blessing from heaven.

And I was completely sick of hearing about him.

Owen kept talking. "You'll have to see it! It's an immersive experience."

"What does that mean?"

"Museums aren't stuffy boxes with just paper documents and walls of photos. The best ones encourage the visitor to interact — touch, sound, visual effects! With the Smithsonian grant we've built an extension where you walk in and experience the storm with sound, video, and holograms. You can be with our ancestors in 1898 and wonder if you'll survive!"

It sounds frightening, and I say weakly, "How exciting."

"The ribbon cutting is next week. Come with me."

No one ever wants to spend time with him, and out of guilt, I agree to do so.

During our conversation, I do not touch him, for his memories are bitter, too fixated on dying and loss. Right now, I'm not up for the emotional drain it would produce. Like Grandfather has for Mom, Owen keeps a shrine, a small one in his room for his wife, Natalie.

He holds out a ponytail of brown hair.

"Stroke it, Zoe. It's your aunt Natalie."

I reach out but my hand doesn't make contact. He doesn't notice my repugnance, as he is lost in the sensation of caressing his dead wife's hair. He presses it against his cheek and begins to cry.

I remember when he would talk about her as if she was still alive. "Natalie will like this — or Natalie wouldn't approve." Thankfully, that phase seems to have faded away with time.

For a moment, there is something in his eyes. Not hang-dog resignation, but something sharper. "You need to be careful. The anniversary will be here soon."

The anniversary of the Gale always did something to us Under-hills. Another reason to be well out of here before that November date rolls around.

"Is the town doing something for it?"

"A party on the grounds. Nolan is arranging it."

Usually, Grandfather leaves the historical stuff to Owen as a consolation prize. Perhaps Owen is sensitive about this change in status, for he says quickly, "Planning parties isn't what I do. Besides, I'm far too busy working with a historian sent by the Smithsonian on a book about Abraham."

Abraham, tamer of the Gale. The one who shouted to the skies that he would give his soul if the town was saved. In the end, not only did he sell off his own, but he bartered his descendants.

"Is there much to write about?"

"There's always something more if you know where to look.

Old wills, newspapers, gravestones. This guy really knows his stuff, and he has online access to research that I could never get into. He's very thorough. Dots his i's and crosses every t. He annoys Nolan."

When he says the last, Owen's eyes have a spark of malicious gleam. I can't blame him for taking pleasure where he can, for Grandfather likes to trample over his brother.

I'm not fond of digging into the past, especially anything to do with Abraham, however, twenty years back does interest me. "Do you remember the last time you saw my mother? Before she vanished?"

"I'm sorry, Zoe. I wish I could help. I was at a conference about bonsai and came back to Nolan shouting the house down." He hesitates before saying tentatively, "I don't want you and Ryan disappointed, but after all these years, I doubt they can solve what happened to her. I was here when the police talked to Nolan, and they didn't have any leads or really anything to explore about what happened to her that day. Nolan didn't take it well."

I'm glad my hands are stuffed into my pockets, for they are shaking. Aiming at nonchalance, I shrug. "Don't you watch those true crime shows? Sometimes the cold cases *are* solved. All they need is a new lead or a fresh perspective."

He spreads his hands out, palm up, in a gesture of conciliation. "You could be right, Zoe. Never say never, right?"

For a moment, I understand why Grandfather is often impatient with him. He is as firm as a melting marshmallow and just as irritatingly sticky.

Six

My old bedroom is the same as when I left at twenty-one to steal memories so I could be other people.

I close the door softly. The room does not smell stale, so Sally must have aired it out.

Since Aunt Belle was in charge of my childhood, the room is plain. *Poor little Cinderella.* I shake that thought away. If I wanted something different, something more than a pale green bedspread, a white dresser, with matching nightstand, and a brass bed, I could have asked Grandfather. It was my timidity that made the room what it was.

You didn't want to be here, so it didn't matter.

Like all the rooms, it has an en-suite bathroom. Pulling open the drawers, I discover everything inside them has been cleaned out. Luckily, though, my clothes still hang in the closet. Aunt Belle's cleaning job hadn't gotten far. I wonder who stopped her?

Someone has brought up my suitcase and I toss it on the bed to unpack. As I flip open the lid, I discover that someone has searched its contents already. Not a sloppy job, but I have a certain way of folding my clothes to maximize the space and they are not the same way I packed them last night.

My bank cards are concealed in the lining of my suitcase, and as my hand seeks the almost invisible slit, I find the hard plastic gone. Someone is cutting me off from my resources. Without money, it would be hard to leave, though not impossible.

My fingers are shaking as I punch the number on my phone for my online banking. "I'd like to report my cards as stolen." The password I give is over twenty characters long with a mixture of numbers, letters, and symbols I've memorized. I answer the three security questions that are so random that no one who knew me would stand a chance of answering them.

Not for me the answer of my favorite pet's name, my first car, or my favorite TV show.

"It looks like someone attempted to use the card online for a purchase, but it is declined because they didn't use the three-digit security code."

Another safeguard to stop someone from accessing my account was that I had scratched off the CVV number on the back after committing to memory. Over the years of playing cat-and-mouse with Grandfather and Ryan, I'd learned a few things.

"Do you want us to send you new cards?"

"No. I'm not settled yet, but I would like to freeze the account until I get a new mailing address."

By the time I jump through all the hoops with the person on the other end of the line, I am sitting on the bed, trembling.

Leaving New Mexico, Ryan had paid off my lease. Movers were scheduled to take my furniture to a storage unit. With ease, my brother dissolved my former life. He hadn't asked if I had money.

Now, someone in the house wants my wings clipped. Wants me dependent, with no chance of bolting. My eyes go to my doorknob where the lock had been removed when I got my first period.

"Young girls can't be trusted not to become sluts. Look at your mother giving us a bastard," says Aunt Belle. "I'll be watching you, young lady, so don't think I won't."

When I was sixteen, Aunt Belle came to my school and

checked me out a few weeks after spring break. She said it was for a dental appointment she forgot, but instead she drove me to a Boston psychiatrist who diagnosed me as having Borderline Personality Disorder.

The smell hit me as soon as we entered that gray block building: urine and disinfectant. She hustled me down the hallway and we entered a waiting room with yellow walls and a nurse behind a shatterproof glass.

When we were admitted, I said nothing. Aunt Belle did all the talking while the doctor watched me while he pretended to ignore me.

"Zoe imagines she is other people. I'm sure there are some drugs or something you could use, doctor, to make her more tractable. She's wild, you see."

What wild thing had I done to deserve that? Probably told some secret memory out-loud and Aunt Belle heard about it. It certainly wasn't running with boys like her imagination thought.

The only benefit to being institutionalized for a week and listening to the doctor's pompous, condescending diagnosis was that I learned new words. Later, I used them to taunt Aunt Belle by calling her a paranoid histrionic.

Finally, Grandfather showed up and rescued me. As my guardian, he had the ultimate authority over my person, and he told Belle and the doctor that I was only a teenager acting out by impersonating people, like actors did. There was no more to it. Belle had no legal authority over me, and he didn't want to involve his lawyers, but if it was necessary—.

It was the only time I had seen Grandfather not give in to something Aunt Belle wanted. It made me feel good, until I learned from one of Owen's memories that Grandfather knew Belle had snuck me out of school and had waited a week before bringing me home. Did he want to play hero? Or had he only pretended to rescue me, to tie me closer to him?

I never trusted him again.

The only thing that is crazy about me is coming back here; I am still too vulnerable, surrounded by sharks.

Distantly, I hear the chime of the grandfather clock that is in the hall at the top of the stairs. It is close to dinner. Grandfather would expect me to wear a dress, not jeans and a casual t-shirt.

There are rows of my old clothes hanging on the rods, boxes of mementos on the shelf above, and shoes on the rack. My room is another shrine to something dead. A shrine to the old me. As I realize this, I start to laugh, and even to my ears, it sounds a bit hysterical. *Overactive imagination said the doctor.*

I select a simple dress and pull on some low-heeled, slingback shoes. None of it is my style anymore, and as I look in the mirror, I see an old-me I've long outgrown.

Putting my toiletries away, I take a moment to splash some cold water on my face, but I'm still feeling shaken about the stolen debit and credit cards and the time-warped clothes closet. Without money I was vulnerable. They could force me back into a box they made for me.

This is temporary, I remind myself, but the eyes in the mirror are wide with fear. *Don't worry, you aren't a child anymore. Find Mother's killer and if you can't, leave anyway. They can't keep you here!*

Except I've committed who knows how many crimes in pretending to be other people. All it would take is a few calls to law enforcement, and I'd be locked up again. Forced to undergo another psych evaluation.

I need an escape plan. I am still thinking about how I can run away when I enter the hallway. My eyes instinctively go to the door to the room next to mine: Mother's room, and I'm surprised to see the doorknob start to turn.

Thinking it might be Ryan, I wait, but no one exits, and I take the knob in my hand. The metal of the knob is almost painfully cold. As I enter, there is a smell in the air of a woman's perfume and memory tells me it is Mother's signature scent.

Grandfather keeps Mother's bedroom the same as it was the day she left. Of course, at the time we thought she'd be back, so that was the first reason. The next was grief, and lastly guilt.

The room is not neglected. It's dusted and vacuumed. There are fresh flowers in a vase: Sally doing what her aunt has done for years. Keeping a dead woman's room ready for her return. Except we know now she won't come back. *Ever.*

It isn't like what you see on television with toys, teddy bears, or posters on the wall. It is an adult's room with a bed, nightstands, a table and chair, dresser, and a door to an en-suite bathroom. But the velvet drapes and the bedspread flower pattern are out of fashion. And at her bedside table is a book she will never finish.

It isn't like there are a lot of places to hide. I check under the bed and in the bathroom, the shower stall, and the walk-in closet, and find no one.

How did the doorknob move? Was it loose? It feels as secure as the one in my room, although it has a lock on it. I wonder if Aunt Belle had ever threatened my mother with removing hers? If she had, my aunt had failed to get it done.

I am about to leave the room when something whispers in my ear.

Zoe.

This house has always had a prankster in it. Some spirit that calls your name, pulls your hair, or tries to trip you on the stairs. Owen said it was Abraham, but I was never so sure.

This time the voice is female.

Is it *her* voice?

Opening my eyes, I look around the room, but nothing is different and whatever it is, doesn't speak again. Overactive imagination. Mother is on my mind and some old memory surfaced, filling in the blanks.

Sighing, I exit the room, and stand in the hallway deep in thought so at first I don't react to the man who passes me. I blink and watch him walk away down the hall to the stairs before I realize it was the man from the ferry. The man who had given money to the old woman.

I go after him and ask him, "What are you doing here?"

"Going to dinner."

"I mean, what are you doing *in this house*? Why are you *here*?"

He starts down the stairs and stops at my words. Behind his glasses, his eyes are brown-mossy green. "I'm researching your family's stories about Abraham Underhill. Your family has him all wrong."

The historian Owen had mentioned.

Before I can demand what he means, he continues down the stairs to the foyer and turns into the trophy room. I am left standing at the top of the staircase, dumbfounded.

What does my family have wrong?

Seven

Entering the trophy room, I notice immediately that more have arrived: Ryan's father, Robert Bancroft, and his wife, Marion. How was Sally going to stretch that lasagna?

The historian walks away from me and takes a seat at the fringe of the group. He opens a book to read, ignoring us all. As no one acknowledges him, for a moment I wonder if he is really there. Overactive imagination.

The married couple is seated on one of the two couches: Robert wears a long-sleeved designer shirt, his company logo prominent, and his arm rests behind Marion with a display of ownership. He surveys the room like he thinks he can buy it, but doubts it is worth the investment.

Marion wears too much makeup with bright Santa-red lipstick, and her hair is as stiff as a corpse because of layers of hairspray. Her brow is stretched tight, and her eyebrows do not move, but her eyes scan the room like a ferret. Both are in their late forties.

Robert is pontificating to Grandfather. "Naturally, it was an accident. Brynn was always exploring the National. Remember that time she claimed a bear chased her?"

A hulking brown-black shape, the musky smell of it, its size shocks my mind. I run. I share the fright from one of my mother's memories and for a moment I am in the woods, and not in this less civilized place.

Ryan touches my arm, bringing me back to the present. He is with an older woman that I don't recognize.

"Zoe. Sabrina Robinson, Mom's old friend."

Sabrina swoops in for a hug and smothers me in a cloud of perfume that is not like Mother's. She rests her hands on my upper arms and examines me. "I saw you last at Kitty's funeral, but I don't know if you'd remember that."

Grandmother Catherine, known by all as Kitty, passed from a stroke a few years after Brynn disappeared.

The scratchiness of a tulle underskirt, and tights that I pull up when no one is looking. My shiny white shoes that I wear at Easter are pretty, but they pinch. I am soon distracted, though, because this is my first funeral. There are many people shining with memories so bright that I go around touching everyone, making a nuisance of myself.

When I reach Grandfather, standing at the grave of his wife, the intensity of his grieving memories overwhelms me. Love-pride-possessiveness-irritation-demanding-wanting-mine, and under the bitter, salty taste of loss.

Feeling his feelings, I start to cry. Aunt Belle grabs my wrist, hauling me away so hard that she lifts me off the ground. "Behave! No one has time for your fits."

"A vague memory. I was only about nine. You wore a hat with roses that a bee took an interest in."

She laughs, her eyes crinkling in a friendly way as she releases me. "Yes! It chased me all over that graveyard! I had to take shelter in the limo."

Behind us, I hear Robert. "I'm just saying we need to get our stories straight, Nolan." *What story does Robert want us to testify to?*

To me, Sabrina confides, "I was in the class behind your mother, and two years behind Robert. I saw it all."

"All?"

"How she stole the high school football star and made him forget Harvard and marry her instead."

I know that story. It is an old one and often repeated with different emotional flavors, depending on who tells it. As if my mother was only this one event in her life. Irritated, I attempt to prevent a replay. "I've heard that one before."

She bends forward, inviting Ryan and me to lean closer. "She also had some older guy chasing her back in high school she never wanted to talk about. I think he was a teacher? Someone in his 40s. Old enough to be her father! I saw him a few times, outside the school, waiting for her."

This was something new, and before I could stop myself, I reached for her hand and asked, "What do you remember?"

A man with a hat pulled down low, trying to hide his face. Khaki pants with a button-down Oxford shirt. He's wearing a slouchy cardigan and brown leather loafers. Brynn, terribly young but breathtakingly beautiful, walks past him, shaking her head. She is visibly upset, and her cry is clear. "Just leave me alone! I told you no!"

"Brynn was so wild, back then! Men couldn't help but want her," are Sabrina's concluding words.

Ryan bristles, his ever-ready temper easily flares, especially when anyone casts aspersions on our mother. "There was a DNA test done, Sabrina. I *am* Robert's son. There is no doubt about that."

"Oh, no! I wasn't implying that!" She appears flustered, but there is a touch of cattiness in that round, friendly face with its dyed blond hair lacquered into submission. "What I mean is, what if *he's* the stalker? The one who murdered her because of an unhealthy obsession? That's what I told the police."

Should we be grateful for this piece of information? She clearly thinks so.

"What's that about the police?" calls Robert from across the room. The man prefers center-stage, with all eyes on him. Jealous or admiring ones, but eyes there must be. He and Grandfather are similar in this department, but while Grandfather easily commands centerstage, Robert is the understudy; not as good as the original, and he often forgets to leave the stage so the other actors can say their lines.

I cast a sideways glance at the stranger, curious to see if he is paying attention to the family drama, but his gaze is still on his book and while I watch him, he turns a page. He has beautiful hands, and his face is untroubled by the rising tension around him.

Well, two could play that game! I fade back, becoming wallpaper, removing myself from what will soon become another family scene I want no part of.

This is Ryan's role. Mother's champion.

"Sabrina was just telling us that Mom had a stalker back in high school. Do you know anything about that?" Ryan moves over to the male side of the room, where they are jockeying to win tonight's crown.

From private conversations, I know my brother has mixed feelings about his parentage. Two teenagers conducting a secret love affair under their parents' noses is romantic until one becomes pregnant.

Robert and Brynn had a shotgun wedding because Grandfather wasn't going to have his only child have a baby out-of-wedlock. Meanwhile, Robert's father furiously demanded Brynn abort it. He had big plans for Robert, and none included a teen marriage and a baby. The two families have been fighting ever since.

"Stalker?" As he considers the possibility of the stranger who visited Brynn at high school, Robert actually brightens. "You mean he returned and killed her?"

Next to him, Marion is lighting a cigarette like an old-fashioned movie actress. She says, "Oh yes, I remember him from when we were all back in school together. Looked like a professor. A nice average face." She utters *average* as if it is the worst adjective in the world, and in her circle, it probably is.

Robert nods. "Brynn was dodging someone back in those days. She kept changing where we would meet up. Didn't like to linger after school let out and stopped coming to my football practices."

Grandfather toys with his Sazerac; he is using it in his hand as a prop. He says nonchalantly, "Brynn took a college class during her last year of high school. Poetry, I think?"

"There, you see!" crows Robert, snapping his fingers. "That's the connection! Some college professor fixated on her."

Amongst all of this speculation, Sabrina asks me, "When do you think the memorial will be? I want to be here for that."

"I'm not sure."

Jennifer knows, though. "Nolan wants to have a meeting in a few days after we get settled to discuss the plans for it. I'll make sure you're invited. He wants to do it before the Gale celebration in November."

Meanwhile, across the room, the topic has moved to discussing Ryan's future.

"No, I'm not moving back. I've told you I have no interest in the family business." Ryan's patience on the topic is worn thin, for we've heard this for over a decade, ever since Ryan turned eighteen.

"I can't keep the door open for much longer," says Robert, oblivious to his son's mood.

Ryan shrugs. "Close it. I have a good business selling and renting real estate in the city." He gives a sideways glance at Grandfather and adds, "Besides, my future is here, at the Big House, when Nolan decides it's time to retire."

Grandfather doesn't speak and only swirls the ice in his glass.

Robert won't let go. "I see you're playing hard to get, Ryan, but I can't make you a member of the board. You'd have to start as a department head, but not over research and development. The laws about how we test our drugs are too complicated for someone to understand right away."

Once again, my brother declines. "I'm not going into the family business today, tomorrow, or next year! Peddle your painkillers to the masses on your own."

Taking a deep drag on her cigarette, his stepmom has the hoarse, deep female voice of a chain smoker. "I don't remember you saying no to our nasty drug money when you enjoyed all the perks of being a frat boy skipping classes without consequences."

Ryan becomes waspish. "Which I've been paying back, dear Marion, or hasn't Robert told you that? You want me to trot out the receipts showing each check I've sent compensating Robert for my college tuition?"

Grandfather throws back his head and laughs, slapping his thigh with the palm of the hand not holding his glass. "You tell them, my boy! Better yet, I'll pay off the balance now. Someone, get me my checkbook."

At the mention of paying off debt, my gaze slips to Owen where he sits quietly, trying to pretend he doesn't exist. Unlike the historian, he is not succeeding, and I am painfully aware of his discomfort at the mention of Grandfather playing Lord Bountiful. He is looking every bit of eighty and his thin lips are tightly pressed together lest he say something he will regret.

Owen pleads with Nolan to help with his wife's bills. Nolan refuses. "I can't continue bailing you out, Owen. You need to stand on your own."

"But the hospital said if I can't make a payment now, they won't treat her. It's an experimental procedure. Cutting-edge. With a deposit, I can get her into the trial group. We've tried everything else—"

"It's a harsh lesson to learn, but you need to keep better control of your finances."

"You don't know a damn thing about my finances!"

"Stay out of it, Nolan. I don't want your help," Ryan tells Grandfather.

"Don't be so prideful. You'll regret dipping into your inheritance, just as my brother did. Let me help."

Owen can no longer contain himself and rises from his seat and leaves. Only I, and the historian sitting with his book, notice his departure. Our eyes meet but his are too enigmatic to read what he is thinking. His gaze lingers on me so long that I grow flustered under his scrutiny, my cheeks growing warm. I don't even know why I'm embarrassed? Because of the family squabbling? Why should I care if he sees it?

Aunt Belle rushes to protect her favorite. "Don't you bring that up again! The trust money is his to do as he wants."

"I should be the one in charge of it," grumbles Grandfather.

Perhaps with the familiarity of decades, Aunt Belle thinks she can argue with him. "The Abraham trust was for future generations to enjoy. You had your share."

The bible-thumping merchant, Abraham Underhill, set up the trust and its rules. When a direct descendant reaches twenty-one, they get their portion. It's managed by a group of trustees, not family, and it is a sore point with Grandfather that he isn't on the board, despite using his gift against them all in an attempt to Charm them to his way of thinking. It was this money which had allowed my flight when I came of age.

Some people like to stir the pot. Others throw the pot in the fire so the grease catches.

"Since Brynn died so young, at least you got to keep her portion, Nolan. Her murder seems to have benefited all of you," says Marion.

"Marion!" exclaims Aunt Belle.

At that moment, Sally enters and announces that dinner is ready, which means we can now use knives to cut each other instead of words.

EIGHT

The dinner table becomes a battleground, but I am surprised to see who the combatants are.

Grandfather takes the seat at the head of the table. What Ryan and I call the king position, as if the table is a chessboard. This places him under the painting that hangs on the wall behind him. The portrait of Abraham with his son Seaborn, Nolan's father.

Abraham, in his senior years with a full beard, dressed in a black frock coat, is seated with an open book in his hand. Leaning casually against the chair's arm is Seaborn. He is probably around eight or nine. With his blond hair tousled as if he just come in from playing outdoors, the boy is uninterested in the book that his father is looking down at. Instead, he is staring at you, his light blue eyes already holding secrets.

It was supposedly painted as a gift to Sarah, Abraham's wife, but if so, where are the other boys? Levi, Matthew, and John? Their lack always irritated me. Weren't they worthy of being immortalized?

It shocks me when Ryan sits in Kitty's queen chair at the opposite end of the table. It has remained empty since her death.

Jennifer takes the seat to his left, and Ryan indicates that I am to take my place on his right. For a moment I hesitate, but when I do, I don't look at Grandfather. Now our alliance is out in the open.

Owen's historian sits next to me, Sabrina on his other side. Across from us are Owen, Marion, Robert, and Aunt Belle. When I lean back slightly, I can be out of Grandfather's line of sight. If Ryan wants to play such games, let him take the brunt of Grandfather's ire.

Sally must have been given a heads-up to expect more guests for dinner, for the lasagna is nowhere in sight. Instead, soup and salad, and an entrée of halibut with a side of roasted fingerling potatoes and carrots, appear. It is served by a teenager who quickly gives us our plates before exiting through the door to the kitchen.

"You really should come to the preview, Sabrina. It's only for donors and special guests. It would be a shame for you to miss it." Owen is trying to convince Mother's old friend to come to the museum's private showing.

"Museums really aren't my thing," Sabrina says, giving a self-conscious laugh. "Instead, I thought to do some shopping now that they've opened that boutique area on the boardwalk. You never know what you might pick up in one of these specialty shops."

"But it's the history of the town. Where you grew up. Surely you want to know about your roots." Owen is hurt, and in his excitement about one of his favorite hobbies, forgets it never pays to show vulnerability at the Underhill table. The sword is quick to fall. From the king's seat, Grandfather tells him, "Stop pestering her, Owen. She clearly doesn't want to go."

Owen is like the dog that won't stop begging for attention from the owner who beats it. "But it's *our* history. It's important. It makes the Underhills who we are."

Ryan's father, Robert, says sarcastically, "Not everyone is interested in stories about the Underhills."

Owen turns bright red, either in embarrassment or anger, I'm not sure. "If we aren't important, why do you think the Smithsonian sent a professor down here to study us? Duncan came here to do valuable research, which means the tale of the Great Gale *is* important! Our family is important."

"Of course, it's important." Grandfather's words drip with condescension. "Otherwise, the museum wouldn't have won the grant that pays for Mr. Crane's salary while he resides here at the Big House, pawing through our personal belongings."

Finally, the man blocking my view of Grandfather has a name: Duncan Crane. He is wearing a dark navy long-sleeved shirt, with stone-gray slacks and a leather belt the shade of weathered horse saddles. The shirt is a slim fit that shows the line of his body to advantage, and he smells of the outdoors, as if just came in from raking leaves or shopping for a Christmas tree. Wholesome. It didn't seem right for a history geek to exude Hallmark boy-next-door sexy.

Maybe I couldn't see Grandfather, but I could still hear him. "The oral family history about the Great Gale is probably the most valuable contribution the museum has."

Duncan finally speaks. "I disagree."

All the wolves around the table stop their conversations and go on alert. Heads turn towards Grandfather, wondering what he will do with this challenge. Even Sabrina has stopped discussing shopping opportunities with Jennifer.

"Disagree with what?" There is surprise in Grandfather's question, for in his arrogance he is caught off-guard.

Duncan's voice never rises above a mild, almost dismissive tone. He speaks as if giving a lecture on explaining composting and can't even be bothered to make it interesting.

"Your belief that Abraham Underhill's story is the most important one that Kingstowe has to offer. He is only one of several founding families that have played an important role in the area's history."

Grandfather's voice makes me shrink smaller. I use Duncan as a shield to dull the blows of his words.

"Without Abraham, there wouldn't be a Kingstowe! He was fundamental in stopping the Gale, turning it aside so the town survived when many others along the coastline did not."

Duncan is unaffected by the emotions swirling around the dinner table and replies calmly, "What Abraham did or said is only a family story. While oral anecdotes are interesting and can give a view of an event, they are often not accurate. If we are to know the real Abraham Underhill, that requires research to find documentation about him. There is nothing in the contemporary newspaper reports about Abraham's behavior during the storm."

I tremble, feeling Grandfather's rage. *Shut up-shut up-shut up,* my brain pleads to Duncan.

Grandfather says with haughty disdain. "Are you calling my family liars?"

"Families lie all the time."

I suck in my breath.

"I think I know the truth about my own family."

Even Owen is awakened to the danger and he is studying his plate with the intensity a surgeon gives during surgery to his patient.

"You know part of the truth. Your pride prevents you from seeing other aspects of it," says Duncan.

"What do you think you know about this family that I do not?" An icy blast comes down the table from the king.

"Your legend states that Sarah's son, Levi, is her firstborn. That is incorrect. She had twin girls before him."

Seated next to him, I can see that Duncan's hands are perfectly steady as he cuts the fish with his fork and brings a piece to his mouth. How can Duncan continue eating while my stomach tries to decide on whether to throw up?

"The family bible—" begins Grandfather, only to be cut off by Duncan. "Is wrong. From the ink and the style of the cursive writing, it's clear the entries listing the children of Abraham and Sarah were put in at a much later date. I suspect it was done in the 1940s or 50s."

Duncan's voice warms to his topic. He is in his element now and excited by finding research others did not know. "The 1890 census records would have cleared this mistake up long ago, but it was destroyed. Instead, by not letting myself be swayed by stories, I found a Kingstowe church record showing a set of twins baptized at age six weeks with their parents listed as Abraham and Sarah."

Grandfather barks, "Then where are they? *Where* are *they*?"

Duncan gives the answer. "Buried in a Portland graveyard. Sarah and Abraham were visiting relatives there when their girls died."

Grandfather is pole-axed as he tries to assimilate this new bit of information. Before he can recover, Duncan continues dissecting the Underhills, pinning us down like dead butterflies.

"Abraham and Sarah had six children: the twin girls who died, Levi, who was with his parents during the storm; Seaborn, Matthew, and John. Levi died in World War I and John in World War II. Neither had children. Only Seaborn and Matthew had families, and Matthew moved from Kingstowe to California."

I couldn't help myself and looked up at the portrait of Abraham and Seaborn. The son that mattered. Grandfather's father and grandfather. My great and great-great grandfathers. My great-uncle Matthew only had sons, and his sons only had boys. I am the only female descendant that is living. It is a strange anomaly, and one reason Grandfather had doted upon Brynn, and later transferred that affectionate pride to me. We were girls. Special trophies.

The first person who is brave enough to speak is Robert's wife, Marion. "Fascinating."

Her bored sarcastic drawl breaks some of the tension. After her foolish remark about Brynn's death in the trophy room, she has retreated behind a mask of silent disdain until now.

As usual, when Robert is brave enough to speak, he is dismissive of our family heritage. "A storm that re-shapes the coastline and removes an entire beach is dramatic enough, don't you think, without adding Abraham Underhill to it?"

"The Great Gale's history is nothing without the Underhills! Nothing." Owen can't help himself from defending our bloodline. To him, Abraham's story of defeating the Gale means we are anointed in the eyes of God. While Grandfather wins trophies to put on his shelves to show the world his superiority, Owen collects photographs, journals, and newspaper clippings that support his theory that we are blessed by some divine force. If he ever lost that belief, I don't know if he could survive the blow.

Ryan, who is not a dreamer, says ironically, "The legend of Abraham's plea to God to stop the storm becomes far less dramatic if you bring facts into it, Mr. Crane."

Grandfather gives a chuckle that to my ears sounds forced. "Not everything in this town has to be about us."

I'm astonished to realize that he is gracefully allowing Duncan to score his point because he knows he is losing the argument. Better to look like the king giving a magnanimous blessing to an inferior rather than appearing bested.

It was all about us. Duncan can talk about stories and what are facts, but the descendants of Abraham knew something he did not. Abraham bartered his soul and ours to turn the storm. We were marked by the Gale, given gifts (or curses), which meant we would always pay the price of saving Kingstowe.

NINE

I escape the after-dinner-coffee talk. Not only would it have been more of the same posturing, but the jiggle of the doorknob of my mother's room still bothers me. Did it move because of some tremor in the house? Was a breeze strong enough to do that?

Standing outside her room, I forcefully jump up and down, trying to get it to move. When it does nothing, I stomp up and down the hall, keeping an eye on it, but it still doesn't budge.

Inside the room, I play with turning the knob. It takes the usual force to get it to turn, as it is not loose, with strong screws holding the plate in place on the door frame. The window is closed as it was earlier. My hand passes over the air vent, but the gentle puffs of air aren't strong enough to even flutter the curtains.

Of course, Owen would say it was our ancestral spirit playing tricks, but even a paranormal investigator would say you need to eliminate a human cause first. Besides, Mother's room had never shown activity before, so why now?

Secret panel? I start to tap on the walls, and when the bedroom door opens, I swing around to see Duncan Crane.

"I'm in the room on the other side and heard the knocking." My fist is still upraised, paused mid-knock, and I quickly tuck it behind my back. He enters my mother's room. "What are you doing? Searching for a safe or a secret passage?"

Feeling like an idiot, I replied truthfully, "Secret passage."

He closes the door behind him. "Do you know what to listen for?"

"Do you?" I ask accusingly.

"Yes. I'll show you." He comes over to where I stand and reaches over my head taps along the wall, demonstrating how the taps can sound either hollow or solid. He is still wearing the clothes from dinner, and still appearing outrageously normal in this house that isn't.

"I guess being a historian you've searched old houses looking for secrets." *You might have found one or two, but you won't find them all.*

He contradicts my assumption, "No. I worked on remodeling old homes in college. You need to know where the studs and utilities run in the wall before you knock them down."

"Are you always so contrary?"

"I don't know what you mean?"

"If I said it was night, you'd say it was day."

"More accurately, I would point out that night is only temporary and is followed by day."

To stop myself from rolling my eyes, I go to the other wall and start tapping. We work ourselves around the room and even into the closet but find nothing suspicious.

"Most likely, if your mother wanted to leave, she'd climb out the window. There's a pretty stout tree branch you can get to."

Instinctively, I glance out the window, but this side of the house shows the sea, and I immediately look away. The pounding of the waves has been in my head all day and it is getting harder to ignore it.

"I've been thinking about what you said at dinner. You don't think the story about Abraham and the Great Gale ever happened?"

"There is a statue of Abraham in the town square, so someone thought him important enough to put it there. But I think the tale got embellished over time. Would you like to see what I'm working on?"

I nod and we leave Mother's room together.

Downstairs, he brings me to a sitting room that is at the side of the house. In my grandmother's day, Kitty used it as her personal retreat, for it has double doors leading into the garden. Now the couch is shoved to the edge of the room, to make space for a long table that is stacked with notebooks, binders, boxes, and papers. He touches the stacks reverently as he talks.

"The Internet has sped up the process of collecting the information, but only if the original records have been scanned and stored for viewing. You'd be surprised to find what is still tucked away, secreted away in attics or cellars. Journals, diaries, scrapbooks, photographs. All of it gives us a perspective of people's lives."

Being an outsider, he intrigues me, and I edge closer, wondering what a touch would discover. But in the end, I'm too chicken and don't take advantage of my gift. Sometimes, you'd rather not know what people are remembering.

Duncan reaches for what looks like a shoebox and explains it is a container designed to store documents without affecting them. He hands me a pair of white cotton gloves and puts on a pair himself. "The oil in our skin can get on what we handle and eventually could destroy or stain the paper."

Outfitted like scientists, Duncan lifts the lid and reveals a stack of creamy paper.

"Letters between your ancestor Sarah Underhill and her family. Some of her cousins in Portland loaned them to us for this project. I hope to convince them to donate them to your museum."

"It's not *my* museum. The museum is about the town, not my family."

He gives me an oblique look, and I feel like we are back on the ferry again with me not understanding what he's trying to say.

Duncan brings out a letter from the stack.

"In this one, she writes about losing her twins to Diphtheria." I lean over to see an ornate script that looks like it should be on the Declaration of Independence. "It's not until the 1920s that vaccinations significantly decreased the mortality rates."

"You sound like a professor."

He chuckles; a nice warm sound that holds no sharpness. "Sorry about that. Both of my parents were academics. Retired now."

I read Sarah's writing:

"The two darlings breathed so hard that I held them upright in my arms, hoping to give them air. Their skin flushed with fever from the disease. I wish we had never come to this cursed city and long for the comfort our home could have given them during this horrible illness that has set their skin on fire."

It is almost like a memory, and I feel a rush of hunger, wanting to consume all that she wrote. "Do you have any more?"

He gives that soft chuckle again, and I take a deep breath of his scent, which is a masculine earthy woodsy blend of cardamom, cypress, and coffee.

"You've been bitten by the bug." He draws a binder over, flipping it open. There is a page marked with a sticky label and his finger draws a line across the page. "This is a printed record of the 1910 census for Kingstowe. Here is the entry for Abraham and Sarah Underhill, and their household of three children: Levi, Seaborn, and Matthew. Newspaper articles confirm that Abraham's profession is now a self-employed shopkeeper and post office manager. He's still a church deacon, but he is spending most of his time now doing city business."

His finger points to a box on the census record that shows a number. "Here you see where the family lists two dead children and three living. The address for their home matches where you live now, and it is listed as a farm, free of a mortgage."

"It tells you all of that?"

By now, our heads are close together and I feel a racing anticipation as the hour is getting late, and it is then when reality slips into romance.

"Yes, this was one of the more in-depth U.S. censuses that were done."

Our cheeks are very close and he turns his head and I see up close one of his hazel eyes with its matrix of green and brown.

If he touches me, what will I learn?

His breath is warm on my cheek, and I close my eyes in anticipation of knowing him both with my gift and my lips. But his next words startle me.

"I came here to find you, Zoe Underhill."

My head jerks back and my eyes open. "What do you mean?"

His eyes are solemn, and it frightens me.

"My father knew your mother."

"How do you mean he *knew* her? Are you saying we're siblings?"

This time he's the surprised one and says emphatically. "No! Not at all! My parents are *my* parents." Duncan's hand is held up in a gesture of helpless explanation.

"I think you need to explain yourself. *Right now.*" My heart is beating fast, and I feel I am standing on a precipice. Who is this man to barge into my life and tell me about my mother? How did he get here? I'm feeling confused, but also hostile.

He pushes his wire-framed glasses back up his nose. Harmless. Hallmark Channel, remember? But I was beginning to think his appearance of normality is in reality a sinister front.

"My father met your mother when she attended a class he was teaching as a summer artist-in-residence at a nearby college. Sabrina Robinson mentioned him visiting your mother at the high school. But she misinterpreted his intentions. They weren't romantic; he wanted Brynn to apply to college, but she refused."

"She got married right out of high school because she was pregnant." *Was he telling me the truth? If not, why lie?*

"You were big on proof at dinner. You'll have to show me something that supports this theory of yours."

"Brynn sent my father a letter a few years later, asking if he would help her apply. She enrolled the year before she conceived you. I have a copy of her transcript. Illegally gained, I'm afraid."

Duncan gets up slowly, as if he is afraid of frightening me away, and goes to the end of the table. Unbuckling a leather satchel, he pulls out a manila envelope and leans forward, extending his arm so I don't have to move closer to him in order to take it.

My hand shakes as I pull the papers out. Like he said, it is a transcript with my mother's name, address, and birthdate on it. There is a letter and as I unfold it, my eyes go first to the signature to see the familiar signature of Brynn Underhill. She wrote this to his father, Philip Crane, about eighteen months before I was born.

I've reconsidered your offer to help me enroll in college and would like to pursue a degree in literature after all. Is there any way you could assist me?

She would have been twenty-one and with access to her share of the Underhill trust. I am pretty sure that Robert, Ryan's father, didn't know about this. Neither did Grandfather nor Aunt Belle. All those times they thought she was sneaking out to see a boy, she was attending classes?

Duncan keeps talking and I stare at him, barely comprehending his words. "From what I've gleaned from your family members, it seems they suspect she was involved with someone romantically."

My tongue is thick, and I hear myself say from a distance, "You know who he is, don't you? My father?"

"It was my father's teaching assistant. His name was Michael Gardner."

"Was?" Everything in the room becomes fuzzy, and the roaring in my ears almost drowns out his reply. I can't catch my breath, and it seems an elephant is sitting on my chest. Far off, I hear the crashing waves of the sea and a woman's voice calls my name: *Zoe*.

"He died in a car crash about two months before you were born."

I put the documents back into the envelope and stood up. This is all too much and in typical Zoe fashion, I need to get away.

"I need time to think about this."

"I'm sure it's a shock—."

Shock? He just turned my entire world upside down. Everything I thought I knew about my mother would need to be re-evaluated.

"So, you came here to give this to me?"

"Yes. I heard about the museum's request and told my boss I'd go. I'd hoped we would meet, and I could pass this information along to you."

Our meeting was all arranged. Planned by him so he could let a girl finally know who her daddy was? How benevolent of him.

"Why now? Why not years ago? I'm twenty-six years old."

Perhaps he expected me to greet his news with jubilation, for Duncan now appears uncertain, his cheeks faintly flushed with embarrassment or shame. "When Brynn dropped her classes, my father came here wanting to convince her to come back. He never saw her, only Nolan. Your grandfather let him know he was unwelcome."

"Are you saying Grandfather knew that Brynn was going to college? That she had dropped out? That she was pregnant with Michael Gardner's child?"

Grandfather had never revealed anything about this meeting to me.

"My father didn't tell Grandfather about Michael. He only

wanted to convince your mother to come back and finish her studies. To achieve her dream of getting a degree."

I pull away, walking to the door in a haze, my hands clutching the envelope.

"If I can help—?"

"Oh, I think you've helped enough, don't you?"

TEN

Sleep usually brings me a welcome oblivion from my overactive imagination. A void to be nothing, hold nothing, remember nothing.

"Zoe."

The woman's voice awakens me. As I slowly come back to awareness, I'm holding myself defensively, hunched around a pillow, my arm thrown over my head as if protecting myself from a blow. I bring my arm down and pull down the covers, straining to hear.

At first, it sounds like a cat wailing.

I throw off the covers and grab my robe off the chair. Peering out the window, all I see is the dark as the nightstand clock tells me it is just past one in the morning. There is no moon, so the only lights visible are dotted spots in the distance marking the location of neighboring houses hidden behind trees.

Thumbing the latches, I lift the window and immediately feel a rush of cool night air and smell the salt of the sea. Distantly, I hear a boat's horn. The wind picks up and there is a whisper of leaves as they rustle from the breeze.

No. These sounds are not coming from outside.

Retreating from the windowsill, I go to the door and slowly open it a crack. It is louder. Some child is upset, and no one is comforting them. My schoolteacher emotions kick in; no child suffers on my watch.

Behind me, I close the door softly, my fingers trailing away on the latch. This side of the hall has my room, Mother's, and the guest room for Duncan Crane. Across the hall are Ryan and Jennifer's suite. Grandfather, Uncle Owen, and Aunt Belle live in the wing on the other side of the staircase.

Should I wake Ryan? If it was only him, I would tap on his door, but I knew Jennifer would make a fuss about his crazy sister wanting attention. Ryan's obligations as my brother have been waived for those of a husband.

What if it turns out to be a cat? Or maybe a fox? They can sound pretty wild during mating season. I'd look stupid if I woke up Ryan over a caterwauling from animals. I'd never hear the end of it.

My bare feet are quiet as I make my way down the carpet runner to the top of the staircase. The stairwell acts as a noise funnel and the sound is even louder, rising from somewhere below.

The child sobs as if her heart is breaking. *Why doesn't someone do something?* Going down the stairs in a sideways crab walk, I look up, but no one is following me, and from peering over the banister rail, the foyer appears empty. I reach the floor, and the stone is cool under my feet.

"Zoe." The whisper is in my ear and I reach up to swat at the tickle, finding nothing but air.

I realize now where the noise is coming from; it is from the cupboard under the stairs where we store winter coats and rain boots.

When Grandfather would host evening parties, Ryan and I would be tucked away in bed for an early bedtime, but we'd creep downstairs to hide in this closet. Each time someone's coat would be hung up, we'd suppress a fit of giggles because they didn't notice two kids concealed in the back under a blanket. Once the party started, we would creep out, playing spies, listening in on the adult conversations.

Is a child hiding in the closet behind the umbrellas?

The sobbing is quieter. It is the sound of someone who has given up hope that anyone will come. *But she's wrong.* I've come.

My hand grips the cool smooth metal of the knob and I twist it, opening the door to reveal the heavy dark coats and rain slickers hanging inside. Reaching forward, I pull them back to see who is hiding, only to face the woman from the ferry, wearing her fisherman's knit cap and overalls.

"You're running out of time to save her, Zoe."

I open my mouth, but my throat is too paralyzed to scream.

Scrambling backward, I slam the door and run for the stairs, but in my panic, I crash into Duncan Crane, coming down them. He steadies me as I am shaking violently.

"I heard you leave your room. What's wrong?"

Not able to speak, I point back towards the closet. He puts me behind him, but when he opens it, there is no woman, only coats.

In my room, I throw my suitcase on the bed and start pulling clothes from my closet. Duncan, who has followed me, says, "The ferry doesn't make a run until six a.m."

That stops me. I'd have to take the ferry. Crossing the sea. I ask demandingly, "You have a car?"

"Yes."

"Would you take me to the bus station?"

Duncan speaks calmly, which infuriates me more. Is he a man who never gets excited, worried? *Screams?* "Why don't you tell me what this is about? Why did you go downstairs in the middle of the night? What did you think was in the closet?"

My bank card! I don't have the money to pay for the bus

ticket. Which is probably the intention of the person who stole it. If Duncan bought me a ticket, Ryan or Grandfather would demand to know where, and they'd track me down and bring me back.

My teeth worry my lip. "I thought I heard a child crying."

Instead of laughing, Duncan becomes thoughtful. "There are things that mimic a crying child, usually to entrap an unwary person to their death. Do you know of any child that has died in this house?"

I gape at him. "You believe me?"

His hand comes up to push his gold-rimmed glasses up his nose. "The depth of your fright tells me something happened. I've been here for about a month, and I've witnessed odd things, to say the least. This house is unusual, as are the people in it."

Pressing the heels of my hands to my forehead as if to hold my brain inside of my head, I say, "Maybe I am crazy, like they all say. But I promise you I'm not on drugs."

"I didn't think you were. Whatever you saw frightened you deeply."

Worried, I asked him, "Did you give that woman on the ferry the other half of that twenty?"

"I couldn't find her after we crossed over, so I folded it and tucked it into a slot on the boat's bulkhead."

"She's here to collect it." *Zoe, you sound hysterical.* I tell my inner voice to shut the hell up. I'll be as hysterical as I wanted to be.

Duncan comes to me and grips me by my shoulders. We are not quite eye to eye, and I look up at a face that looks immensely sane. *At least one of us here is.*

"Is that what you saw?" I nod my head mutely. "Did she say anything?" My voice trembles as I repeat it to him. He frowns in concentration, as he replies, "It said *her*? Do you think it was speaking of your mother?"

"How can I save my mother? She's dead." My voice cracks on the last word as I begin to cry. It is the first time since I heard the news from Ryan that I've allowed the dam holding back my grief to crack. My mother is dead. *Really dead.*

Duncan's arms come around me, and he brings me close to his chest. It is not sexual, just sorely needed comfort. I gain a vague memory of a princess in a castle, some Renaissance faire nonsense, but I am too upset to focus on what weird Disney memory Duncan is recalling.

Eventually, my nose drip becomes more embarrassing than the need to cry. I pull away, saying, "I need some tissues from the bathroom."

The honking sound into the tissue isn't the most elegant, but it is effective in clearing out my nose. Calmer now, I return to the bedroom. "Maybe I imagined it? Like sleepwalking."

"Do you have such an active imagination?"

Yes, I do, Duncan Crane. I have such an overactive imagination that I can create a whole person just from stolen memories. "Hm. Yes."

Taking the chair next to the window, I bring my knees up, hugging my legs. "Since it doesn't look like I can leave right now, tell me what else you know about my mother."

He does not sit on the bed and since there isn't another chair; he takes the floor, sitting cross-legged. The envelope with the documents had fallen to the floor from the bed when I was sleeping, so he puts the paperwork back into order and slips it all back inside it.

"My father was invited to be an artist-in-residence the summer before Brynn's senior year of high school. She was one of three selected to experience college life before their senior year. It was a program to encourage students to commit to college and help them become comfortable with the campus."

"Was your father an artist?"

"A writer."

That makes far more sense. I had never seen any evidence that Brynn was into drawing or painting, but writing? Yes, I could see that. A dim memory of her writing in a journal drifted through my thoughts.

"He was really impressed by your mother's writing and thought she would be continuing her education at the university, but at the last moment, she withdrew her application. He came here to Kingstowe to reason with her, but she rejected him without telling him why. It was not until much later when he learned about your mother's marriage and Ryan."

Why did she have to give it all up because of a baby? Grandfather had money. She could have gone even with a husband and a baby. *But would Grandfather have permitted it?* Would Robert have allowed it?

Robert and Brynn had lived at the Big House after their marriage. What a hell it must have been for them both, for Grandfather and Aunt Belle would have watched them both like hawks. It was probably a big reason their marriage failed.

"How does this Michael Gardner figure into this story?"

"A few years later, your mother wrote to my father. They met, and he helped her with the paperwork and acted as her sponsor. By the spring semester, she was in love with my father's teaching assistant, Michael Gardner."

"The guy you believe is my father?"

"I have a picture of him. Do you want to see it?" I wave that idea away. Let's focus on the parent I know, and not some stranger who I was finding hard to believe existed. "I'm afraid my father was furious with both of them. His TA for what he felt was taking advantage of his protégé, and his protégé for getting pregnant again."

"Sometimes birth control doesn't work," I snap. I had heard many times how I was an unfortunate accident and really didn't need Duncan reminding me of it. "How many girls have you been with? Did you ever worry if they got pregnant after you strolled away? I doubt it!"

Like when he dealt with Grandfather's anger, Duncan became

still and quiet. His voice was kind and soft. "One day we can go over all the girls I've been with because I think I'll owe that information to you, but for now, I'd like to help you."

"Why?" I ask bluntly. It is almost four in the morning by the bedside clock, and the night's events had not made me feel generous and welcoming.

"My father felt he failed your mother. When I was a kid and begged for bedtime stories, he'd tell me about a beautiful princess trapped in a castle on an island, who was guarded by a troll. It would take the right prince to free her from the spell."

"Michael. But he never did come, did he?"

Duncan's fairytale had no answer to that. He looked down at his hands, avoiding my accusation.

"Dad only found out a year ago, when he was talking with an old student who lives in Kingstowe, that Brynn had disappeared. He couldn't believe that she'd leave her kids when she gave up her dream of being a writer for them. He couldn't come, but I'm here for Brynn and Brynn's daughter. If you'll take my help."

ELEVEN

An hour before dawn, I finally fall asleep. It is such a heavy, dead-to-the-world crash that I don't wake until well past noon.

After a hot shower, I find a note slipped under my door. It's from Duncan stating that he went into town for some scheduled interviews. It gives his cell phone number, which I immediately put into my phone.

My stomach growls, and hunger forces me to emerge from my lair and go down to the kitchen, where I find Sally. She gives me several choices for a meal, and I settle on a chicken salad sandwich.

"Let me toast the bread for you. It will taste better that way. Trust me." She leans over the toaster, a household goddess focused on creating nurturing food.

"I meant what I said yesterday. I'd love to see Happy and catch up. She was very kind to me when I was a kid."

"I'm sure she'd love to see you." Sally rattles off her phone number and I add it to my cell. "She's never home on Tuesdays and Thursdays. Those are her garden and book club days. And in the morning, she's a teacher's helper at the elementary school."

"Ryan tells me you have kids?"

"Yes, two boys. They're at school right now."

"One of them wasn't serving us dinner last night?"

She laughs. "No! That was a high school kid who helps me out when we have guests. Mine are in middle school. One wants to be a physicist and the other a professional baseball player."

Neither sound like boys who'd cry in a closet. Or dress up like an old woman to play a prank on me.

"They never stay the night here, do they?"

Her open countenance shifts to one that is clearly uncomfortable with what she is about to say. "No. Because of Abraham."

Ah. She means the resident ghost that everyone thinks is our ancestor, the founder of the Gale-blessed.

"So, he's still about turning on and off lights, is he? Slamming doors? Rattling doorknobs by chance?"

She makes my sandwich, something I could have done myself. It felt weird having a servant again after all this time of living on my own. "I'm afraid he's gotten a bit worse."

"How so?"

"Nolan doesn't want us to talk about it."

"Because then he'll go away? Fat chance."

She hands me the plate with my sandwich and gives me a weak smile. Sally won't say more if Grandfather commands her not to so I abandon the topic and after thanking her, I take my plate and a glass of lemonade through to the dining room. I find Ryan and Jennifer in the middle of their lunch.

Ryan greets me with an interrogation. "Where have you been?"

"I slept late." What he really wants is an accounting of my detection plans. "I'll probably be meeting Sally's aunt tomorrow to reminisce about old times. And plan to meet our old gardener after that."

"Good."

The sound of something crashing interrupts us, and we all

exchange surprised looks. Ryan exits to the hall, with Jennifer and I following behind.

It is easy to locate where the noise came from, for Grandfather is shouting. We find him in the trophy room arguing with a stranger that Jennifer identifies to me. "Ben Summers, the mayor."

"That land was promised to me!"

Summers is clearly uncomfortable, as anyone would be when you are the focus of Grandfather's rage. "I can't control who sells their land or to whom they do."

Grandfather's face is red. "I forbid it!"

Summer again denies any responsibility. "The sale is between Robert Bancroft and Seamus Covington. You'll have to ask one of them to back out of the contract."

Ryan involves himself. "What land deal?"

Summers answers because Grandfather's is too busy gnashing his teeth. "It's an undeveloped eighty-acre tract just north of the golf course."

The description rings a bell with Ryan, and his face illuminates with understanding. "I do remember Mr. Covington promising Nolan first dibs, but that was like over a decade ago. Was it listed for sale recently?"

"It was done behind my back!" retorts Grandfather's. He paces to the windows and looks seaward. His hands are clasped behind his back, knotted together in frustration.

"It was a private sale. The land was never listed publicly," explains Summers to my brother.

"Covington must be ancient?" Ryan muses.

"Ninety-two," Summers supplies.

"This is *your* father's doing," says Grandfather, still showing us all only his rigid back.

Ryan doesn't disagree. "If Robert knew you wanted it, he'd grab it out of spite."

Ryan's dad has certainly cut Grandfather off at the knees. It was probably why he had looked so smug at dinner.

The mayor edges toward the doorway and says in a hesitant, awkward rush, "I'll be going now. I just thought you should know before the sale goes through." For a moment more, Summers stands awkwardly, shifting from foot to foot as if he is at a starter's block and the gun hasn't gone off yet. When Grandfather doesn't respond, he makes a run for it.

After the echo of the front door closing fades, Grandfather spins around to face off with Ryan. "What do you know about it? Were you in on this deal?"

Ryan shakes his head. "As I said last night, I stay out of my father's business. You should go over there and Charm Covington. At his age, he should be easy to persuade."

Grandfather doesn't like failures, especially any he is involved in, so he admits the next bit reluctantly. "I tried. He wouldn't budge. Said he was keeping it for his grandchildren to enjoy hunting on it. What a liar!"

The broken vase on the floor suddenly has a matching one as Grandfather sweeps its mate off the sofa table to crash onto the wooden floor. I flinch, pulling back, but Ryan leans in, as if Grandfather's rage feeds something in him. We were always this way as children: Ryan thrived on the confrontation; I wanted only to retreat.

"I heard that the new exhibit building at the museum isn't being named after Grandmother Kitty like it was supposed to be. What is going on around here? Are you losing your grip?"

Grandfather snaps, "I don't know what you mean."

Ryan's response is just as terse. "This town is ours to look after."

Even though it is true, it feels wrong to speak of owning a town, like talking about sex outside the bedroom. I look down at my feet, embarrassed for everyone.

Grandfather's posture reminds me of Ryan's at the gas station. Tall, legs spread slightly, shoulders back, with his chin at an arrogant tilt. "Of course, it is still ours. Never doubt it."

"I do doubt it." My brother is calmly self-assured; the young lion facing off with the old.

Grandfather cuts the air with the flat edge of his hand. "You haven't been back home for more than a fly-by visit, so don't preach to me about the state of things around here. What do you care? Or about me? The man who raised you after your mother ran off?!"

Ran off to die. Let's get the facts straight.

I am forced to admire my brother, as he is not intimidated, but matches Grandfather's mood and raises it. "After Mother's disappearance, Kitty died. It's been one disaster after another. Haven't you made the connection, yet? We're being punished."

Grandfather is stunned, as if Ryan's words are the ones with a punch. "That isn't why—? Kitty had a stroke."

Ryan is relentless. "We need to know what happened to Mother and until we do, nothing around here is going to go right! Was Marion's accusation last night, right? Did you murder my mother for her trust money? Or was it because she dared to tell you no?"

I gasp. Grandfather's fist goes flying, but Ryan must be expecting such a move, for he steps aside like some sort of ninja before it can connect. There is a tense and silent stare between them before Ryan storms past me, grabbing Jennifer by the arm, and going out the front door, slamming it behind them.

Before I escape, Grandfather notices me. His nostrils flare as he is breathing hard, like a racehorse who has spent it all. He shouts, "Are you going to accuse me of harming my own daughter?"

You knew she was at college, so why did you let me believe she was chasing boys? Why did you keep your princess locked up in the castle?

How I wish to touch him and taste his memories, but I fear what they will tell me. I say lamely, "I'm sure Ryan doesn't think that."

"He does." Grandfather steps toward me and I instinctively back up. While my grandfather had never touched me with violence, I'd seen what he could do. My movement causes his face to break into pieces, and his voice cracks as he pleads. "Zoe. I would never hurt you! Or her!"

Thinking of all the times he hit my brother with such force that it sent Ryan to the ground or slammed him into walls, it is hard to respond without lying. Perhaps it is way past time for some honesty.

"Sometimes your emotions do get away from you."

"I would never ever have hurt Brynn. Get that notion right out of your head!"

Instead, a silent film of exactly how that could have happened rolls through my mind. *Too easy to see Brynn defying her father and Grandfather striking her. He's strong and causes more harm than he ever intended. Conceals the evidence so he won't have to face what he's done.* The images seem so real that my stomach lurches and I blurt out, "Was it an accident—?"

"There was *no* accident! The last time I saw her was the night before."

"I remember the two of you arguing." I hadn't meant to consciously mock him, though that phrase seemed to do so.

"Yes, but that was earlier in the week and has nothing to do with her death. Trust me on that."

"What was the argument about?"

He shakes his head like a befuddled bear. Grandfather doesn't want to think about it. "Nothing important. Brynn was being disrespectful of her mother after Kitty had asked—" Grandfather's mouth clamps shut.

"Asked what?" Caught, he knows he must answer if he wants me to believe he didn't harm my mother.

"Who your father is. That's all we wanted to know, but she wouldn't tell us."

How I want to throw it in his face that I know my mother was going to college and had abandoned it when her lover died. But why tell the man who told me for years my mother was a tart who ran off to be with some man, abandoning her children?

A wave of weariness comes over me. I tire of these games and think again about how easy it would be to leave and become someone else, like I've done so many times before. *Was this how my mother felt? Exhausted from fighting to defend her right to exist as herself?*

"I hope you are telling me the truth."

"I am. Tell Ryan what I said because he'll believe it if it comes from you."

Oh no, I wasn't going to clean up his mess! It was time Grandfather learned how to do that himself. He'd relied upon Charm to get him out of trouble, but that would be ineffectual against Ryan, who knew how it worked from the inside out.

"What do you think really happened to my mother?"

Grandfather is quick to answer. "A lover. No doubt in my mind. She Charmed the wrong person and paid for it with her life."

I glare at him. "Are you saying it was her fault that she's dead? Because she was pretty? Or wore the wrong dress?"

"No! That isn't what I meant." He lowers his voice and moves closer to confide thoughts he doesn't want to be overheard. This close, I am aware of his age that hollowed his cheeks during these last five years of my absence. His voice is hoarse with emotion.

"You have no idea what happens when a Charmed person finds out they've been coerced into a relationship. It can put them into a dangerous rage. I've lived decades with a woman who, when she learned she had been coerced to be my lover, hated my guts. If Ryan is smart, he'll never let Jennifer know how he won her."

Ryan and Jennifer's courtship had happened away from the family and while I hope he hadn't wooed her with Charm, I couldn't say.

"I don't think Grandmother hated you."

At my statement, he sighs. "She loved me more than I deserved."

Grandfather is in a confiding mood, so I think it was time to ask a question I'd always wanted the answer to. "What does Aunt Belle know about our gifts?"

"I had to tell her about you when she tried to put you away. She wanted an explanation about why you were the way you were, and why I was fine with that."

My mouth opens, but nothing comes out. He sighs and puts his hand under my chin to force me to look at him.

"I had to tell her. After your mother died, the older you got, the more erratic your behavior became. To an outsider, it looked like you were ill, sick in the head. Going to class and insisting you were Mary, and the next day Teresa! Of course, I knew it was your gift manifesting, and that you'd eventually figure out how to work with it. It's a confusing, intoxicating time. I know. The same happened to me. And Ryan. I knew you were just experimenting. Pushing it to see how far you could go. Like a girl, trying on different outfits to figure out who she is. Realizing her potential as her body awakens."

We are touching and snapshots of Grandfather's memories flood my mind, like someone's highschool yearbook. Girl after girl. Long hair, short; brunette or blond, slender or curvy. He took them all like others do collector cards, just because he could. Stretching his talent. *Experimenting*.

No wonder the man at the convenience store had told the clerk to run. Grandfather hunted women like they were deer.

I knock his hand off me. It doesn't even register with him that at this moment, he disgusts me. His mind is still elsewhere, living in the past.

"Brynn was reckless with her gift, as I had once been. I tried to warn her; to make her see sense. That if someone's Charmed that deeply, it marks them forever. They crave you like a drug, and if you deny them, they hate you just as deeply as they once desired you. Look at Robert Bancroft. He still wants to punish us all because Brynn divorced him."

"*He* divorced *her*. When he found out she was pregnant with me."

Grandfather gives me an odd look. "No. Your mother initiated the divorce. It was the one thing that really angered Kitty. She thought Brynn should lie in the bed she made. Make a go of it with Robert for the long term, but your mother used her trust money to pay a lawyer and did it all behind our back."

I recalculated things in my mind. Divorcing Robert must have been one of her first steps in making an independent life. Plans for college and becoming a writer. Falling in love with someone else. These thoughts roll around in my mind, but I'm not ready to reveal them to Grandfather.

"After Brynn disappeared, Robert wanted Ryan to leave with him and fill that hole that Brynn left him with. But of course, it wasn't enough. Ryan never would be."

I'm offended. "Ryan isn't a consolation prize!"

"I know. *I know.* That's why I moved heaven and earth to keep him here during the school year. He shouldn't carry that burden for Brynn's reckless actions in seducing Robert back in high school."

That was the pot calling the kettle black!

TWELVE

After Grandfather's revelations, I want to be alone, so I go back upstairs, intending to return to my room. But in the hall, seeing my mother's closed door, I ask myself: Who was my mother? What was she really like? Did she know her murderer? The answer was probably here, among her personal things. I had never dared, but wasn't it time I found her out?

Was she an arrogant seductress taking and discarding boys? Was Michael Gardner just another one of her victims, like Robert? Or was she just a young woman trying to discover who she was away from a suffocating household?

I seize the doorknob and enter her room, closing the door behind me. The room looks the same as it did yesterday evening, even though I now have several startling revelations to deal with.

My mother had plans. She wanted to go to college. She had fallen in love with someone new. But those futures were cut short, and she returned here to be a mother to two small children. When I was six, she vanished. And now, when I am twenty-six, on the one-hundred-and-thirtieth anniversary year of the Gale, her body is discovered.

From Ryan's argument with Grandfather, he doesn't think it is a coincidence, and I am coming to the same conclusion.

I need to know her. Who she really was because I instinctively feel that will be where the answer to who murdered her will be found.

I start my quest by searching her lingerie drawer. It's usually where women put things they care about, but I don't find any letters or jewelry, only undergarments. She liked nice things, but I find nothing super expensive or excessive, even though I know she had the money to buy the best of anything.

It makes me wonder: if she was the slut my family believed her to be, wouldn't she have bought more racy things? Instead of pale blues and pinks, shouldn't there be black and red bras and pantie sets?

Or am I letting stereotypes cloud my thinking?

Next, I go through her jewelry cabinet, and I'm surprised to find her wedding ring and engagement set. The last features a blue topaz so big it looks like glass. It is something a kid would buy because it was big and would be noticed. Robert's choice, I'm sure.

If she had wanted the divorce, why keep it?

A memento, or is it a trophy?

The other jewelry is thin gold chains, delicate pendants, and slender earrings. I select a gold chain with a pendant that holds two small stones: a diamond for April and a sapphire for September. Her children's birthstones. I put it on and continue my investigation.

After going through her desk, I realize there are no convenient diaries or letters. Because of what Duncan told me about her wanting to be a writer, I find it odd. Don't writers write? Where are her musings?

Probably anything like that was removed long ago.

The only thing I find is an address book from back when people would actually write down phone numbers. Sabrina's old number is listed, along with a few other names I don't recognize.

Since it might be worth reaching out to them, I slip it into my back pocket.

There is an appointment book, but not much is in it. Probably something Grandfather gave her to keep track of her charity appointments because, after all, a substantial gift of money always got a photo of an Underhill in the newspaper. Except for me, all Underhills are expected to do their civic duty. Me, they can't risk, because I might say something odd or become someone other than Zoe.

Opening the wardrobe closet, I sort through the clothes left behind. Her tops are made of hemp, silk, or cotton. No polyester. The slacks are mostly linen. Knit dresses all in simple, clean lines so they could be pulled on and off without fuss. She liked a certain shade of peach and blue, colors I also wear because they go well with the deep red brown of our hair.

I've worn many types of clothes, all suited to the personas I assumed, so I have experience in how they reflect the inner nature of a person. Everything my mother owned is the vibe of someone who likes simple, uncomplicated things. A rich taste, but nothing ostentatious. Not someone greedy, crass, or loud.

It occurs to me that one day I will be dead; will someone go through my things trying to figure out who I was? Loathing the thought, I am about to close the door when I notice the luggage stacked in the corner. It is a set of three matching cases, along with an overnight bag all in a dark navy with a designer emblem on the latch. If she was running away to meet her lover, as everyone insists, why are they here? Why is her closet still full of clothes

Because she didn't run away.

Her lover was dead.

And her body was waiting to be found for twenty years.

The bathroom is harder. Like the rest of the room, it is Sleeping Beauty's chamber frozen at the moment the curse from the wicked fairy begins.

Unlike my bathroom, Grandfather made sure that no one desecrated the shrine by cleaning anything out.

The drawers reveal a simple beauty regime: cleanser, toner, lotion. Her make-up was shades of rose, smoky blue-grays, and a deep purple eyeshadow that sparkled. The last was probably for the evening.

In the cabinet, I find a razer, tweezers, and a bottle of over-the-counter painkillers, mostly full. Behind the can of shaving cream, there is a prescription bottle. *Huh?* I examine the label. *Take as needed.* Using my cellphone, I snap a picture, as I don't remember her taking medication or going to a doctor.

I can't stop smelling the contents of her shampoo bottle, and as I return it to the shower, I wonder if it would be morbid to buy my mother's brand of soap, shampoo, and skin lotion? Just to smell her?

Obviously, others have looked through her things many times, but there is one thing no one else but I can do. I could become her. *Be* her. Why not try it? Replaying all the memories I've collected about her over the years might reveal something important I hadn't noticed before.

There are many ways to get into character. For example, dressing the part.

From the lingerie drawer, I select a cotton set of bra and panties in peach. Shedding my own clothes and pulling them on, I notice we are now almost the same size. It is disturbing to know I am about one year older than Brynn was when she died.

Returning to the closet, I shuffle through the hangers to decide what to wear. There is a comfortable dark blue dress with a v-neck and long bell-shape sleeves, shaped like some sort of cosplay Renn-faire princess or maybe a girl from the 1970s who would be going barefoot to rock concerts.

As I hold it, a very old memory of her wearing this dress comes to my mind. *Yes, she liked this one.* I pull it over my head and fasten the ties around my waist. The fabric is soft under my hand and the skirt swirls as I move. Looking in the mirror that hangs on the bathroom door, I realize her skin was the last to touch it.

In the bathroom, I use her perfume: a blend of lilac-vanilla-clove. Yes, this is what I smelled yesterday when I entered her room. The very same.

With a little water I resuscitate the violet eyeshadow, use the lightest bit of barest blush, and a coral lipstick to complete the sun-kissed, barely there look that I remember my mother favoring. Not for her the layers of foundation and red lipstick that Robert's current wife, Marion or Jennifer, favored.

Tilting my head back and forth, I examine my finished face in the mirror. If you don't account for the gift of Charm, my mother had, which enhanced her features, we look superficially the same: fawn colored eyebrows, scattering of freckles, wide forehead, and apple cheeks. But my nose is shorter with an upturned tilt at the tip, and my mouth is thinner, and smiles less. My eyes are as blue as hers, but mine have a haunted stare.

This superficial likeness is probably why Aunt Belle hates me, and Grandfather dotes on me.

On the bed, I lie down and stare at the ceiling, thinking about how to approach my goal. I'll draw on every memory I have of my mother and the ones others have shared with me. From these recollections, I'll build her brick by brick back into a living person.

Many of Grandfather's memories are connected to the sea, so I am not surprised that one of his favorites is about Brynn on the water. Brynn is about nine years old, and she sits next to him on the *Lady Kitty*, the sailboat named after Grandmother.

The wind flaps the sail, and it is a beautiful day to be out on the water. He looks down at Brynn's head with its dark brown hair and the red highlights brought out from a summer spent outdoors. She wears a coral swimsuit with large stripes of navy blue and yellow across the chest.

Suddenly, she stands up and Nolan instinctively grabs her around the waist to stop her from falling into the ocean. When they had left, his wife insisted Brynn wear a life vest, but as soon as they had pulled past Fishhead Island, Brynn ditched it with his silent permission. So, if she went over, Kitty would give him holy hell.

"Look!" His daughter points to the side where a trio of dolphins are keeping pace with them. "Daddy, they're racing us!"

Brynn's excited face turns to look at him, and he grins back. He wants her to love the sea as he does. "Do you want to race them?"

"Can we?"

"Sit tight!"

He doesn't remember if they won or lost the race because that wasn't what was important about that day.

Next is a memory I picked from Sabrina's mind when we had met before dinner, when I brushed against her during her tale about my mother.

They are in Mother's bathroom, experimenting with makeup. A beauty magazine is spread out on the counter, which shows steps to line the eye.

Brynn is sitting on the counter so she can lean close to the mirror. She hands Sabrina a case of eye shadow. "This plum would look gorgeous on you."

"That sounds like something the saleslady we met at the mall would say."

I hear my mother giggle for the first time. From the clothes she wears and her skinny frame, I think she's about fourteen. In four years, she would be pregnant with Ryan. And in eleven years would be dead.

Thinking about it breaks me away from the immersive experience I need, so I force those dark thoughts away and return to Sabrina's recollection.

She leans close to the mirror and carefully draws a line above her eyelashes.

"What boy do you like?" At her friend's question, Brynn's hand goes askew and she mutters a mild curse. Grabbing a tissue, she tries to correct her mistake, while Sabrina presses her for an answer. "C'mon, isn't there a boy you like?"

Brynn's hand steadies as she draws the line around the other eye. "No. They're too silly."

"Well, they sure like you." Sabrina's memory is tinged with envy. "They aren't asking to sit at our lunch table because of me."

"It's not me they like. Not the real me. So don't feel jealous."

"The real you?"

Owlishly, Brynn stares back at her reflection, her eyes wide. "I make them sit with us because it makes me laugh inside to see them acting stupid."

Robert's sharpest memory of Brynn is when they discussed the divorce. A memory he gave me when I was a child and was incapable of understanding it.

"Why? Just tell me why?"

Brynn emanates a glow of unnatural beauty. In Robert's memory her eyes are luminous, her long hair lustrous, and her form is more curvy. It is Robert's vision of her: a seductive goddess who he worships but, at the same time, wants to control.

Brynn tells him, "We don't love each other. I don't think we ever did."

Robert grabs her by the wrist and forcibly brings her against his chest. He is taller by a good six inches. "I own you. You're mine."

When Brynn sighs, her breasts tremble against Robert's chest. Her eyes are getting a faraway look that angers him because he can't go to what she is seeing.

Robert knows her weak point — their child, Ryan. "My parents would love for me to take Ryan from you and your family."

Brynn's eyes are hard and dangerous. Suddenly, she looks much older and colder. She looks like Nolan. "You will have him over my dead body."

Aunt Belle's memory drips with sanctimonious smugness, for she is righteous in her role as enforcer. Even though she has been waiting for hours, the desire to catch Brynn doing something wrong strengthens her resolve to stay awake as the night drags on.

The first time her sister and her brother-in-law go out of town, and what does Brynn do? Run off telling no one where she was going or with whom. Leaving the housekeeper to watch her children.

Annabelle knew the girl would come in late. It's how she got in trouble the first time. This is because Kitty and Nolan are too lenient with her. It was time someone taught that girl how life really worked!

Brynn is trying to come in quietly, but Annabelle's ears are sharp. She slides off the kitchen stool and turns on the kitchen light. Brynn gives a guilty jump and Annabelle crosses her arms, pleased. "Did you enjoy yourself?"

Brynn takes off her sneakers, which are wet from the night's rain. Her hair lies limp against her skull from being soaked. "Matter of fact, I did."

"Don't you talk back to me, Brynn Denise Underhill."

Brynn shrugs. "Don't ask for an honest answer, then, if it upsets you so."

Her niece attempts to go by her, but Annabelle shifts and blocks her path.

"Who have you been with?"

"Is that your business? I don't think so."

"I'm telling your parents about this as soon as they return."

"I'm twenty-two and with my own money. So go ahead."

This close, Annabelle finally notices what a wet dress plastered to a slim body cannot conceal. She says flatly, "You're pregnant. Again. Is it Robert's?"

"No."

Annabelle hates that dreamy cream-fed-cat look on Brynn's face, and the slap makes a red handprint on her cheek. "Slut! Your father won't be pleased when I tell him!"

"Go ahead, but it still won't win you any points. He loves Kitty, not you. You're like the carpet - a bit worn but serviceable. A bit more useful than Owen."

"How dare you?!"

Brynn is an Underhill, and she uses her words like a machete, making brutal chops upon Annabelle's fragile ego. "You've hung around here for decades trying to catch his attention. Mom might forgive it, but I think you are a dried out, pathetic husk. You've never lived."

"Shut up!" Annabelle raises her hand as if to give another slap. Brynn juts her chin forward, putting her face closer to the open palm.

"Go ahead. And I'll tell Mother all you've been up to. There's only one hussy around here."

Panic. Sheer panic. The memory ends with a tidal wave of explosive emotion of impotent rage.

THIRTEEN

"What are you doing in here?"

As if my thoughts conjured her, Aunt Belle is standing in the doorway. She never did learn to knock despite all the times we've asked her to. Aunt Belle continues barking, like one of those irritating small dogs that women carry around in purses. "Answer me, young lady! Why are you in here?"

I sit up from the bed and swing my legs over. Bending down, I pull on the sandals I had chosen from Mother's closet.

My silence angers my aunt, and she comes forward and slaps me, just as she had Mother so long ago. In that brief moment of contact, I am given a memory that lies on the surface of her mind.

She frantically searches my mother's room and finds letters under the mattress. Yes! Now, she'd know who the girl was sleeping with. She quickly flips through them before stacking them together and sliding them under her shirt, tucking them in her waistband. Annabelle opens the bedroom door and peers out to see if anyone is in the hall.

After last night I didn't think I had any capacity to be shocked. I am wrong. I am horrified and angry at Aunt Belle's arrogance in taking something so intimate of my mother's and never sharing it with her children.

She denied a part of our mother to us.

Suddenly, I am as furious as Ryan can be. I stand up and say in a voice that thunders, "Where were you when my mother was murdered?"

My aunt is not used to being confronted and she sputters, "I was here looking after Ryan on the day she left and know nothing about what happened to her."

"Liar." I grab her old lady wrist. She writhes in panic, bucking in her attempt to escape me. But it is of no use, and I finally show her that I can be a ruthless Underhill after all, for she can't hide what she is remembering.

She whispers, "Do you love me? More than her?" The kiss is his answer and while it is sweet, it does not slake her thirst, her need, for him to tell her she is the one he cares for above all others.

Stunned, my grip releases her as if I was holding a rattler. "You and Owen?"

The repulsion on her face at my words lets me know I have the wrong brother. I am speechless, my mind a whirling carousel, trying to reconcile this new knowledge with the old. Many things I've heard or were given as a memory over the decades fall into place.

From Happy: *Poor thing. She just doesn't understand that some men move on to the next flower when they get all the pollen.*

From Marion: *The old goat fouled his own nest. I can't imagine why Kitty put up with him.*

Aunt Belle rubs her wrist, and says viciously, "Reading my mind, you little freak? You should be locked up, and your brain given to science! In the old days, they'd have burned you and your mother as witches!"

How did she keep this information from me for so long? *Because she doesn't touch you except to punish you.*

I can't understand such a betrayal, and worse, living with the loved one she had deceived. How could she reconcile it? What type of sister could do that? Grandmother wasn't here to say it, so I did. "You betrayed your sister by sleeping with her husband."

"Nolan seduced me," she hisses.

Perhaps she is right to give him the motherload of the blame. Earlier, he admitted to the dangers of using Charm, and here was the woman he abused with his gift. "How long did it go on?"

"It stopped when Kitty became pregnant with Brynn." Even though it was a long time ago, the rejection still stings. She probably blames the pregnancy for ending her love affair with her brother-in-law. No wonder she hated Brynn and the daughter who looks like her.

"You accused my mother of being a tramp, and what are you? *What-are-you?*" The last three words I yell back in her face and distantly there is a sound of thunder. There is a storm brewing, and I hear the rattle of rain against the windowpane.

I'm barely aware of it, but our fight draws an audience. Jennifer is watching us from the doorway in wide-eyed fascination.

"You're the evidence that she was what I named her!" Her accusing finger comes up to point at me and I slap it down. There is one thing I want from this old woman. "Where are my mother's letters? Her private papers you stole?"

"I burned them all! They were wicked nasty things."

My hand reaches out again for her wrist, but she is too quick and puts it behind her back. "I don't believe you. You keep everything, even bits of old string and rubber bands. Where are they?"

"You'll never find them."

Something comes over me, so hot and fierce, it fills me like a possession. I shove her back on the bed and straddle her, pinning her down so she can't move. At that moment, I feel like I could break her neck.

"Tell me *where-they-are!*"

Aunt Belle cannot stop herself and a memory surfaces. I jump off the bed and run down the hallway to the other wing of the house. She comes after me, screaming at me to stop; Jennifer is behind her, shouting for Ryan.

I throw open Aunt Belle's bedroom door and enter a room filled with antique furniture, turn-of-the-century pieces that are massive and solid. Frozen soldiers guarding a stagnant, joyless life. The air is stagnant and there is a strong smell of lemon polish that fills my nostrils.

The box I'm looking for is at the bottom of her oak wardrobe. I toss out the clutter that is on top, not caring what happens to her bric-à-brac junk, until I find the blue box she remembers. Taking off the lid, I see a stack of slim journals, and a packet of letters tied together with a ribbon.

Someone grabs the back of my head, viciously yanking my hair.

"I won't let you have them. They're mine! I need them!"

Being on the run, I've learned plenty of down-and-dirty self-defense moves. In a heartbeat, I reach behind me and pinch her elbow. She lets go, screaming, and I throw her sideways to the ground where she rolls on her back, clutching her arm.

I replace the lid and step over her prone body to leave. Ryan pushes past Jennifer, standing in the doorway, and looks down at Aunt Belle moaning on the floor.

"What is going on here, Zoe?" says my brother.

"Ask your darling Auntie Belle."

Hugging the box protectively to my chest, I go by him, leaving them all behind.

I cannot be inside, for the house is choking the life out of me. But when I exit the front door at a trotting run, I am facing the Majestic, and further off in the distance, the sea.

Zoe.

I barely notice the sprinkles of rain as I run in a panic toward the stand of trees, the opposite direction of the water.

"Zoe!"

My focus is on moving forward and getting as far away as possible as quickly as possible, so I startle when Duncan steps in front of me, blocking my path.

"Are you alright?"

"No."

He looks down at the box I'm clutching so hard that I've bent the cardboard lid.

"Would you like to go for a drive?"

"Not to the sea!" I almost scream my fear. The desire to run is all I feel.

His voice soothes like aloe on a burn. "How about we take a drive down into the National? I found a great pull-off picnic spot last week."

I nod my head, as I've exhausted my ability to speak. Duncan doesn't touch me as we walk back towards the house to where his car is parked in the drive with the driver's side door open. He must have been coming back from town and seen me run out of the house.

Duncan opens the passenger door, and I slide in. When he returns to the driver's side, he starts the engine and reminds me, "Seatbelt."

Pulling blindly at it, I bring it across my chest, which forces me to put the box in my lap to get it to click. He turns on the windshield wipers. and as he circles the drive, I stare only at the Majestic. The form of the grand old tree is a smeared blurry image as the wipers try to clean the windshield.

The state highway takes us through the heart of the peninsula with the forest on either side. We enter the National, where the tree canopy shadows the road, and a small bit of my tension releases.

We have driven for half an hour when he says, "Do you mind if I stop for something to drink?"

Staring out the window, I shrug and in a moment, he turns into a gas station convenience store. It's a small place with hand-written cardboard signs covering the glass windows that declare they carry bait and beer. A license to hunt or fish. And stand-up paddle boards to rent.

When Duncan returns, he sets a bag between us. I'm too tired to be curious, so don't bother looking inside. It's another fifteen minutes before we get to the pull-off he mentioned. I know it. It's a lookout point between Bullnose Cove and Shallow Bay, but he parks putting our backs to the ocean.

Being in the middle of the week, and well past the lunch hour, with rain blurring the world, we are the only ones in the lot.

From the bag, he pulls out two bottles of water. "I don't plan on getting pulled over with out-of-state plates by a state trooper with alcohol in the car or on my breath."

Duncan is so sensible. Does he ever act irrationally? Wild? Lose his temper? I can't imagine it.

The next thing he pulls out from his magic bag is a candy bar. "I hope you aren't allergic to nuts?"

"No. No, I'm not." My voice sounds hoarse, as if I've been screaming.

As I bite into the caramel and chocolate, I realize I haven't eaten today. Grandfather's fight with the mayor means my chicken sandwich is still sitting on the dining room table, unless Sally has already swept it away.

Duncan tells me what he did today. He interviewed local people who told him stories passed down from their ancestors about the Great Gale. If some of those referenced Abraham Underhill, he didn't mention him.

Instead, he tells me about the deaths of families, buildings swept away into the sea. How terrifying the storm was when it blew in quickly and unpredictably. The days of rain which put most of the town underwater when the levee broke, the wreckage left behind and the clean-up of those who survived it.

The stories made me shudder. Maybe I'd flee to landlocked

Kansas. Flatter than a pancake, I hear, with just a river or two on the edge of the state.

"Are you going with Owen to the museum opening? The new exhibit is pretty amazing. It uses all the latest technology to give you a feel of the times. It will be fascinating to see how people react to it."

Stop talking about the museum! Who cares?

"Aren't you going to ask me what's in the box?"

"I figure you'd tell me if you want me to know."

My fingers stroke the broken lid, and I feel the urge to cry seeing the damage. "Inside are journals and letters my mother kept and that my aunt stole from my mother's room. I'm guessing it was after Mother vanished because she'd have raised holy hell about it if she'd found them gone and that I would remember."

"I'm glad you got them back." Duncan's arm comes around the back of the car seat, behind me, but not touching. He's giving me a circle of protection. "Have you read them yet?"

I shake my head.

"You don't have to read them right away. You have all the time in the world to make that decision."

But I do want to read them. I want to know her.

Slowly, I lift the lid. On top are stacked envelopes. I pick one of them up and see they are addressed to my mother but were mailed to a post office box, not one in Kingstowe, but in a town nearby called Wellston.

Hesitantly, I pull a letter out from its envelope and unfold it. I immediately flip the page over to see the signature. *Oh.* It's a letter to her, not from her. "It's from Michael Gardner."

I slowly read through it and, when done, set it between Duncan and me. There are only about twelve envelopes and looking at the date, they were sent about five months before I was born.

Each piece of paper tells me more about the man who is my father. Still, he feels remote, like some character in a story that wasn't necessarily my own. "They loved each other and planned to get married. But she wanted to run away and elope. Do you still have his picture?"

"It's on my phone." He removes his arm, and swipes through images and stops on one, turning the face of his phone to me. "Michael's parents are still alive. He has a younger sister who is married, and she's a mom to a couple of girls and a boy."

The photo must have been taken at some formal event, for he is wearing a button-down plaid shirt and a navy blazer. He stares, not smiling, directly at the photographer. What sucker punches me is he looks a little older than I am right now. Too young to die.

This is my father.

"Do you want me to send the photo to you?"

I nod, mute. I send him a text on my phone giving him my number so he can send the file to me.

"How did he die?"

"He was on his motorcycle in someone's blind spot when they swerved into his lane. They were on the interstate and the high speeds caused a pretty bad smash-up."

"Did my mother know about it?"

"That I can't tell you for sure, because by then she had stopped communicating with my dad. They had a big row about her leaving college during the mid-terms. When I talked with Michael's family, they knew he was seeing someone, but didn't know her name. It's okay. I didn't tell them about Brynn or you. I figured I'd leave that up to you, for when you were ready, if ever."

I have grandparents, an aunt. Cousins. It is hard to wrap my mind around the idea that these mythical people exist.

Underneath the letters are a few slim volumes. They are in my mother's handwriting and look to be journals. I feel sick knowing Aunt Belle had read through these. Feeling violated, I replace the journal back on top and close the lid. I'm not ready to read her diaries.

A horrible thought crosses my mind. "I can't keep these in my room. She might steal them again or destroy them."

"If you trust me to store them, I'd be honored to."

"You can't keep them at the house. Nothing is safe there."

Not even people.

"I won't. I've got an office at the museum."

"Okay." Although I agree, I can't hand them over to him just yet. I want to read all the letters, touch the paper, and trace the pen strokes of the father I would never know.

Duncan seems to know my thoughts. "If you need more time, I've got emails to respond to."

I nod again. From the back seat he pulls over a bag and removes a laptop. He turns on his phone's hotspot to connect, while I return to the letters. The journals are too much for me, but the letters? I want to make their words into memories.

FOURTEEN

Last night when we returned, I went straight to my room. Maybe there wasn't a lock on my door, but that didn't mean I couldn't drag my nightstand in front of it to prevent anyone from entering. There was a soft tap on the door around eleven, but I didn't answer.

The next morning, I am in the middle of eating an omelet when Owen enters the dining room. Seeing me, he does a double-take before walking over to the buffet where he pours himself coffee from the carafe.

As Owen does, he immediately stomps all over matters others would have avoided mentioning. "I hear you and Belle had quite the dust-up yesterday."

"Hm-hm." I continue eating.

"Her arm is in a sling."

"Too bad for her," is my answer.

He grins. "That's the spunk! I didn't know you had it in you, Zoe. You've always been a quiet little shadow around here."

I'm still irritated from yesterday and give him a direct stare, my face solemn. "You don't really know me, though, do you?"

He blinks, taken aback by the bluntness of my response. "I guess I've not seen much of you—"

Ashley, the teacher, corrects him: "Little of you."

"Little of you these last few years—"

"Five years." I take a swig of orange juice, freshly squeezed. Sally really takes care of us. It can't be out of affection, so Grandfather must pay her really well.

Owen reaches across the table, his gesture conciliatory. Well, if he is going to offer it, so be it. I rest my palm on the back of his hand. "What do you remember about the day my mother disappeared?"

"Like I told you, I was at a bonsai convention. I didn't know your mom was gone until I got back."

Owen excitedly walks through the aisle of a convention room lined with vendor booths on either side. Displays of miniature trees are everywhere. Other booths have banners selling source material, cutters, and clippers for shaping your tree, or decorative stands to display your specimen to advantage.

I draw my hand back and pick up my cloth napkin to wipe my mouth. "I'd never have the patience to do your hobby."

"You need to appreciate the long game. Do you know they have a bonsai in Japan that is considered a national treasure? It was trained as a bonsai in 1610 and is over 500 years old!"

"But is it as old as the Majestic?" I challenge him, lifting an eyebrow.

Owen takes my jest seriously. "The Majestic is at least as old. It was here before Kingstowe was a town. Before Abraham settled here."

"Speaking of which, Sally told me old Abraham has been making trouble."

"As the founder, he doesn't like being forgotten."

I gaze at the portrait of Abraham and Seaborn, and not for the first time wonder what Seaborn's expression is trying to convey. "So, having your bedsheets pulled off you in the middle of the night makes us respect him more? I'd like him better if he'd let me get a good night's rest."

Owen bristles. He doesn't like anyone joking about Abraham, even if it is about his ghost. His bloodline was the one thing that Grandfather could never take away or mock and Owen embraced the family heritage with a vengeance.

He is about to say something when Ryan enters the room. I haven't seen him since the row yesterday with Aunt Belle, and I stand up to leave. My brother demands abruptly, "Where are you going?"

"Into town with Duncan."

"I'll walk out with you."

So much for me evading a discussion about yesterday.

Exiting the front door, my brother walks to the Majestic, which places us away from the house and listening ears. The old oak had once been a rendezvous spot for our games of pirates, but I was in no mood to play make-believe.

Ryan's energy is tigerish. "Learn anything yet?"

A lot of things. Things I'm still struggling to understand or believe, but nothing I am ready to share. "I just got here. You need to give me some time."

"Why? Isn't your gift up to the job of finding Mother's killer?" His emotions snap-crackle-and-pop. I say nothing, which forces him to rein in his frustration, for he knows that if I dig my feet in, nothing will move me to speak. He switches to a more conciliatory tone. "I just want to know what happened to her. Which one of them did it? Don't you want to know?"

"Have you ever thought maybe it wasn't one of them?" The look of disbelief on his face makes me persist. "It could be someone unknown to us."

"Perhaps." But I can tell he really doesn't believe that possibility. "Robert seems set on it being that stalker, Sabrina mentioned."

I squirm, but Ryan doesn't notice because he's thinking of his dad. "Obviously, he wants attention directed elsewhere. His company board isn't pleased about Mother being found. That's why he wants me to come work for him. It will quell rumors that he murdered our mother."

I'm surprised at Ryan's cold-blooded thinking. This was his father, after all! "Surely not!"

"I know it's hard for you to understand because you think having a dad would be great, but I'm not sentimental about our relationship. It took him two years after Mom disappeared to finally start acting like a father, and it was too late in my book. But is he a murderer?" Ryan pauses and shrugs. "Maybe. The jury is still out."

If he will consider the possibility, I have questions about Robert. "By the time Brynn disappeared, they were three years divorced, and he was remarried. Why would he still care enough to kill her?"

My brother rubs his chin and doesn't meet my eyes. "He talks about her in a weird way."

"How so?"

Ryan says slowly, his face pensive, "He talks about her like she was some sort of fairy princess he has to save. There's a wistful note in his voice, like he knows he missed out."

A princess in a castle tower, guarded by an ogre who was never rescued by her prince.

Involuntarily, I reach out to Ryan, touching him. "She was something special." In a moment of mutual loss, we share memories of our mother. *Frowning over Ryan's homework, helping him sound out words as he struggles with his vocabulary list. Leaning towards me with a spoon feeding baby me. Her eyes startling blue, with an outer ring of black. A smile filled with magic and secrets you wanted to know.*

My hand drops away, and he gives a melancholy sigh. "He never understood her."

"None of them ever did, not even Grandfather. But still, I find it hard to believe anyone would hate her enough to kill her."

Ryan gives a humorless smile and surprises me by saying, "Oh, I think Marion could. She's an excellent candidate. What you probably don't know is that she's fixated, obsessed, with Mom. Jennifer pointed it out to me, and now I can't unsee it. Like last Christmas, Jen complimented her on how pretty the tree looked and Marion bragged that Mom never had a tree as pretty. Why mention Mom at all? But she does it all the time. The car she drives is better than Brynn's car; the vacations she takes are more exciting."

Creepy. "So, Marion killed Mom because she wanted to have Robert? But they were already married."

"That means nothing. Maybe she thought Robert would go back to Mom? Or that Mom was some sort of threat to her happiness?"

If we were going to consider that, I suggest, "What do you make of Sabrina?"

"Mom's best friend? Seems nice enough, but I've only seen her a few times when we've visited Kingstowe over the years. On the street, a wave and hello, with a promise to get a coffee together. But we never do."

I bite my lip and decide to broach the subject, going sideways to the topic of my father, Michael Garland. "She seemed gleeful about that guy who she thought was stalking Mom. It's almost like she felt Mom deserved to be harassed because she was pretty."

"Jealousy? That doesn't seem enough to murder someone for."

"Girl jealousy. It's real. To shine more, the popular girl pairs with someone not as pretty."

"Mom would never have done that!"

How little my brother knows about women.

"Mom wasn't a saint, and high school is hell. What I find strange is wouldn't Sabrina be the one Mom would confide in if she found a new love? Or tell when someone was bothering her? You'd think she'd know more."

"They were out of school for years by the time Mom disappeared. Almost a decade. Maybe they weren't as close anymore?"

Suddenly, all this speculation sounds ridiculous. No one we knew could be a murderer. "Maybe it was just a horrible accident, like your dad suggested."

"You can't really believe that?" I look down at the ground as Ryan continues, "She wouldn't have fallen down some stupid well. She was woodwise."

Hiding behind a tree, Mother covers my mouth. We watch a doe with twins. In my ear, she whispers: Ryan and Zoe.

"It's long past the time you and I step up and take control. The old regime is fading. Aunt Belle says Nolan's been selling off his boats. Yes, that surprises you, doesn't it? I'm going over to Fletcher Marina today to get more details. It's all part of Mother finally being found."

"Mother is dead. She's part of nothing," I say flatly.

"Mom's murder, the Gale, the family. It's all connected."

When I don't respond, he switches tactics, probably voicing what he really wanted to ask me when we came out here. "What happened yesterday with Aunt Belle? She won't say."

I tell him about my attempt to learn something about our mother by wearing her clothes and remembering. That my attempt was interrupted by Belle. How I learned about the theft of Mother's letters and retrieved them. By the end, he is not happy with either of us.

"Understand, Zoe, she depends financially on Grandfather—"

"Because she didn't get a job. Her choice."

"Her job was raising two small kids! And what thanks does she get for it from you? A hair-pulling fight and a sprained arm."

I dig in, feeling mulish. "We've had this discussion before. We have two different experiences with this woman. You were always her favorite, while I was nothing. Worse than nothing!"

When Ryan was a child, he'd Charm her for extra cookies and a late bedtime. He kept her sweet for both of us, but as soon as he left to visit Robert for the summer, Aunt Belle's attitude towards me changed. For years, I was told it was my *overactive imagination*, or was too sensitive, so eventually I stopped telling anyone about her abuse.

Aunt Belle stays here because she hates her former lover. I open my mouth to say those words but shut it. If I shared this new information, it would change how Ryan felt about Grandfather and Belle forever.

The Majestic's heavy branches sweep low to the ground, almost touching the earth. I bend over and from the ground pick up an acorn with its little hat still attached. When we were kids, we always believed they were magical and were often used as tokens, pledges, and payments.

I hand the nut to Ryan. "Forgive me?"

He hesitates, but in the end takes the acorn and my apology about Belle. "I admit I'd like to see those letters myself."

"Hm." I am not agreeing with anything until I am ready. "Aunt Belle says she was home looking after you the day Mother went missing." *When she wasn't stealing Mother's letters.*

Ryan frowns in concentration, tossing the acorn up in the air and catching it with one hand as he thinks. "It's a bit of a blur to me, but yeah, I think I was home from school, sick that week."

When Mother disappeared, none of us knew that it would be an important date until days later when she didn't come home. Ryan and I, being children, probably didn't even realize she was truly missing until weeks had gone by since the adults hid that information from us.

She went to visit a friend. She'll be back home soon, Zoe.

"Do you think the school will still have your attendance records so we can check the date?"

"Doubtful. That was over twenty years ago. Why would they keep that stuff? What else have you learned?"

"Grandfather says he would never have hurt her." I don't tell him about the powerful scenario I imagined yesterday, or how Grandfather could have done it.

"You and I disagree about Aunt Belle, and I take issue with your defense of Grandfather. You're fine with him because he knows you worship him, but for everyone else, if he can't Charm you, he beats you until you agree with him that the sky is green."

"Our relationship is more complicated than that." My need for a father figure, and Grandfather's spoiling me because I was a girl, had led to a relationship that stayed infantile, but I don't want to argue with him about it. "Owen shared a memory with me of a Bonsai convention he was attending. Could you check the dates?"

Ryan scoffed. "You think that rabbit is guilty of murder?"

"Who knows? I didn't ask any of them if they killed Mother, only what they did that day."

"So just ask them," says Ryan, impatiently.

I sigh and explain it to him all over again. "I can only lift memories when I'm touching someone. And then only the memory that rests at the top of their mind. If I asked that question, do you think anyone would let me touch them? Certainly not Grandfather or Owen, who know what I can do? And Grandfather told me that Aunt Belle knows about me, too."

Ryan threw the acorn to the ground in frustration. "Then what good are you?"

Robert and Grandfather had coddled him like a young prince, and Ryan sometimes acts like a three-year-old needing a nap. But we are adults, and I'm tired of being shoved around. "Maybe you should have left me where I was happy if you don't like the way I do things?"

"I don't know why you'd want to be anyone else, anyway. Every time I find you, you're alone, barely scraping by, and living in some hole-in-the-wall backwater."

"Maybe I like my little apartments that I don't share with a bunch of male egos trying to crush me every day? Where I don't have to hear about our precious ancestors and what we owe Kingstowe?"

Ryan crosses his arms and says, "Nolan could get you committed again or locked up in jail if you keep this up."

"How did you know about that? You were gone with Robert and Marion when that happened!" Again, I'm thrown off balance, learning something about the past that my memory gift should have shown me long ago if I had only known to ask the right question when touching him.

At least he has the decency to look ashamed. "When we were skiing in Switzerland, Robert told me that Grandfather had put you under medical care for your own good."

"Actually, it was your precious Aunt Belle who did that!" I'm so angry, I can't look at him. Past him, I see Duncan waiting patiently beside his car, which I am beginning to think is the getaway car. We had arranged last night to leave about this time, and I am more than ready to go. "I'm not wasting any more time arguing with you. I have other stuff to do today."

Walking away, I feel a sharp poke in my back. *He's thrown an acorn at me!* Swiveling around, I pick up a handful of acorns and raise my arm as if I'm going to return the favor. When he ducks, I taunt, "Ha! Fake out!"

I scatter the acorns on the ground and walk to where Duncan opens the passenger side door.

Fifteen

Duncan has an easy way of driving. His hands on the wheel are relaxed and while he is alert to the road and other drivers, it is not in a nervous or tense way. *Elegant.* That was the word I was looking for.

He does everything calmly, competently, without the drama that I'm used to from males. You can breathe when you are with him. I don't need to walk on eggshells around him or fear that he will jerk some emotional choke-chain around my neck.

Because of my request, we are going the land route and avoiding the ferry. Going through the National means we take much longer to get to Kingstowe, but I don't care.

Duncan tells me, "Your box is on the back seat. I thought you could check it out before we get into town."

I reach back and get it, and taking a deep breath for courage, open it. Removing one of the leather journals, I'm surprised to discover that they aren't private diaries, but stories and poems. My mother's words quickly draw me into her world, and I read a few of them out loud just so I can hear them spoken.

At the end of one of them, Duncan says, "My father was right about Brynn. She should have pursued a degree. Have you ever thought of going to college?"

My fingers go over the page, feeling the ink made from a ball-point pen. "I went until I was twenty-one. But I didn't stick to it. I liked the open road better." A road far, far away from Abraham, Grandfather, Belle, and Kingstowe. "I'm guessing you went to college?"

"Of course. You can't get out of it when your parents are both teachers. It's the family business."

"Your father teaches writing. What does your mom teach?"

"Psychology. But they are both retired now. I'm an only child, born late in their lives."

"Do you find it lonely being an only?"

"Not at all. I've got dozens of cousins and they are always nosing into my business in the family chat room. Asking me when I'm going to get married; am I dating someone?"

No one in my family asked those questions. They were satisfied that sensible, charming Ryan would carry forth the Underhill name. The only thing that surprised me was that Jennifer didn't have a couple of kids already.

We passed the exit to Wellston, where Mother had kept a post office box to get her letters from Michael. I'd have to go over there soon and wander around, seeing what she saw.

In this area, there were some luxury home neighborhoods because it was right outside the National with quick access to New King Harbor. Just a few days ago I was in New Mexico where homes were one-story tan adobe, not two-story boxes with white-gray-or green clapboard wood siding, white framed windows, and shutters.

After we go by the white church with the tall steeple, the countryside returns to forest.

"How long will you be staying?" I ask.

"At least until the new museum exhibit opens. Maybe longer. It all depends."

On what? But I didn't want to ask. Asking meant I might have to divulge my plans too.

After we cross the King George River, I warn him. "It's a speed trap through here. Ryan's got caught plenty of times back in high school."

He adjusts his speed without speaking.

"Do you know where this Italian restaurant is?" Sabrina and I had discussed meeting for lunch today and that is why Duncan is bringing me into town.

"Yes, I know where it is. I've made a study of every restaurant and fast-food place in Kingstowe."

"You like to research things, don't you?"

How much do you know about me? And about the Underhills?

We were starting to pass the black iron lampposts and the white picket fences of the houses on the south side of town. Instinctively, I slump down in my seat, hoping not to be seen, which makes Duncan ask, "Are you embarrassed to be seen with me?"

"I'm doing you a favor," I inform him.

Probably word was out that I was home and it wouldn't do him any good if people knew we were together. There was the burden of being an Underhill, but also specifically Zoe Underhill, the one who imagines herself to be other people. The one who knows things about you when you didn't tell her. After a few bullies jumped me on the playground, I was left alone when I revealed secrets they hadn't told to the adults.

Don't mess with an Underhill.

We go around the one-way main square, passing the statue of Abraham and Sarah with their baby, Levi, in her arms. The baby who grew up only to die in the first World War. Frozen in brass, Abraham is still shouting to the sky, imploring God to intervene on the town's behalf while Sarah weeps. Always weeping.

Duncan tells me, "The sculptor is James Earle Fraser."

"I know."

He continues, as if he didn't hear my mumble. "He made it right after World War I ended."

"1952."

Duncan laughs. "Of course, you know! I'm sorry. I got caught up in the facts."

"That's alright. It's really well made, and I understand your love for it."

"Do you love it?"

"I did once." *Now, I fear it.*

Sabrina suggested we meet at the Italian restaurant in town that I remember being a family-owned place which, in the afternoon, serves pizza and pasta. In the evening, it transformed into fine dining.

Since my last visit over five years ago, they have put in a patio and since it is a mild fall day; it is here that I find Sabrina. She already has a menu and hands one to me when I sit down.

"I've ordered us an appetizer already. Some calamari and stuffed mushrooms."

"Sounds good. Thanks for meeting me."

"I'm happy to. It will give me a chance to chat with the adult Zoe. Find out how well Brynn's daughter is doing."

The server interrupts us so I can place my order. When she leaves, Sabrina says, "When I heard the news about your mom, it gave me such a weird feeling. Like everything from the past was yesterday instead of twenty, thirty years ago. I've been thinking a lot about her since then."

I nod and set my forearms on the table so I can easily touch her when I need to. "I know what you mean. Yesterday, I realized I'm two years younger than when mom disappeared."

"It's funny how I feel like I'm still in my twenties, and then you say something like that, and I realize how ancient I am!" Her smile holds a bit of sadness as she contemplates the reality of time.

"I mean, next semester my oldest will be graduating from college."

"Congratulations. How many kids do you have?"

"Two boys and a girl. We don't live here, although we do own a beach house so we can come for vacation. It's where I'm staying this trip."

She seems nervous and keeps talking, telling me about her husband, each child, the sports they enjoy, the awards they've won, and their plans for college or jobs. Our appetizers arrive, as well as a drink for me and a refresh for Sabrina.

It is when our entrées arrive that Sabrina finally broaches the topic of my mother.

"I brought some things for you to see." From a capacious designer tote bag, she removes a thin book and when I take it from her, I realize it is a high school yearbook. Yellow sticky notes mark certain pages. "This is from the year we graduated, and I've book-marked all the pages that mention Brynn."

I'm not sure what I'll see, but I put my finger on the first place-marker and opened it. The hair and clothes throw me off a moment before I recognize her.

Sabrina tells me about each photo as I look through the pages. "That's the club she formed in her senior year: the Dead Poet's Society. It's from the movie of the same name. Of course, I knew nothing about poetry, but she insisted that I join."

The girl standing next to Mother is Sabrina. Sabrina is thinner and, of course, much younger, but her round face and apple cheeks are recognizable even in this incarnation. I notice the group is all girls.

"No boy would admit he liked poetry back then. To tell you the truth, I don't know if they'll admit it even now. The age of the great Romantic poets is long gone."

I flip through the other pages she's marked and find pictures of Mother as part of the newspaper staff. One of Robert in his foot-ball jersey on the football field, lifting her up to his shoulders; they are both laughing and it looks like she is about to fall. The pages of the high school mug shots aren't very many, for the graduating class wasn't very big at all.

I ask her, "Do you mind if I keep this for a few weeks? I promise I'll get it back to you."

"I thought you'd like it. And I've brought these for you today. Some photos you might want for the memorial." She pulls out a large envelope and gives it to me. Inside are photos. Some are candid shots of my mother, others with her and Sabrina. Robert is in a few. There are a couple with Sabrina and my mother on a sailboat with Grandfather. It reminds me of how much she loved the water.

"I'm surprised not to see more photos of her and Robert."

"They didn't start dating until the last semester of our senior year."

"Do you remember how you met my mother?" This time I touched her hand because this is a memory I want to keep.

"It was in middle school. We were assigned by our teacher to do a group project together, and that's when we really became friends."

The smell of school paste, the swish-swish of scissors to cut images out of magazines, and the action of the fingers rubbing over the images trying to flatten the wrinkles the paste has made when they are stuck down on a poster board.

"It seems like a dream that my mother was ever that young."

Sabrina gives me a smile. "Sometimes it seems like a dream to me, too."

"*Zoe?* Zoe Underhill?"

A woman about my age comes over to our table calling my name. This is exactly the situation I wanted to avoid. Of course, I remember her as I remember everything.

Except the day your mother disappeared, a voice whispers in my ear.

"I thought it was you." The woman approaching our table is a former classmate; we didn't get on then and I expect that isn't going to change today. "I guess you're in town because they found your mom. Who do the police think did it?"

Her rapacious inquisitiveness is disgusting. But like many faced with someone who embraces rudeness, I find myself unable to speak. Sabrina asks, "And who are you?"

"Beth Carnegie. Zoe and I are old buddies from school."

Sabrina's voice is as loud as Beth's and by this time, everyone in the restaurant is watching us. "Beth Carnegie, did you say? Your dad isn't Victor Carnegie by chance?"

"Yes, he is. Do I know you?" Beth's voice is sharp, imperative, but it's obvious she is punching above her weight, so I remain silent.

"I know your dad. It's so sad that he's still an alcoholic." Beth starts to sputter something, but Sabrina ignores it as she adds with false sincerity. "Very sad. I thought he might learn his lesson after he drove home drunk from the prom and hit that poor cyclist, but I see from the *Beacon* he's been cited again with DUI."

Sabrina tut-tuts and shakes her head sadly before picking up her menu and addressing me. "I think we both deserve a dessert, don't you?"

Beth stands there, blankly, before casting a dark glance at me and muttering, "Freak." She storms away, back to her group of friends at another table.

Sixteen

At the end of our lunch, Sabrina chooses a slice of Tiramisu while I pick gelato. As we eat dessert, I ask the questions that have been on my mind.

"Did you see my mom that week before she disappeared? Or that day?"

"I'm afraid the last time I saw your mother was a few months before that. We were living in different places by then and she had come down to Boston on a weekend getaway. She seemed the same as always, with nothing bothering her."

I open my phone to show her the pill bottle photo. It unsettles her, and she puts her dessert fork down, discomfited.

"I didn't know. When she was pregnant with you, I was in Boston with Max doing his residency. She had her ups and downs and at one time I did wonder if she didn't have peripartum depression." At my confused expression, she explains. "Sorry for the fancy term; my husband is a pediatrician. It's like postnatal depression but can happen when you are pregnant."

"But she never talked about—?"

She shakes her head vigorously.

"Brynn would never kill herself. She adored you and Ryan, and she feared what would happen to you both if she wasn't around. Nolan and she always had a contentious relationship. When Ryan was born, Annabelle was always undermining her authority, playing pretend-mommy. Then there was the situation with Robert. She'd never do anything that would give him sole custody."

"Why?" She gives me a look grown-ups give to their children, wondering if they are ready to be told bad news and I am quick to reassure her. "I'd like to know. Honestly."

"It was over two decades ago, and I don't think it would have any relevance to what happened to your mother. I don't think he's capable of *that*."

She meant murder.

"What was Robert like back in high school?"

"It was inevitable that he and your mom would get together. Brynn was always wildly popular, and he was on the football team, a star player and not doing so bad academically either. His family expected great things from him. But then, she got pregnant, and that ended that."

"It happens." I try to say this without anger, and barely succeed.

Sabrina continues as if I haven't spoken, for she is lost in the past. "The thing is everyone blamed your mom for the pregnancy. Of course, that's what society does. Blame the woman as if men have nothing to do with it." Her mouth purses in a grimace before she takes the dive.

"Robert knew she could have anyone, and after spring break, she started pulling away. She had applied to several colleges, but not to the one where Robert was going. He feared losing her."

I am beginning to fear where this is going but can't get off the ride; I've bought my ticket, and the rollercoaster is already beginning its ascent.

"He pressured her into it. Having sex. I don't think she was — willing. You kids have a name for it."

Yeah, we have a name for it.

This time it is she who reaches over and puts her hand over mine. "Please don't tell Ryan. I shouldn't have told you, but you have an odd way of getting me to blab my head off."

"Those bruises look bad! Did you fall down the stairs?" Sabrina says it jokingly, but she is thinking that Brynn's father must have struck her again. The man might be good-looking, but he has the devil's own temper.

Brynn is uncomfortable with her question. "No, it wasn't my dad. Let's drop it, okay?"

They were at her house because Sabrina's mom was at work, and they could raid the fridge and watch a show without being nagged about chores or homework.

"How did the date with Robert go? You two slunk off pretty fast from the crab bake last night."

Brynn starts to cry.

"Don't worry, I won't tell him." Ryan would not take the news well and really, in the long run, did it matter? This was over twenty-five years ago, and they were teenagers. His relationship with Robert was bad enough already without me telling him Sabrina's theory of forced sex and sexual assault.

"I've always thought getting Brynn pregnant was Robert's way of getting out of responsibility," Sabrina says.

My mind is still reeling from the information and the memory she shared, and I have to yank it back from wandering away. "What do you mean?"

"He could always blame Brynn for why he didn't go to that Ivy League college." Sabrina puts her fork down and her cheeks are a bit pink with shame. "Please don't tell anyone what I've said? Robert has a lot of influence in Kingstowe, and he could make it very unpleasant for me during my visits."

"No worries."

What I don't tell her is if Robert killed my mother, I wouldn't keep anything secret.

With my cards still missing, I don't have any money, but Sabrina gladly pays for our lunch. Afterward, she drives me over to the museum where I am to meet up with Duncan.

The last time I went through the county museum was in middle school during a field trip. Attendance was mandatory for a passing grade in my state-required history class. I spent the entire visit being teased because of my last name being found everywhere in the exhibits.

It didn't help that I had already developed contempt for Abraham and his progeny, Seaborn. They had saddled me with this 'gift' that made me a freak.

Today, what was once a little poky museum run out of a dilapidated brick building next to the railroad tracks was now triple the size. It still has the old 1900s brick front of the train depot, but the dull brick is now bright as a shiny penny with a mural painted on the side of the building showing an oversized wave about to crush a tiny town.

The place used to smell of dust, mildew, and mothballs, but it has completely changed. The exhibits are new and slick, with huge photo blow-ups and professionally made interpretative signs. Instead of taxidermy specimens losing their fur, and a box of chipped fossils you could handle, there are pristine artifacts, all labeled, in glass cases.

There's even a model of the town of Kingstowe and its harbor, complete with a water tank where kids can play with the boats. A few young kids are making them sink repeatedly while their moms stand by chatting over their baby strollers.

I go through the Native American part of the exhibit, the early colonial American area, and as I turn the corner, I'm in the 1890s and facing a sign announcing the Great Gale exhibit which will open the week before Thanksgiving close to the 130th anniversary of the gale.

"Do you want to go in?" Duncan's voice makes me jump in place.

"When did you get here?"

"Just now. I stepped into the lobby to see if you were back and saw you go down the hall. What do you make of it all?"

"It's changed a lot."

"For the good, I hope."

"Oh yes, definitely. I didn't expect something this professional from our town museum."

"Money helps, and a professional adviser." Duncan unchains the sign and, with a wave of his hand, invites me to come past the barrier. "Come on. I'll give you a VIP tour."

Feeling guilty and seeing a few of the other visitors give me a glare, I ask, "You sure?"

"I'd like your opinion of it. As a family member." After re-hooking the chain, he opens the swing door that looks like the entrance to a movie theater. We enter a dark room, and he reaches over and turns the lights on.

Duncan gestures for me to go to the right, and as I walk by, a wall display comes to life and starts speaking. It is a vertical computer screen, and the image is of my ancestor, Abraham Underhill. I recognize it from a family photo, but it is spooky to see his mouth move as he begins to speak about the events of the day prior to the Great Gale.

"The day starts out quietly, and the sea is calm. It was not until the evening when it began to snow that we started to fear..."

I can't stop staring in horror as Duncan tells me how they did it. "AI technology. We manipulated one of his photographs to make a moving image and wrote the script from his diary and letters. An actor did the voice."

"Eerie," I say softly, barely able to speak and fighting the urge to turn around and run out of the entrance. "I've seen so many still photos of him, seeing him move like he's a living person is— bizarre."

Abraham's imagined voice continues, "*We were at the church celebrating a wedding and became trapped in town by the bad weather...*"

Next to Abraham's animated image are large black-and-white photos of Kingstowe before the gale hit. Main Street, neighborhoods, picnickers on the beach that would be removed by the Gale, women sitting on blankets next to hampers while men with their pants rolled up are wading in the sea. Photos of hardworking men with their boats, as they unload their catch of the day. Main Street with wagons and horses. A woman wearing an enormous saucer-shaped hat that is crossing the street is blurry as the camera didn't freeze her movement.

This exhibit is about life before the storm and how people made a living in Kingstowe. There is plenty of information about the sea trade, the type of ships and the fish they caught, which kept the town thriving.

The people in the photos don't know what was coming. How their life is about to be destroyed one autumn day.

From there you turn a corner and enter the Gale exhibit. There is a sound of whistling wind and a breeze over my face. At my look of surprise, Duncan points out a red light on the wall. "Fans are placed at the right place and are triggered to start by a motion detector. The same with the sound recordings."

The speakers are all painted black and hidden near the ceiling. But this doesn't explain why I can smell sea salt or feel the fine misting spray on my face. There is more here than illusion, and I lick my lips, tasting salt.

I feel like I'm going through a house of horrors instead of a museum.

The sound of the wind increases, and the special effect of a creaking building is added. That's a subtle touch for when the seawall broke and the town was flooded, those trapped at the Congregational Church of Kingstowe were forced to go up.

They used a ladder and climbed into the church tower; all the children, women, and men were caught in a building that the wind was trying to tear apart. The gale hammered at that tower, taking off the wood cladding piece by piece, while Abraham prayed aloud, beseeching God's mercy.

Resulting in the bargain where he gave his soul and those of his children if the gale would retreat.

Zoe.

I realize that someone is missing in all these photos and signs. "Where is she? Sarah Underhill?"

"Unfortunately, I couldn't find a photo of Sarah to use."

It's been a while since I've looked through the old family albums but the only one I remember of my great-great-grand-mother is a grainy, slightly out-of-focus, photo of Sarah sitting in a 1930s automobile wearing a saucer-shaped hat that puts her face in shadow. Levi is in the driver's seat, and Seaborn, about the same age as the portrait in the dining room, is standing on the running board.

Owen's comment that you would feel "in the storm" is pretty accurate. The noises are giving me a headache and the tilting floor effect isn't helping. Did the museum not consider what this would do to people susceptible to migraines or vertigo?

"You have Sarah's letters. Couldn't you have quoted some of them?"

"The only letters I have of hers are before 1894. We really don't know much about her at all, which isn't surprising of a woman living during those times." What Duncan tells me next startles me. "We haven't even been able to find her grave."

"Isn't she buried next to her husband, Abraham?"

"No. He's in the Congregational cemetery and so is Nolan's father, Seaborn, beside his wife, Daphne. But no Sarah. Levi was buried overseas during World War I. Matthew is in a cemetery outside Boston, and John's body was never found after his ship sank during the bombing of Pearl Harbor."

The sea took back its own.

"Why wouldn't she be buried here?"

Duncan tells me he has some ideas.

"I thought she might want to be buried near her twin girls, but I've checked that church graveyard, and she isn't there. Another possibility is her gravestone was lost or destroyed. That does happen with older burials that have been vandalized over the years. And some cemeteries get moved because of development, but I checked the church records and there's no record of her being buried here. Maybe she was traveling when she passed away?"

"When did she die?"

"That's another strange thing. I can't find any record of the date. No death certificate issued by the state, and your family Bible doesn't record it either."

I rub my temple, wishing my headache would go away. I could feel the pulse jumping beside my eye. "Can you turn that wind machine off? It's really too loud. And how did you get the floor to tilt?"

Duncan gives me an odd stare. "It shut off about five minutes ago, and we haven't entered the storm experience hall yet with the motors controlling the floor. That's ahead of us."

Overactive imagination. That label from the psych doctor I couldn't forget. "A woman as well-known as Sarah Underhill doesn't just disappear."

Duncan shakes his head. "Sorry. I've just hit nothing but dead ends. I've searched newspapers, graveyards, and church and state records."

Behind Duncan, there is the sound of someone wearing heels coming down the corridor. I imagine we going to be reamed out for being in the exhibit before it opens.

When she turns the corner, I see a woman whose face is shadowed by a huge saucer-shaped brim. Her 1910-era dress fits her from neck to toe and her form is fuzzy, like I'm seeing her through oily glasses. She stops about eight feet away and I can see the glint of her eyes flashing in her hat's shadow.

I swallow hard before asking Duncan, "Has anyone said this building is haunted?"

"No one has mentioned it."

Zoe.

Seeing ghosts is not my gift.

"What do you want?"

Duncan isn't an idiot. He knows I'm not speaking to him, but he is puzzled and looks from me to where I am staring.

Memory Keeper.

"What do you want?"

"Do not forsake me, O Lord! O my God, do not be far from me! Make haste to help me, O Lord, my salvation!"

I snap at the male voice emanating from the weather display, "Shut up, Abraham!" But he keeps rattling on with his prayer for the Lord to save him.

She laughs. *"I should have told him to shut up long ago."*

"Why are you here? What do you want?"

"You need to fix things, Memory Keeper."

"What things?" I demand, my lips dry.

"Get the memories right. All the memories."

The figure is gone, and I rub my eyes with the heels of my hands and rake my fingers through my hair, which is wet against my temples.

Oh. It's not sweat, it's sea water.

Seventeen

Maybe Duncan thinks I'm crazy seeing ghosts, and I'm upset because, for once, I know I'm not. Rushing out of the emergency exit to get outside, I feel as though I'm having an anxiety attack. Maybe I am.

"Here. Take it slowly." Duncan puts his hand on my shoulder, and I take a deep breath.

"This is going to sound wild, but I saw her. Someone or something that looked like Sarah from the photograph I remember of her. She was wearing a long dress from the early 1900s and an enormous hat." My hands go out to either side of my head to show him.

Duncan doesn't even blink as I tell him this. "What did she say?"

Trying to concentrate calms me down. "She wants me to get the memories right. Something in the story we know about the Gale must be wrong."

I am surprised that he is listening so calmly without contradicting me. Wasn't he all about facts?

He suggests, "In your family legend, Abraham is always the

one credited with turning back the Gale. Maybe people got that wrong."

"Like you said at dinner, maybe the family played with the truth and changed it to be what they wanted. Because Abraham wanted to be the hero." As I say this, it feels right. Abraham the blowhard. The big man about town making his handshake deals that earned us a reputation. That made us money. The man Sarah has wanted for years to shut up.

Duncan tries to reassure me. "Don't let it bother you, Zoe. Everyone knows Abraham conquering the storm through prayer is an apocryphal story. A modern parable encourages the idea that there is a higher power that can be reasoned with, that cares about humanity being saved. It's just a bedtime story."

How could I explain to Duncan that Abraham's tale was no mere story? His pact with the storm was the reason the Underhills were gifted. It explained why the town turned to us to fix their problems—and why they tolerated it when Grandfather claimed his tribute from their women.

They believe we have the power to save them.
But what if we don't? What if it is all a lie?

"Do you have our family Bible here?"

He shakes his head. "Not the actual Bible. That's at your grandfather's house, but I do have scans of certain pages, such as the family tree and some other entries on my computer."

I look back at the museum, not wanting to return. "I think we need to look at that first."

Taking my arm, Duncan brings me around to a different back entrance marked "Employees Only." From his wallet, he takes a card and scans it to release the door lock. The offices are deserted, and the clock on the wall reads half-past six. Where did the last few hours go?

We come through a hallway, past a few offices, and follow it to a dead-end where a door is marked "Records." Duncan scans his pass again as I say, "It's strange. I know nothing about Sarah but her name. Grandfather didn't know her or Abraham because they were gone before he was born. And all I've ever heard were stories about her husband and their sons."

"She was born in Connecticut, and she met Abraham through one of her Portland relatives. He traveled to do sermons and was in the area because of an invitation to preach. They married about two years later and had six children: a set of twin girls and four sons. At the time of the Gale, she had one living child, Levi, and was pregnant with Seaborn."

That surprises me. I thought Seaborn came later. "When was he born?"

Inside the room there are several work desks with computers, and in the middle is a conference table with several chairs. Along the wall is an architect's storage file, made up of long shallow drawers which are perfect for oversized flat documents that won't fit into standard files. The bookshelves that line the walls are about half-full of books and boxes.

Duncan goes to his desk and turns on his computer. He grabs an office chair and wheels it over for me. We sit down side-by-side and in a moment, he has the information on his screen.

"He was born seven months later, according to the dates on his gravestone. That's cross-referenced with the 1910 census, the church record of his baptism, the birth announcement in the newspaper, and your family Bible. Let me increase the image so you can see it."

He hovers the mouse over the entries as he describes them. "The Bible itself is old. I'm guessing it's from the early 1800s. Definitely, pre-Civil War, what with the cover design and the gilded pages inside. Here is an image of your family tree and I've noted the dates in a red circle on the jpg of those I thought were done at a later date."

I lean over, cheek-to-cheek. I'm careful not to touch him. Right now, I don't need anyone else's thoughts. Mine are enough.

"I can tell you that isn't Grandfather's handwriting. Did

Seaborn do it? Maybe his wife, Daphne? Or would it be one of his brothers? Or even Abraham himself?"

Duncan goes into his logical mode and I rest my chin in my hand and listen as he recites the information.

"This Bible was passed down from Seaborn to Nolan, and it was probably Abraham's, considering the age and his affiliation with the church. The handwriting is more modern in style and was written with a ballpoint pen, not a fountain pen, so post-World War II. I'm no expert, but you do get a feel for such things after looking after so many historical documents."

It's obvious what is missing: anything about Sarah.

Duncan is having the same thoughts as he goes back to the computer and, pointing with his mouse, shows me image after image. "Abraham has both a birth and death date, but the Bible only gives us Sarah's birth date. No listing of the twin girls, but all of her sons are there: Levi, Seaborn, Matthew, and John, with all of their wives. For Seaborn's line, there is a listing for his son Nolan, and wife, Catherine, and their daughter, Brynn."

The Bible notes that Levi died in 1918, and John in 1941, while Matthew's family ended up moving away from Kingstowe.

I nibble a fingernail, thinking. "Grandfather didn't know about the girls, so maybe Seaborn didn't know about his sisters? Maybe he just forgot to write down the date of his mother's death. Maybe she died away from home." I hesitate before asking, "You don't think she killed herself?"

He shrugs. "We simply don't know. But you are right that suicide isn't something people would acknowledge readily. And neither is divorce."

I feel it in my bones that there is no way Sarah would have divorced and walked away from her children. "I feel that Sarah and Abraham wouldn't have divorced. Family pride wouldn't have allowed it."

Duncan's historian mind rattles off more data. "Abraham was forty-one when the gale happened, and he died at eighty-two.

Sarah was younger, and records put her at twenty-nine at the time of the storm. Of course, women didn't live as long as men because they often died in childbirth. Perhaps that is what happened?"

I seize on the part that I feel is important. "What records? I thought you said there weren't any about her?"

"Naturally there are census records which are mandated by the US government," he explains. "They list the head of household, spouse, and children, along with their ages. Since they were done door-to-door sometimes they aren't always correct and have misspelled names or the dates are slightly off, but if you compare several decades, you still get a pretty accurate picture of the family."

Duncan leans closer to the computer, and the light illuminates his face with a bluish-white cast, making him almost Mephistopheles in appearance, and his glasses go opaque. "The last census record I have for Sarah is in 1930. She isn't listed in the 1940 or the 1950 census. Something must have happened between 1930 and 1940."

A shiver runs up the back of my spine and gives me a brain freeze over the back of my skull. "1938 happened."

"What does that mean?"

I shake my head, chiding him. "Where were you raised? Surely not around here? In September of that year, a category 1 hurricane hit New England and killed over six hundred people. The weathercasters always bring it up whenever we have hurricane weather. It's state history."

"You think she died in that storm?"

I'm thinking so much that I almost forget to use words. "No one was killed in Kingstowe in that storm. No destruction. It skipped us."

Did Sarah make a bargain that cost her life?

There is a buzz behind me and the library door unlocks but I am caught up in my thoughts, and ignore it.

"Sarah's been written out of the story, trampled and thrown

away. Abraham lied when he made the story all about him, and he knew it was a lie. And this museum exhibit is built upon that lie. He's a fraud," I say rather loudly, feeling the rightness of it down to the souls of my feet.

My uncle is here and staring at me with his mouth agape. He licks his lips and clears his throat. "I'd thought you'd already be gone for the day, Duncan."

Duncan shuts his computer up and grabs the strap of his satchel from the back of his chair. "Just wrapping up."

EIGHTEEN

A week later, the leaves are now bright yellow, and the reds are emerging. I feel the urgency of the season, of letting go of the old. Even though I've only been here for about ten days, I'm already fearing getting stuck. Boxed in. Labeled.

It took me a week to finally get a hold of our former house-keeper and make a date to see her. Sally is right, the woman is never at home.

Duncan and I stand outside the door of Millie Farmer's home. It is a 1980s brick ranch in a faux-colonial style of red brick, white trim, and black shutters, which doesn't match the older part of town, but it probably is free of the leaky plumbing or the drafty windows that the two-hundred-year-old Kingstowe houses have.

Still, the facade jars with the Hansel and Gretel cottage I had pictured her living in when I was a kid.

The doorbell brings her, and upon seeing us, she throws open the glass storm door. Before I can speak, she pulls me into a hug, and my stiffness melts. There are too many memories of this woman's lap, and her arms around me teaching me how to brush my teeth, or of her braiding my hair, for me not to enjoy this embrace.

I see little-me from her eyes: a skinny thing with enormous eyes that watches everything carefully, and a mouth that seldom speaks. A wave of sympathy and love from Happy as she braids my long hair and ties it off with a silky blue ribbon.

"Look at you, all grown up!"

Millie Farmer beams from a well-remembered round face that is almost froglike in appearance with its wide mouth and small chin and forehead. Her eyes are startlingly blue, bright against the white hair and the pale pink of her skin. Her body is the shape of a well-loved teddy bear.

She was a better foster mother than Aunt Belle to me; in the last five years, I haven't written to her once. Shame makes my face burn.

Her attention travels to my companion, who enters the house after me. "Now, who did you bring with you today?"

Reaching out, he shakes hands with her, while introducing himself, "Duncan Crane. I'm doing some work for the museum."

She nods while I smirk. Duncan probably doesn't realize that town gossip already knows all about him, including the brand of his shampoo, and whether he takes his coffee black or with cream. People are probably already speculating who they should match him up with, for Kingstowe doesn't like to let anyone go.

"Come along to the kitchen. I've just pulled fresh muffins warm from the oven."

The inside is filled with friendly clutter. Photos all over the walls of children and grandchildren, school pictures, wedding photos, and holiday candids from the Fourth of July and Christmas. I even see one of me: a school picture from my elementary days.

We pass through the living room with its large comfy, family-sized sofas and China cabinet full of porcelain-white figurines to the kitchen. This is the heart of her home, and it reflects a French country farmhouse style with blue cabinets, a yellow and white checkerboard backsplash, and countertops of white marble.

She gestures for us to take seats at the breakfast table while she pulls out plates and silverware from the drawers. "Would you like coffee, milk, orange juice, or a soda?"

I chose orange juice, and Duncan coffee.

"I was sorry to hear about Mr. Farmer."

Her husband died of a heart attack about three years ago.

Millie grimaces and shakes her head. "That was a terrible day, but he went peacefully, out in the garage, surrounded by his vintage cars and tools."

The serving plates are all decorated with dainty pink flowers, and she sets them in front of us, along with forks and blue gingham cloth napkins. A butter dish is whisked from the fridge, and a knife set alongside it. The muffins are blueberry, and they are full of homemade deliciousness.

When she settles in a chair next to ours, she asks, "Tell me everything you've been doing since I saw you last."

"Traveling a bit. I saw the Grand Canyon."

"Oh, I've always wanted to go! But couldn't convince Harvey. He said visiting Vermont during the fall foliage was as far as I would ever get him, and he was right. Was it as lovely as they all say?"

I tell her about landmarks I've seen, but not that I was posing as different people when I was there admiring them.

She tells Duncan, "That's good Irish butter, so don't skimp. Hot muffins crave butter." My companion takes her advice and puts on another pat. To me, she asks, while probably already knowing it all from Sally, "How's everyone up at the Big House?"

She doesn't know that Owen hasn't spoken a word to me since he heard me say Abraham was a liar. I say diplomatically, "Owen is very excited about the museum opening."

Her eyes crinkle, and the folds on her face shows she smiles often. "I can imagine! It's taken years for this project to come together, what with fundraising, getting permits, and builders. It's his pride and joy and deservedly so. Have you been to see it?"

"Yes." *It's haunted and built on a lie.*

"I saw in the paper your grandfather is still opening up the grounds for the Gale's anniversary. I wasn't sure he'd go through with it after your poor mother was found."

Grandfather wouldn't hold off being the center of attention because of a dead daughter.

When I remain silent, Duncan steps in. "I gather that the caterers and tent had already been arranged. Mr. Underhill didn't think he could disappoint the town, considering it is such an important anniversary."

Millie cocks her head and says behind her coffee cup, "He's always put Kingstowe above family, but perhaps it's time to pass on the baton? Step down and let Ryan take us? Do you think he would do that?"

Ryan says he wants to put the old regime out to pasture, but is he really ready to do all the work that Grandfather does? And what would happen to his real estate business back in the city? Would Jennifer be happy living in Kingstowe, seeing Aunt Belle and Grandfather every day?

I say diplomatically, "Ryan's thinking it over, but I'm not sure Grandfather is ready to hand over the reins."

"He'll have big shoes to fill," says Millie. "Back in the day, Nolan was always go-go-go. Meetings, building projects, committees. He never sat still. Neither did Catherine. Cutting ribbons, hosting parties, starting up clubs and societies. Never a moment of peace in that household. They kept us all busy."

Duncan thinks like an interviewer and asks, "How did you come to work for the Underhills, Mrs. Farmer?"

"It was a friend of a friend. Told me to go up and tell them I could bake. They were looking for a cook then, and I needed money to set up a house with Harvey. Of course, my mother didn't approve of me leaving the family restaurant to go work for

Nolan Underhill, but the money was better, and the hours were regular."

"Why didn't she approve?" I knew Duncan would ask that, so I toy with my glass tumbler as Millie answers, "You may not think it now, but Nolan was quite the rascal back in the day."

The idea makes me sick, but after learning about Aunt Belle and Grandfather's affair, I force myself to ask her. "He never—?"

She shakes her head. "Oh no, not me. I was already engaged to Harvey and was head over heels in love with him. True love. That's the only protection against a man as charming as the devil."

I can't stop myself. "How could Grandmother put up with it?"

"People chased after him and he couldn't say no. Girls couldn't take their eyes off of him. I figure it was like being married to a rock star. You'd forgive a lot if you were married to Mick Jagger."

Coerced by Charm.

I shake my head, still mad at him for old affairs newly learned. "I'd never put up with being cheated on."

Her bright blue eyes shift sideways to my companion, and Duncan responds as if she has asked him a question. "The men in my family are deeply monogamous once they fall in love."

The two of them exchange a secret smile. If I stay much longer, these two will have me married off to him with a kid or two.

"I wanted to ask you about my mom, because I barely remember her. Since you came to work for us before even Ryan was born, I thought you might have some stories about her."

"She was such a darling girl, your mother. You take after her." She reaches over and pats my hand, and I get another sweet taste of loving memories: *my mother stuffs an English muffin in her mouth as she grabs her school backpack. Racing out the back kitchen door, which bangs behind her. She gives a wave over her shoulder to Millie, who is wiping hands wet from washing dishes on her apron.*

"A lot of girls grow into their beauty, but your mom always

had a glow about her. A laugh and a smile. She attracted friends like flowers do bees."

Charm. I wonder if my mother ever grew tired of this adulation? Did she ever wonder if someone loved her just for herself? Does Ryan?

"Brynn was the apple of her father's eye. The first girl born in the Underhill line in three generations." *Another family lie.* "Nolan was always showing her off at the Harbor Club and having her play the piano for his friends. He loved taking her out on the water in one of his sailboats. They'd come back sunburned and hungry, and Catherine would scold them for being gone all day telling no one where they were going."

She takes us through many more reminiscences and occasionally I make a point of touching her hand when she refills my glass or hands me a muffin so I can capture the feel, smell, and touch from her thoughts. I tuck it all away like an old greeting card into the box of my heart.

Eventually, Millie starts to talk about the others in the house.

"Owen really didn't know her as a child. Brynn was already married to Robert and had Ryan by the time your uncle moved back home after Natalie's death. But Annabelle? Brynn and her were oil and water from the very beginning. I'm afraid she took some of that dislike out on you, Zoe."

Her sympathy makes for an awkward silence; how can I acknowledge the truth without sounding pathetic? I decided not to address it. "I was wondering what you remember about that week leading up to my mother's disappearance?"

Her frog face folds into deeper lines of sadness.

"I've been thinking about it ever since the news of them finding your poor mother broke. When she was pregnant with you, she got pretty low, but after you came along, you were her little ray of sunshine. She was starting to perk up and take an interest in things again."

Was she? My mind went back to that bottle of pills in her bathroom. She was coping, but how well? Did anyone truly know? She'd lost her lover and her dreams, had two small children, and was living with her parents and aunt.

"What do you remember about that day, in particular? Did anything happen that was unusual? Where was everyone?"

Happy answers me readily enough. "There was tension in the house all week long. To the point Brynn and Annabelle were giving each other the silent treatment. They were always quarreling over Ryan because Annabelle wouldn't stop giving unsolicited advice. Women who haven't had children can get that way — become possessive about a niece or nephew. It got so bad that even Kitty snapped at her to leave Brynn alone."

Millie shook her head. "But it was more than suggestions. It was just plain interference! That week, Annabelle had signed Ryan up for a sports team and his practice was the same dates Brynn had enrolled him in a scouting summer camp."

Probably Ryan fulfilled some fantasy of Aunt Belle being a mother. He was Nolan's grandson, so did she imagine he was hers if fate had been different? How did Kitty put up with her?

"That day Ryan complained of a sick stomach, but his mother was going to make him go to school anyway, as she thought he was faking it. Annabelle insisted on him staying home, and by the time the two had exhausted themselves by arguing, it was too late to send him. Brynn told Annabelle she could play mother if she thought she was better at it. She stormed out, and that was the last I saw of her."

"Was Ryan really sick?" asked Duncan.

Millie considered his question before answering. "Now, that I don't know for sure, but I reckon even if he was, he got over it quickly enough. He spent the day playing video games and found reasons to come into the kitchen, begging for cookies. That day I was pretty frazzled because the plumber was there trying to fix the drains, so eventually I had had enough and ordered him a pizza."

"So, Aunt Belle was home that day?"

"Only in the morning. By the time Ryan complained for the umpteenth time about the Internet being too slow for his video game, she found someplace else to be. Said she would pick up Nolan's dry cleaning, but that was a lie. We always had it delivered to the house." Millie shook her head in mirth. "Being a mom is tough work, and Brynn was right. She wasn't up for it."

"Was anyone else home?" I ask.

"Catherine. When Ryan was driving us all mad, she asked him to fix her sewing machine."

Duncan was curious. "Was he able to do that? Seems like a big job for a kid."

Millie slapped her palm down on the counter, laughing. "You know he did! No one was more surprised than Catherine, for the old thing hadn't worked for over a decade. He took it all apart, cleaned and oiled the parts, and by dinnertime he had it whirling away again."

I prompt her. "Nolan and Owen?"

"Both gone. I think because of business or club meetings, but I don't really remember exactly where. I'm sorry, Zoe."

There was one person we hadn't discussed — me. My memories of that day didn't include a plumber or Ryan fixing a sewing machine. "I remember nothing about a sewing machine. I just remember making chocolate chip cookies with you."

She shakes her head. "No. You're wrong, my dear. You weren't there."

I blink. "No. I was home that day. I remember the letter C on Sesame Street."

"Well, you were back home for supper, but you weren't with us in the morning or at lunch. Maybe you were at daycare?"

I am stunned speechless. I'd never gone to a daycare.

Nineteen

For the rest of our visit, Duncan asks Millie general questions about her life and the town, but he avoids any further discussion about the Underhills and the day my mother disappeared. Maybe it is the frozen look on my face that clues him in that I don't want to talk anymore about it.

Leaving, Millie gives us spine-crushing hugs and a box of homemade cookies. Walking to his car parked at the curb, Duncan says emphatically, "You look spent. I'm taking you out for lunch."

"I don't want to be around people."

"What if I grab something and we go back to my office to eat?"

"Okay." Even a haunted museum is better than a busy cafe.

Duncan isn't kidding that he knows every Kingstowe drive-through and restaurant. He rattles off a list and gives an opinion about each. We end up with lobster rolls and some French fries.

We go through the back door of the museum. Duncan seems popular, for we meet a few people in passing, but since they are busy with phones or visitors, they only give a smile or wave.

He sets the bag of food down on the conference table and, from a mini-fridge, pulls out a couple of sodas. Sitting across from each other, I put the food into my mouth mechanically, not tasting any of it.

Duncan's appetite doesn't seem to be affected, but he is sympathetic. "It must be disturbing not to know where you were the day your mother disappeared."

My voice is flat. "You think?"

"You'll figure it out. You're resilient, Zoe."

Irritated, I snap, "You don't know me!"

"You're right, I don't. But I'd like to."

Which version of me? He said he came here for me. *Why?*

"Why did you come here?"

"I already told you. My dad used to tell me stories about Brynn."

Duncan crumples up his empty sandwich wrapper and puts it back into the sack before going over to the trash can to throw it away.

He's being evasive. I feel it. "What did your dad tell you about us? About Brynn and the Underhills?"

He comes over to my side of the table and leans against it, crossing his arms and his feet at the ankles. "I grew up being told bedtime fairy tales about your family. The royal Underhills, who all lived in a castle, surrounded by water. A beautiful young princess who was the fairest in the land, but whose father refused to let her go unless a prince could accomplish the three tasks."

Duncan gives an exasperated laugh. "My dad is a bit of a dreamer, and he really can weave spells with his words. I developed a bit of a crush on your mom. Maybe I even thought I would be the prince who finally won her."

"My mother isn't a sleeping beauty. She's dead. There's no one here for you to rescue." I stand up putting us face-to-face. "It's easy to hide behind a story. Abraham is hiding, and so is your dad."

"I'm telling you the truth. He did come here and try to help Brynn."

"Let me guess, Grandfather scared him away." By his expression, I know my theory is right. Did he call the sheriff to escort Mr. Crane off the premises? Or was there a night spent in jail to give Mr. Crane time to think?

"You haven't answered what I've asked. You knew there wasn't a princess to save when you took the job, so why come here?"

He starts to blush and avoids my gaze as he speaks. "When I was in graduate school, I drove up here one summer to see the place my dad always told me about. It was only after I got here that I realized I picked the worst time to visit because it was the Fourth of July weekend."

"Oh God, you didn't come on parade day, did you? It's a madhouse around here."

He gives a self-deprecating chuckle. "Yes, unfortunately. And it was packed, but I enjoyed it. It seemed so old-fashioned with men walking around dressed in colonial coats and knee breeches. Women in petticoats and brass-buckled shoes. Something out of a museum."

I touch his arm and his memory sweeps me away. *The street-lamps are hung with red, white, and blue banners; and there is the smell of gunpowder in the air because there is no way to stop the kids from setting off fireworks within the city limits; the taste of ice cream melting on your tongue.*

"I saw you in a bookshop and after you checked out, I asked the clerk who you were."

We were so close I can see the day reflected in his eyes. Our breath mingles, and as our lips touch, I fall into his memory.

He elbows past the crowd standing on the sidewalk chatting. Why don't people move?! Blocked again and feeling hot, he enters the bookstore. The bell tinkles and someone from the front desk cries out, "Don't let the door slam!" and Duncan catches it just in time.

There is a crowd in the bookstore, but not as much as the one outside. He goes down an aisle sideways, making his way to where the history section might be. Duncan always checks those shelves looking for something special.

It's easier to move back here because there is only one girl who stands alone, like an island.

If you saw the sunrise for the first time, it would be this girl. Dark brown hair streaked with red highlights, a pale complexion with the faintest tinge of pink - like the highest-grade porcelain when you hold it to the light for it to shine through. She is reading a passage in a book, with the knuckle of one forefinger pressed against soft rosy lips that he would like to know himself.

"Oh, excuse me," says someone behind him and he is pushed forward. He would have touched her except she glides out of his way with the ease of a swan on the lake. His approach breaks her concentration, and she looks at the gold watch on her wrist. She must have been late because she closes her book and starts toward the counter to pay for it and everyone steps out of her way, never touching her.

After paying for her book, the girl exits the door, letting it close slowly when Duncan pushes up to the counter. "Who is that girl?"

The clerk is already checking out the next person and says without breaking the rhythm of his tap-tap on the cash register, "That's Zoe Underhill."

"You followed me that day."

"I did. You were so lovely. I was surprised that I found a princess after all." His mouth moves over my cheek to my earlobe, his teeth nibbling it like it's Easter chocolate you're trying to save but can't resist.

"Why didn't you say hello?" I whisper.

He tells me as he strokes my cheek gently, "I don't know. It would have ruined things."

Things can be spoiled so easily.

The door clicks open, and my uncle Owen enters the room. He is flustered and looks away. It is déjà vu, an appearance in some repeat pantomime irks me, but Duncan shows not an iota of discomfort at being found kissing me. With his arm still around my waist, he asks my uncle, "Did you want to do some research, Owen? We're heading out."

"Oh, I don't want to put you two out. Take your time." Owen turns his back to us, to give us time to become decent or because he is embarrassed catching us.

Exchanging looks, which makes me cover my mouth to stop from laughing, Duncan tells him we are heading out. After telling Owen goodbye, we enter the hallway, shoving each other like children as we make our way out to the parking lot.

On the way home we say nothing as we hold hands across the front seat. But when we pull down the driveway, I sigh. *Back to reality.*

As if he's reading my thoughts, Duncan says,

"I mean it. You're stronger than you know."

That's the type of thing you say to someone right after you tell them they have a horrible disease that they may not survive. I raise my hand and dismiss his comment with a wave. "Don't."

He parks the car and turns to me, one arm across the backrest. "You don't believe me? Why not? I think you'd admit that a weak person wouldn't be able to stand against your family. Even my father couldn't do it, but here you are, doing it."

"In the past, I've run away, and I'd run now if I had the means to do it. That's not standing up to them."

"Isn't it though? You left. Something your mother was never strong enough to do. And by leaving, you've denied them the battle they want. They love fighting so much, imagine what it is like for them to be denied it?"

They must have heard the car, for Aunt Belle is coming out the front door. She calls to us, "Dinner is already on the table" and then stands there with her hands on her hips, waiting.

"Ready to enter the lion's den again?" Duncan jokes.

Rolling my eyes, I give a mirthless laugh. "C'mon, lion tamer."

. . .

That evening after dinner, I read a book in Kitty's garden room while Duncan sorts through his stacks of papers. Occasionally, one of us looks up to smile and the other stops and returns it before returning to our reading.

Being together is like sharing a secret, but in this house, you can't speak of it or it will be stolen from you.

At my bedroom door, we have an awkward parting because Ryan and Jennifer are coming up the stairs and will be in the hallway any minute. The back of our hands touch each other, the tips of his fingers caressing mine as they rest concealed from view by our bodies.

"Tomorrow?" he says.

"Yes."

Ryan is here now, so I open my door and enter my old bedroom, a place I outgrew when I was twelve. Before undressing, I shove my nightstand in front of my bedroom door. I wasn't going to risk her or anyone coming into my room without me knowing.

Would Duncan know how to install a lock?

After the shower, I pull on a t-shirt and slip between the cool sheets and their faint, comforting smell of fabric softener. Nothing like a well-made bed after a long day. Turning off the light, I have a few moments to think about Duncan before I'm deeply asleep.

The next time I know consciousness, I'm still half asleep trying to figure out where I am. Something hits my head with a light thunk. My hand comes up to my cheek, and something small hits my shoulder and then my hip. I roll over, holding the coverlet up, and several acorns roll off, making plunking noises as they hit the floor.

What are acorns doing in my bed?

Even as I puzzle over it, about a dozen come raining down from the ceiling like raindrops, and I quickly raise the covers over my head to protect myself. Did a squirrel get in? Is there a hole in the roof?

When I moved the nightstand, I had put the lamp on the floor beside my bed. I slide a hand out from under the blankets and fumble for the switch. When it comes on, the rain of acorns stops.

Slipping out of the covers, I find the floor is covered with acorns and I accidentally step on one, causing me to give a yelp. There aren't any holes in the ceiling and my window is closed.

"Abraham?" I ask, but no one answers. "Ha-ha, your prank is hilarious. Are you mad because I know you're a liar?"

Making an apron out of my t-shirt top, I collect the small brown nuts scattered all over. They feel a little cold as if they've been outside; some even have a few flecks of dirt or grass on them.

Oak trees have unique caps on them, and it helps to identify the tree they come from. These all have a light brown, oblong nut about half the length of my pinkie finger, with a thick, bowl-shaped cap. I've seen them many times, and suddenly I know. These are from the Majestic.

Rolling an acorn between my fingers, I remember.

Ryan and I are in the front yard under the Majestic's green canopy for it is summer. I'm eight and he must be around eleven. Ignoring him, I continue to hand-gallop my plastic ponies through the dirt path I've carved out for them in the grass.

"I'm sorry I Charmed you, Zoe." He tries again. "I never meant for Aunt Belle to see you take that money out of her purse."

I refuse to look at him. "Maybe you should have done it instead of Charming me to do it. Now she thinks I'm the thief, not you!"

He gets down on the grass, rolling on his back so his face is under mine. Ryan isn't trying to Charm me now, but persuasion is his tool-in-trade, and he thinks a smile will solve everything. "I won't do it again."

"Yes, you will. You're just like Grandfather. You'll do anything to get your own way."

"What can I do to make you believe me?"

I pull some tops off the grass and make a pile of them. Dipping the head of my toy horse, Blaze begins to eat.

"Here." Ryan thrusts his hand under my nose, holding an acorn. I ignore him and keep playing. "It's a Majestic acorn, so it's magical."

Laying Blaze down for a nap, I pick up the acorn from where it rests in Ryan's palm. It looks like all the other acorns in the grass. Nothing special. I am about to toss it away when Ryan grabs my fist to stop me.

"It's from the Majestic, the strongest tree in Kingstowe, so these acorns are from the best tree ever."

"You say it's magic?"

"Of course it is!"

"Then put your hand on it and swear to the Majestic that you will never Charm me again." His hesitation proves me right. He has no intention of keeping his promise. I sit up and start collecting my horses to leave.

"Wait! Okay. I'll swear."

My brother puts his hand over mine, the acorn sandwiched between our palms. "I promise that I'll never Charm you again unless it is to save your life. Or my life. Or the life of someone we love."

"Hm. That sounds like a fairy promise."

"C'mon, Zoe! Believe me. I really mean it."

I pocket the acorn and tell him, "Now go away because I'm still mad."

He gets on his knees, rolling to his feet. "Happy wanted me to tell you she made brownies, but I guess if you're not interested—."

"No!"

We both jump up at the same time and sprint toward the house. Ryan even lets me win this time.

TWENTY

A few days later, after dinner, Grandfather informs us he wants to plan Brynn's memorial, so we are to join him in the trophy room like good little soldiers.

When Duncan moves to leave, I grab his hand. "C'mon, lion tamer. If I'm going in, you are too."

"I'm not family," he protests.

"Ryan has Jennifer to back him up. So, you'll have to be my partner in this circus ring."

In the room, we sit side-by-side on the loveseat across from Jennifer and Ryan on the opposite sofa. Sabrina, who was invited to dinner, takes the chair next to Jennifer.

Owen trails in behind us all, taking a spot off to the side where he won't be noticed. He's like the old family dog, a bit slow and forgotten, but familiar, and always there to trip over.

One conspicuous absence is my aunt. You might think it was because of shame, but Aunt Belle never backs down from anything unpleasant, especially if she can use it to cause more pain. Grandfather tells us she is working on the committee for the homecoming queen. Convenient. Maybe Grandfather planned to do this tonight for a reason?

Robert and his wife aren't here, but I doubt they were invited, and no one misses them.

As the meeting starts, it's clear Grandfather merely wishes us to hear his plans. "I've booked the Episcopalian church for the last Thursday of the month. We don't want to interfere with the Halloween festivities and if we leave it until November, that means we are competing with the museum opening and the Gale celebration."

The Gale celebration. The last few days there has been a woman in a suit and heels walking around the front lawn with a laptop in hand. Grandfather hired her to manage the celebration. He wants it perfect, and he obviously doesn't trust Owen to do it, but it doesn't stop my uncle from following the woman around and giving her advice.

Ryan interrupts Grandfather. "Why the Episcopalian church? Mom wasn't a member."

"Their sanctuary is the largest in town and can seat the most people," explains Grandfather, clearly irritated at Ryan's questioning of his choice. They have been two tom cats ever since the squabble about Robert stealing Grandfather's land deal.

"Of course, I'll be the primary speaker."

Ryan is determined to challenge Grandfather's every statement. "Why?"

When Duncan speaks, even the simmering resentment in the room listens. I can't figure out how he does it because, unlike the Underhill men, he doesn't yell or use Charm.

"It would probably be best for someone in the religious or civic community to lead the memorial. They only introduce the important guests and it would diminish your role, Mr. Underhill."

"Humph," mutters Grandfather. Even he can't go toe-to-toe with Duncan when he states things in such a logical way.

It's strange no one but me seems to realize Duncan dislikes Nolan. I figure that dislike is because of whatever Grandfather did to Duncan's father when he visited so long ago, but still. Had

Grandfather not tried to Charm him? Was his Charisma failing like Ryan suggested? Or was Duncan simply immune to it for some reason?

Sabrina makes a suggestion. "What about that English teacher from high school? She thought a lot of Brynn, and I know they stayed in touch after graduation. Is she still around?"

"I'll find out tomorrow," said Grandfather. "Now, can I get on with this, unless you have something else you want to complain about?"

Jennifer gives Ryan's hand a gentle warning squeeze, and he says, "Not at this moment."

Grandfather asks Sabrina, "Can you think of any music Brynn would have liked that we can use?"

Memory supplies a tinkle of melody, but I can't place the name. Sabrina does, though. "Oh, she had several that would be good for the memorial. I think *I Will Always Love You*, and *Somewhere I Belong* would be good choices."

"Don't know them," says Grandfather.

Sabrina sings a bit of the melody, and I'm surprised to hear a voice with some training. It fits the tune in my head, and Ryan and I nod in recognition.

"Perhaps Sabrina can put together the music?" Jennifer suggests, and Nolan readily agrees, probably because it is a topic he knows nothing about. It was Kitty who was the music lover, and it was she who taught Mother to play the piano.

"What do you think?" Duncan's question to me makes all the heads turn toward us. Surprised at having everyone's attention, I speak disjointedly. "Harp and cello. Grandmother."

Ryan immediately understands me. "Kitty loved that combination. But we should add a piano."

Sabrina and Ryan plan the music, and I think this is making Grandfather grumpy, but at one point he rubs his temple and mutters, "Damn storm front giving me a headache."

Instinctively, his words make me look towards the sea, but it is getting dark, and I can't see if the sky is clear. Well, the air pressure around here changes rapidly and Grandfather, the great-grandson of Abraham, is very sensitive to weather. He always knew when it was a good day to go sailing, and the winds always favored him much to the ire of those competing against him.

The tides move in our blood, our words make lightning, and the storms play in our heads. *We are as changeable as the weather.*

Sabrina keeps talking about the memorial. "There should be poetry. Brynn loved the power of words so much."

Immediately, I think of Mother's journals stored at the museum; something from those should be read. Selecting one would be my contribution. I was about to suggest this when Grandfather says abruptly, "I have a passage picked out."

We all become silent and turn to attend to him. Grandfather is an excellent orator and when he speaks, his baritone rolls out the poem *Crossing the Bar* by Tennyson as if he is standing on the deck of a ship.

> *Sunset and evening star*
> *And one clear call for me!*
> *And may there be no moaning of the bar,*
> *When I put out to sea,*
> *But such a tide as moving seems asleep,*
> *Too full for sound and foam,*
> *When that which drew from out the boundless deep*
> *Turns again home.*
> *Twilight and evening bell,*
> *And after that the dark!*
> *And may there be no sadness of farewell,*
> *When I embark;*
> *For tho' from out our bourne of Time and Place*
> *The flood may bear me far,*
> *I hope to see my Pilot face to face*
> *When I have crost the bar.*

There is a deep silence afterward, as if we are waiting for the amen at the end of a prayer. In the room's stillness, the only noise is the whistling of the wind as it moves around the house, rattling the window latches as if it is a thief trying to find an entry point.

Owen looks away from the group, and one hand dabs at the edge of his eye. Jennifer squeezes Ryan's hand and, for the first time, my brother says nothing clever or hostile. Even though I want to, I do not reach for Duncan's hand, as I'm trying to be circumspect even though I suspect Owen has probably already told everyone about what he saw at the museum.

"Yes, er. I plan on reading that," Grandfather says in a tone that isn't its usual brusque self.

He really misses her, I think. Followed by the more cynical thought: *some killers are sorry later about what they've done.*

Sabrina asks tentatively, "Would it be all right if I say something at the service for Brynn?"

"Of course you should!" Grandfather says, regaining the strength of his voice. "That's why I invited you here. I'm also wondering what flowers Brynn would have liked."

"Not lilies. She hated them," I speak up.

After flowers, the discussion moves to who to invite and how to manage the reception so the family could meet visitors. Jennifer and Sabrina say they will select the photographs to be displayed.

While Ryan, Jennifer, and Sabrina are making these plans, I watch Grandfather, who is becoming increasingly distracted. His forehead contracts in pain and, at one point, he winces. "That was close."

Confused, I lean over and ask him if he is feeling okay.

Grandfather asks, "Didn't you hear that last thunderclap?"

I hadn't, and Ryan, who overhears our exchange, says, "Maybe you have your hearing aids turned up too loud?"

"I don't wear hearing aids!" barks Grandfather. "It's you who must be deaf if you didn't hear that loud bang. It might as well have been in the room with us!"

"There doesn't seem to be any rain," observes Sabrina, who has gone over to the windows to peer out.

Owen launches into an explanation of how a layer of warm air above a cold layer makes a temperature inversion. For esoteric information is his stock in trade. "The warm air makes a layer that pushes the sound of thunder down to the surface even if you don't see rain or thunderclouds."

"But why didn't we all hear it? Why only Nolan?" Sabrina asks the room.

"Maybe it's *you all* that needs hearing aids!" Grandfather quips nastily.

There is a rattle against the windows as if hailstones have hit the glass. Ryan's head jerks sideways to stare. He admits, "Something is blowing in."

"What's the weather report say?" No one tells Sabrina that Underhills don't listen to them. We *are* the weather.

Duncan's words from the day I met Sarah at the museum echo in my ear: *Sarah was holding one baby, and pregnant with her next. All of her boys have good Biblical names. Why did you name him Seaborn, Sarah? What did you give birth to after the storm?*

Suddenly, there is a tremendous, violent crash and we all jump to our feet. Ryan says, "That sounded like glass. Did some windows blow out?"

Owen's eyes grow round, and his face drains of blood. "The conservatory." He rushes out of the room, with Ryan quick on his heels. Duncan, Grandfather, and I are next, with Sabrina and Jennifer lagging.

Owen's conservatory is reserved for his hobby of bonsai. It is on the opposite side of the music room, and it is south facing. I haven't been there in years, despite Owen's recent invitation. I have the sinking feeling it won't look like I last saw it.

A horrible scream pierces the air, like a rabbit caught in a snare.

In a moment we see why Owen is wailing. The conservatory is destroyed. Every pane of glass is shattered and in the middle of this disaster, he stands. Owen is so shocked that he is physically swaying side to side, as if the room is tilting under his feet like the deck of a ship in a storm.

The bonsai are scattered around him on the floor amongst the broken shards of glass and piles of potting soil. Each tree is wrenched from its pot, leaving its hairy roots bare of soil. Their trunks are snapped, and some are limply bent, like the broken neck of a swan.

His feet slide on the sheets of glass beneath his shoes, and he almost falls. Grandfather reaches out to help his brother, but Owen slaps his hand away. "Don't touch me! You've never cared about this! Or what it means to me, so don't pretend now."

"We can fix it," Grandfather assures him.

Glass can be repaired, but decades of devotion cannot be replaced so easily. Owen pounds on his chest, his voice shrill. "No! You can't repair this! Fix a decade of work with money."

He reaches down and picks up one of his broken trees. In doing so he has cut his hand on a piece of the glass and a bright rivulet of blood starts to flow down his palm.

Grandfather starts to say, "I'll pay for—"

Owen snaps at his brother. "Don't make me laugh! You didn't help me with Natalie, and you won't now. You'd rather keep me under your boot, so don't pretend you care, *brother*." I can't believe Owen is screaming in his brother's face, or how old and tired Grandfather looks under the onslaught. Even a rabbit with Underhill in him fights when cornered.

Owen's face transforms, and his resemblance to Grandfather is uncanny. His light caramel eyes are bulging, his nostrils are flared, and his lips have thinned, showing his teeth.

"All of you are against me! Trying to destroy me and the things I care about. Undermining the family reputation." At the end, he glares at me so fiercely, that I shrink back. Duncan steps between me and Owen, and I hide behind him.

Never tell. Never remember.

Ryan tries to get him to calm down to no avail. "It was some freak storm." That doesn't explain the plants pulled out of their pots or the little tree trunks snapped like a chicken's wishbone.

Owen continues his screaming tirade. It is as if the decades of being trampled on by Grandfather have fed a dormant volcano that is now erupting and raining hot lava down upon us all.

"You've crippled us all— Belle, Ryan, Zoe. You and your pride. Do you think Kitty didn't know you were seducing her sister? She wasn't stupid! But you're so arrogant and selfish that you didn't care how many times you broke her heart, as long as you could add another woman to your collection. You soured Belle until she's nothing but hate— she made Zoe's childhood a hell, and spoiled Ryan so badly that the boy is a brat!"

My heart is pounding like a bird, and my hand goes up to my throat but nothing issues from it but a whimper. I am gripping Duncan's arm hard, and he steps forward to block my view of Owen.

The crisp white sail snaps in the wind. It is a beautiful day with thunderheads far overhead.

Owen's harsh breathing is like a bellows. It is loud in the room, for we are all quietly stunned by Owen's rage. It is as if the docile family pet has gone savage.

He scoops up several more of his trees, loudly smashing more glass under his shoes, as he drips blood all over the floor. But there are too many to collect, and he drops some. Frustrated, he cries out and throws all of them back down to the floor and storms out, casting an angry glower at each of us.

The water laps, laps, laps, and there is a sharp scream that makes a wound in my mind. When it ends, there is only the vastness of the sea, the whistling of the wind, and the snapping of the sail.

TWENTY-ONE

The man asks, "Who are you?"

But Grace Morgan ignores him, humming a little tune under her breath. She knows where there are toys and climbing the stairs two-by-two goes to retrieve them from Zoe's room. She takes the little horses to Mother's closet where she can be safe and they can run free as wild mustangs.

She scoots under the hanging clothes and on her stomach, sets up her little herd of four. The stallion, Midnight, will protect his three mares, Sienna, Dakota, and Stormy. They know Midnight will always protect them from the bad things.

"What are the names of your horses?" The nosy man has followed her, and Grace tries to ignore him. Grown-ups aren't good at playing.

"Do you think they have enough grass?" he asks.

She dips her horse's heads to show they can nibble the carpet.

"Oh, I just thought they might like a piece of candy. Someone told me that horses love peppermint." Across the carpet, he slides a plastic-wrapped round piece of red and white. Not until he moves away to sit at the door does she gallop Dakota over to it to sniff it and accept the treat.

Grace goes back to playing, totally absorbed and lost to the outside world as only a young child can be. There are no angry voices here, no shouting, no sound of the wind or the sail. That all fades away.

I wake up to find myself rolled into a ball in the corner of my mother's closet, hidden under hanging clothes, with her suitcases stacked in front of me like a castle wall.

Duncan is sitting in the closet's doorway. His head is nodding forward from sleep, and he jerks awake when I ask, "What are you doing here?"

"I followed you."

I become frightened. My memory hasn't blacked out like this in years, not since high school.

Moving the suitcases, I stagger to my feet, using my hand on the wall as one leg has fallen asleep. Duncan slowly stands up to move out of the doorway so I come past, carefully stepping over the scattered horse toys on the carpet.

At the bathroom sink, I soak a washcloth with slightly warm water and cover my face with it, patting my skin. I'm acutely aware of the smell of sweat and how my armpits are slick with perspiration, as if I've broken a fever.

Duncan tries not to look worried, but his eyes and mouth are failing miserably. I ignore him and the image in the mirror of my pale face with its purplish shadows under the frightened eyes.

I tell him, "I'm going to my room now."

He keeps following me, and we are standing in the hallway. Things are quiet and I have the feeling it is quite late— or maybe very early— in the morning.

"I'm going to take a shower and go to bed. I'll be all right now. Thank you, and goodbye, Duncan Crane."

His hand comes up but falls away before it can touch me.

I don't go back to sleep. Instead, I am down before Sally arrives and everyone in the house is still in bed. Collecting the newspaper from the doorstep, I read the obituaries as I fix myself oatmeal. A young woman who died of cancer has a funeral service scheduled today in Wellston. Didn't I want to go there for Mother?

Happy always kept money in a tin in the cabinet above the fridge to tip the delivery men and to buy treats from the kids raising money for their clubs who go door-to-door. It seems Sally is keeping the same tradition, for I find almost a thousand dollars in petty cash. That is a lot of Girl Scout cookies.

I gather up the backpack that I took from my closet and quietly exit the house through Kitty's music room. From that door, there is a path that cuts through the woods, and by taking it, no one coming up the drive will see me leave.

The sun is just starting to rise, and the birds are already getting noisy. The path isn't overgrown because Grandfather likes things tidy. It splits at one point, and I take the more narrow path which leads you to the highway that goes through the National.

Walking down the state highway, I'm about three miles along when someone pulls over to offer me a ride. I refuse at least two cars driven by men before a woman with two kids slows down. She is worried for me seeing that I'm walking alone.

"I missed my ride to work this morning," I told her. It is probably the ironed crease in my jeans that decides that I'm safe. No killer presses their jeans. She says, "We're heading into the National to meet up with a mom's playgroup so I can take you as far as the park office. Will that work for you?"

"Perfect."

I grab the door handle and climb into the front seat as her children are in the back. The ride only takes a half an hour, and with my teaching experience, I keep the two boys entertained with questions about dinosaurs and explaining to them how rainbows work.

By the time their mom drops me off at the park's information center, she's ready to hire me as a nanny. "If you ever tire of working at the park, call me."

"I'll definitely keep you in mind."

I've already contacted a taxi to meet me and in the short time that I have to wait, I go into the bathroom stall and change into a dress, hose, and low-heeled shoes. Around my neck hangs my mother's gold chain with the two birthstones. Ryan and Zoe.

My ride isn't here yet, so I get a bottled water and a packaged muffin from the vending machine.

Behind me, someone calls, "Hey! Are you the one wanting a ride?"

It's a gray four-door sedan that matches the description the app gave me. Walking around the back, I take a pic of his plates and send it to the Cloud, before climbing into the back.

"Where do you want to go?"

When I tell him, the driver says he'll take me to Pickard, which is halfway, but when I tell him what I'm willing to pay, he changes his mind and agrees to go all the way to Wellston.

"Why are you going to Wellston?"

"A funeral."

"Oh. Sorry for your loss."

My answer gets him to be quiet, as no one likes to talk about death or be around someone mourning. The driver turns the radio on to a classical station and I settle my head back for the two-hour drive. It is easy to slip into a light doze when you refuse to think about anything.

◆

Vanessa Dickenson's funeral is well-attended. From experience, I know those who die young usually have a good turn-out as the tragedy of a life cut short seems to demand that people show up to share in the grief.

There is also a morbid fascination of "this could be me" in the rubbernecking, but who am I to judge, for I could be accused of it myself?

"How did you know Vanessa?" asks one of the older ladies that I meet at the front of the church. She is handing out programs and I am one of the last to arrive. She is wearing a black dress and pinned at the shoulder is a lily of the valley.

Mother doesn't like lilies.

"We went to elementary school together, but I moved away and lost touch. I could hardly believe it when I read about it in the paper."

There is an awkwardness to funerals that serves my purpose. Unlike a wedding, no one expects a gatecrasher. Why would anyone demand to know who you are if you are respectful? And no one questions you too closely because they fear causing more pain.

She pats the top of my hand, and her hand is cool against my hot skin. "You don't know anyone else here?"

"It's been years since I was here last as a child," I murmur, making myself look nervous, but inside I'm serene. I've done this before many times and the old familiarity of the routine comforts me.

"Come sit with me," she urges. She introduces me to her pew mates as Vanessa's school friend and it doesn't take long before my credentials as a childhood friend of the deceased are well-established because of her sponsorship.

The service is beautiful and uplifting, but the graveyard is sad, for the finality now cannot be avoided with heartfelt songs and speeches. At least the weather is fine, a few say before they wander away back to their cars.

My new friend, Mrs. McGuire, invites me to come with her and her two friends to the family wake. "Her mother will want to meet you. She wants to talk with everyone who knows her daughter."

After a slight show of resistance, I agreed to come with her. Though I am a wolf in sheep's clothing, there is something I can offer Vanessa's family that no one else can, and this will be my gift to them.

There is food and drink, and I find a paper plate but don't get a cup, as I need one hand free. My gift requires touch, but that isn't hard to do at a funeral. People want their hand held; the embrace and pat on the back; the light touch on the upper arm. My role as an unknown mourner releases them from any shame that social constraint would normally demand.

But I am no ordinary mourner. I'm a Memory Keeper and so when I touch them, each thought they have of Vanessa takes on a special glow in their mind that will never leave them. This healing is what I can offer to her friends and family.

In exchange, I collect bits of memories that will eventually form a new Vanessa, one that will rise from the ashes with her dreams and hopes all intact and which will enable me to pursue a new life in Kansas.

"She planned on attending college to study nursing. You see, Vanessa wanted to help others like she'd been helped in the hospital." I touch the speaker's elbow and in a moment that memory takes on a softer realness, all the jagged corners rubbed smooth, leaving not the pain of remembrance but only the emotion of deep love.

It is not long before there is whispering among the visitors. Mourners are telling others they should come to me and share their stories about Vanessa. "You'll feel better after you talk with her," they promise.

Still, I don't approach the parents or the siblings yet. I need more information about who Vanessa is before I do that. Memories from her former high school friends who sat in class with her, marched beside her in band, or ate at the same lunch table. Her cousins give me more intimate knowledge: the food she likes (lasagna) and dislikes (Brussels sprouts), the names of her pet cat

(Sugar), and how she was afraid of spiders, though she liked snakes.

"Come sit with us," insists Mrs. McGuire. I follow her to the back porch where the older generation sits. It is a coven of crones with Vanessa's grandmother and her sisters, and it is this generation who gifts me Vanessa's childhood. She was a difficult birth, but a happy baby. How she took to swimming like a duck. One of her first words was 'crazy', and as a toddler, Vanessa loved to chant it all over the house, which almost drove her mom to that state.

But when they mention cancer, I do not take it. I don't want to know about the disease. Yes, it shaped her, but it drained her vitality, and I want my Vanessa free from the shadow of illness.

My Vanessa is taking shape. She will be determined, with a strong will, and a goal-oriented person. Focused.

"Ms. Hill, this is Mrs. Dickenson." I immediately stand up and shake hands with the deceased's mother while the elders behind me gently nod their heads, endorsing me.

Mrs. Dickenson takes me away, as she wants to introduce me to her husband. It's been hours since the graveyard service happened, and the living room is almost empty. The visitors have voided their sorrow and returned to their world of work deadlines and school obligations.

Vanessa's mother still clings to the few who remain, for once she is alone, the ending of this day will make another ending.

"You knew Vanessa at school?" Her voice is soft and a little hoarse. She's probably been speaking and crying all day. Her reddened eyes hold a bone-weary exhaustion that will not let her sleep.

I'm on firm ground now and give her the name of the elementary school and the teacher Vanessa had in fifth grade. "My family is military, you see, and we moved away before the end of that year. I really liked your daughter, Mrs. Dickenson. I wish we could have remained friends, but the distance made it difficult."

She is trying to place me, and her mind supplies a tentative suggestion. "Are you the girl who loved unicorns?"

It's a pretty safe bet that any girl at that age is crazy about unicorns. I smile. "Probably. I was pretty horse crazy about that age. Still am."

Usually, I have to prompt people to remember when I touch them, but there is no need at a funeral and certainly not with a grieving mother. I ask, "Can I give you a hug?"

She nods mutely. Perhaps she has heard the whispers about this stranger who gives an odd comfort to those who mourn. Embracing her, I know everything that Vanessa's mother has ever experienced with her daughter. Gathering it together, I put it in a gold picture frame, with Vanessa's thin face glowing, her graduation cap on her head.

Before we break apart, Mrs. Dickenson cracks and gives a cry of grief that comes from her splitting heart. Her husband apologizes for her, saying wearily, "It's been a long day."

"I know." *How I know.*

I can't hold him as long as it wouldn't be socially acceptable, but I do the best I can with the time I am given. Society holds that men aren't supposed to need any help in their grief, but I know what a lie that is.

Wellston isn't a big town, and I don't have my credit card, only cash. But Mrs. McGuire takes me to a bed-and-breakfast in town that is run by a friend. When she explains that I'm from out-of-town and here for Vanessa's funeral, the innkeeper quickly agrees to give me a room at half price since I'm paying in cash.

"Only for one night," I tell both of my gray-haired angels. "I missed my train or wouldn't be putting you both out."

"No problem," says the innkeeper. "It's the middle of the week and I have the room."

After saying goodbye to Mrs. McGuire, I follow the innkeeper to the bedroom. On the way, she opens a cupboard and grabs a bar of soap, toothpaste, and toothbrush. "Do you need anything else, dear?"

"No, this is more than enough."

Tucked safely under the covers, I fall asleep, and my dreams start to weave myself a new personality.

Twenty-Two

Two men enter the café. The first has an arrogant swagger and is dark-haired, with a hard jaw. He's handsome but almost in a cruel way, for his eyes assess and dismiss everyone in the room. If Vanessa was casting him in a movie, he'd be the bad boy executive who preys upon hapless innocent girls who are visiting the city for the first time.

Mr. Cool.

The second one, though, he's an intellectual, everything boxed up and organized. But a woman would want to break that reserve. Take off his glasses, bite his lip, put her hands on those shoulders to enjoy the feel of those firm muscles.

"As I told you, she's here," says the arrogant one.

"Why don't you get us something to drink?" says the smart one.

The professor comes over and sits at a table next to hers. In the café, there are plenty of open tables and so his seat is a deliberate choice.

Vanessa is on alert now, but she pretends to keep scrolling through her phone. She doesn't have the money or a credit card to get a plane ticket, but she could start out on a train. There is a bank in the city that has an agreement with her online banking account, so she could withdraw funds in person using her old ID.

"It's a beautiful day."

She glances outside the glass windows. His statement is obvious, for the sun is shining, and there are a few fluffy clouds, and the temperature is mild.

Vanessa returns to her phone and checks the train schedule. There is one pulling out in two hours, so she has plenty of time. Instead of that information being reassuring, she begins to feel anxious.

We need to leave.

The guy with the sharp corners is done at the cash register and brings two coffees to the table and sits down next to his companion. Vanessa can't help but overhear him, as he doesn't even try to moderate his voice. "She won't recognize you, Crane. I've been down this road too many times before. Zoe's tuned out."

Vanessa shuffles in her seat, blocking them both out with her shoulder, as she pointedly turns away. They are irritating her, and she hopes the two men take the point and leave.

"Go ahead. Ask my sister about the dead girl. She'll have all the answers. Zoe will know where she went to school, what happened at her third birthday party, who her secret crush was, and if she liked tea or coffee."

If Vanessa wasn't such a nice person, she'd dump her drink in Mr. Cool's lap. She considers leaving, but with two hours to kill, where can she go? And what would she do if they started to follow her? At least in the coffee house, she can scream and the staff would come to her aid. *Hopefully.*

"I don't think we should rush things," says the guy with the gold-rimmed glasses. You want to hear that voice call you an endearment. *Baby. Lover.*

"You think because your mother is a psychologist you understand my sister? Trust me, you don't have the slightest idea what Zoe is capable of doing. She's got an Underhill gift. If we let her go today, it'll take an army of private detectives from across the United States to track her down."

Vanessa notes the beautiful hands of the professor as he cradles the cup. "Owen really frightened her last night. I have to admit, he even made me uneasy. The guy is totally unhinged."

Mr. Cool is wearing a wool cashmere overcoat in a trendy cut. *Money.*

"Zoe doesn't like people fighting. She always hid under the bed when Nolan got going, but I admit Owen even surprised me last night. I didn't think he had it in him."

Clearly, Mr. Cool, with his sunglasses and expensive clothes, would never hide. He's more the type that does the punching, Vanessa thinks distastefully. She returns to studying the fees and the requirements for enrolling in nursing school.

It's over. He'll make us go with him.

"Just because your sister is sensitive to her environment doesn't mean you should treat her so rudely. Some don't enjoy living with drama, and from the little I've experienced, your family rolls around in it like pigs finding a new mud hole."

"You don't think I've tried to understand her? She's my sister! Of course, I've listened to what she had to say, but you don't understand how complicated this all is. She has real problems, Crane. The shrink Aunt Belle had her see back in high school called it dissociative amnesia."

"But when did it start? And why?" The professor can't keep his eyes off of her, but Vanessa isn't taking his fascination as a compliment. He probably thinks I'm like an exotic creature in the zoo.

Overactive imagination. Dissociative amnesia. Freak.

The other doesn't respond immediately. He is staring broodingly at the coffee in his cup. His checked shirt of navy blue and white, fits him well.

He'd look really good in a sweater.

"Zoe's always had a pretty good imagination with make-believe friends but by middle school, she took it to a whole new level coming home insisting we were to call her Trish or Grace. We all played along, thinking it was a phase, but posing as other people only grew worse. By high school she was running away, disappearing for weeks at a time. Nolan became frantic. We've spent a small fortune in finding her and bringing her home."

Professor says gently, "Maybe home isn't the best place for her."

The serving girl who clocked the two when they entered comes over to me and asks, "How are you doing? Do you want anything else?"

She looks barely out of high school; too young to be this distrustful of men. Vanessa reassures her she's fine, and no, she needs nothing more.

Before the barista can leave, Ryan says something to her in passing and the girl's frown becomes a smile. *Don't trust that one. He'll collect you and you'll be a trophy on the wall, a name in a black book. Eventually, you'll hate him, but you'll always need him.* But the barista cannot read Vanessa's mind and, slightly blushing, she leaves to get Mr. Cool a piece of cheesecake.

"Leave that girl alone," Vanessa orders him.

The man turns his hazel eyes her way. They are light brown with a hint of orange. Eyes of a predatory bird. "I'll do nothing to her if you come home with me. Otherwise, I make no guarantees."

Vanessa tosses her hair back. "Maybe I should just scream for the police?"

"Why don't you?"

They exchange glares, but Ryan knows I won't call the police. There would be too many questions and things could get very complicated, very quickly.

"Of course, we won't hurt her. Or you," says Crane, casting a glance at his companion that clearly tells him to stand down. "I think we should do something to show our goodwill, Ryan. Give Zoe her cards back."

Ryan shakes his head. "That wouldn't be smart, Duncan. With money, she could go anywhere. As it is, she got this far by just using her wits. Don't underestimate her."

Duncan says sternly, "When you stole her bank cards, you took away her agency. How do you expect her to trust you? Or trust me, if I associate with you?"

Irritated, Ryan pulls out his wallet from his back pocket and opens it, sliding out two cards and passing them over the tabletop. "Fine. But when she runs again, you can find her next time. We were just lucky I put that tracker on her phone, and she didn't remove it."

"Have you ever thought that maybe she wanted to be found this time?"

I don't make a move for my bank cards, so Duncan picks them up and puts them down on my table.

"On the drive over, Ryan told me he took these from your suitcase because he was afraid you wouldn't stay unless you were without options. Now you have options."

I slowly reach over and pick them up.

"Still, I'd like for you to stay," says Duncan.

Ryan interrupts this nice sentiment with a demand. "Don't you want to know who killed Mother?"

Screw him! I stand up and stick the plastic in my back pocket and grab the strap of my backpack filled with my dress clothes and shoes. I'm at the door when Duncan calls after me, *"A bird with feathers made from stars flies away with my heart."*

"What's that drivel?" demands Ryan.

I'm caught by a line of poetry. I sigh, turn and come to sit back down, letting the backpack slide off my shoulder to the floor. "It's something Mother wrote."

Vanessa is like a fog and she slips away from me. Not even fully formed, I say goodbye to her. Maybe one day I can live her dream life, but for now, it isn't meant to be.

"I can't say I'm happy to see you both; Kansas was beginning to look very nice."

"I thought you'd go to Nevada," said Ryan. "Las Vegas would be an easy city to disappear into."

"I'll keep your suggestion in mind for next time."

The barista returns with Ryan's cheesecake. She notices we are now talking to each other. "Do you all know each other?"

"This is my brother and a friend." I stumble over the last word. When she leaves, I ask with some irritation, "Don't you two have something better to do today than drive to Wellston?"

Ryan says, "Being away from home today was a good idea. Nolan has called a crew to get the conservatory cleaned up, and Owen is still prowling around the house like a raging bull with a stick up its rear end. So yes, it is a perfect day for a drive to admire the fall foliage."

My brother looks at his phone. "It's a long drive back, and I'd like to be back before dinner. Jennifer is alone with *them* and without a car." Without waiting for our reply, he gets up to leave, shaking down his overcoat to remove the creases.

Duncan suggests, "Why don't you collect your car, and we'll meet you out front?" Ryan pauses a moment before grabbing the door handle. He cast me one last look before exiting. Outside, he bumps into a mom trying to wrestle her stroller over the curb; he apologizes and helps her navigate it up on the sidewalk before strolling off.

Duncan asks me, "Do you really want to go back? If you don't, I can give you some money and help you leave."

I open my mouth to say something, but nothing comes out. No one has ever offered to help me leave my family, and this I need to digest fully. Finally, I shake my head. "No. Ryan is right. I owe it to my mother. If I don't go back and help him figure out what happened to her, I'll be haunted by the what-ifs forever. There is also her memorial to go to."

Duty. Responsibility.

I rise, preparing to leave, but Duncan gets up from his chair more slowly. Grabbing his arm, I pull him along. "You're acting like you're the one who ran away."

He is not amused and pushes his glasses up his long nose, examining me. "You shouldn't be forced or coerced. I'm beginning to regret going to your brother for help, but when I found you gone, I was worried."

"Need another princess to rescue?" This idea has been rankling me for some time.

"I would like to win you, but the only person who can give me that prize is yourself." His hand comes up and slips up my neck to cup the side of my jaw. It's warm and his fingertips are slightly rough. "Look, I want to know you. Everything about you. And along the way, I hope you feel the same way about me. Don't let your family take that away from us."

I press into the warmth of his fingers, closing my eyes for a brief moment. A horn honks, and I open my eyes to see the expression on Duncan's face. He looks ashamed. "You've had enough men shoving you around, and now I've joined forces with one. So, I'm asking again, are you sure you don't want to run? I can throw myself in front of Ryan's car while you make your getaway."

Ryan hits his car horn again.

"Didn't you say I was strong?"

Still, Duncan doesn't move. He's good at being a solid while I'm a liquid. "You decide, Zoe. Do you really want to go?"

"I'll go, but only if my lion-tamer comes with me. You can keep Grandfather in line, and I'll do the same with my brother."

He nods. "Okay."

Arm-in-arm, we exit the coffee house. Ryan's car is at the curb right in front and he shouts through the rolled-down passenger window at us. "This is a no-parking zone, so could you two geriatrics hurry it up before some Deputy Dawg gives me a ticket?"

I get in the back seat, and I'm surprised to see Duncan circle the car to the other back door and climb in beside me. Before we can even buckle our belts, Ryan is pulling away, quick to put the town of Wellston in his rear-view mirror.

"Fair warning, I'm using the ferry, Zoe. I'm not driving out of the way for hours because of your fears."

By strength of will, I keep my hands relaxed in my lap. "On your head are the consequences."

Twenty-Three

Ryan pulls something out of his coat pocket and hands it back to me. "Here. Take a look at this. It's the list of all the sailboats Nolan sold in the last three years. I got it from the harbormaster. Only *Kitty* is left."

My eye scans down the list, reading the fourteen names. It's pretty much Grandfather's entire fleet. With them gone, it means he's given up his racing days which is something I never thought I'd see. "What about his crew?"

"Disbanded."

I really don't want this to be Grandfather.

Perhaps my brother senses my mood, for he meets my eyes in the rear-view mirror. "Like I've been trying to tell you, sister dear, the old regime is on its way out. We need to be ready to make our move, save the family, not run away from opportunity."

"What do you want, exactly? Grandfather's position? Being on the City Council? Going to the town's potluck dinners on the third Thursday? What, Ryan?"

"The town is in trouble, Zoe. You may not care about that, but I do. Safeguarding Kingstowe is our legacy. Our job."

"In trouble?"

Ryan's voice becomes acidic. "I tracked down good old dad and demanded to know why he wanted that land promised to Nolan."

This isn't a mystery, and I don't understand why he brings it up. "To spite Grandfather, of course."

"More than that. Money and lots of it. Robert wants to put in a condominium complex that will pack people in like sardines. Expensive vacation condos for snowbirds, which means Kingstowe will be a ghost town for half a year when they go south to escape the winter.

Kingstowe tolerates the fall foliage fanatics because the tourists are only around for a couple of months. Even so, when old man Garrison's dairy barn was featured on a traveling website as the hottest spot to get the best fall landscape photo, he ended up in court after shooting at some trespassers who had crossed into his fields for a better selfie. I can only imagine how the town residents will feel about permanent vacationers.

"I drove by the plot yesterday with Jenn, and it's even worse than I thought. That acreage borders on the sea's bluff area. Robert's plans will completely ruin the view of the natural coast-line and do who-knows-what type of environmental damage."

"The city will never agree to that."

"When I told him there was no way the city council would agree to that type of explosive growth, he admitted that he had paid a few of them off to vote yes. They see only dollar signs and are already fantasizing about how they'll spend the property tax they'll collect."

"Why hasn't Grandfather stopped it?"

Ryan is impatient with me. "Because he can't! That's what I'm trying to tell you, Zoe. He can't Charm them."

Duncan gives a discrete cough into his hand as if clearing his throat. "I'm afraid your brother is right about your grandfather's influence waning. The name of the museum's annex was changed from Catherine Underhill to Robert and Marion Bancroft a week after I came here."

The road sign says we are twenty miles out from Kingstowe and the sky is filled with clouds. A smattering of rain hits the windshield and Ryan mutters as he turns on the wipers, "Looks like a storm is blowing in."

It would do no good to tell Ryan about my pounding headache or beg him to not take the ferry, so I say nothing. Duncan reaches for my hand sitting between us on the car seat and squeezes it.

He talks to the back of Ryan's head. "Zoe and I met with Millie Farmer the other day. She insists that Zoe wasn't at the house on the day Brynn disappeared." Duncan tells my brother all the other things we learned during that meeting with our old housekeeper, as my hand grips his.

Ryan uses the rearview to check my expression. "Millie must be wrong. You were home with me that day."

I challenge him. "The day you fixed Grandmother's sewing machine? Do you really remember me being there?"

"I remember the machine because I was pretty proud of what I did. But are you sure that was the day mom left?" Ryan's fingers drum out a quick beat on the steering wheel.

"Millie remembers it because the plumber came out, and Mom had a fight with Aunt Belle over you staying home from school because you felt sick."

His fist suddenly pounds the steering wheel. "I don't remember that!"

Duncan says quietly, dropping his words like stones. "Millie thinks Brynn took Zoe with her that morning on the day she disappeared."

"Maybe Mom came back, dropped you off before she left again."

Duncan expresses the horrifying thought I'd had in Millie's kitchen, "Or the murderer brought Zoe back."

Something I can't remember.

Ryan is frustrated and worried. The worry he ignores, as it doesn't fit with his self-image of being in command. The frustration means he makes plans for everyone. "You need to read Robert and Marion."

"I don't see them letting me get close enough to do that."

"Mother's memorial would be the best time. I'll arrange it."

I swallow hard, for I wasn't looking forward to either the memorial or touching Robert and Marion. "Okay."

Ryan is full of suggestions about things I should do. "Have you reached out yet to Nolan's old gardener, Mack Matthews, yet? Working outside, he may have seen someone leaving with Mother. Or you."

"Okay. I'll reach out to him."

I lean my cheek against the coolness of the glass window and look up. The clouds are spinning, stormy gray.

When we get to the ferry, there is a line of cars of those who have taken the long commute from the city. By the time the ferry pulls out, we are full. Drivers and passengers get out to stretch their legs, while I exit just to breathe. Behind me, there is a double-door slam as Ryan and Duncan also get out.

Leaning my rump against the door, I close my eyes. Duncan comes to stand next to me, his thigh touching mine. The back of our hands bump and I slide mine into his warm one.

"Whale!" Someone shouts and it is quickly followed up with other excited cries. Anyone standing on the deck at the opposite rail rushes over, holding up their phone to capture the large gray hump gliding through the water.

My hand in Duncan's tightens. "What's wrong?"

"Ryan," I say urgently.

Ryan brings his hand over his eyes to shade his vision even though the cloud cover gives the water little glare. "It's about the size of an adult humpback. It's not unusual to see them passing through at this time of year. Stop being paranoid, Zoe."

Over the loudspeaker the captain announces the ferry is stopping for the whale's safety as it is coming too close, and we will give it the right of way. He advises the passengers to get their pictures while they can.

Underneath our feet, the thrumming of the powerful engine starts to slow and in a moment it shuts off. Except for the kids shouting about seeing the whale it is quiet. Overhead, there are no birds who like to follow the whales and feed on the same fish. It is as if we have been put under a giant dome of glass.

Duncan immediately notices the same thing. "We are halfway between each shore. Neither at the start nor the end. It's a threshold between."

Zoe.

Duncan says in his deep voice which seems to write in fire on the air, "*I felt that my true vocation, the sole end of my life, was to chase this disturbing monster and purge it from the world.*"

Ryan asks, "What's that from? Hermann Melville?"

"Jules Verne."

"I think the monster is going to breach," says Ryan.

I don't want to look, but I can't close my eyes. It rises from the water, its leviathan body cresting through the waves as its long narrow head touches the sky, showing us the pleats of skin underneath. Along its skin are the round mounds of the barnacles whose mouths pulse open and close, gaping holes.

It spins slowly. Its pectoral fins are longer than they should be, and at the end of each are long finger-like fronds that no whale has. When its body mass hits the water, a splashing wave washes over those standing at the rail. The ferry passengers screech, some in fear and others with happy laughter. Most turn away, checking their phones for the picture they just took, as the tail of the beast comes up.

Up comes the tail, but this is not the broad tail flukes of a humpback, but squid-like tentacles as thick as a man's leg, and half as long as the creature's body. The arms sweep across the ferry's deck, searching. It finds its victim, a woman standing alone and wraps her body with its arms, embracing her tighter than any lover, and drags her over the railing.

I'm screaming as we all rush forward. Duncan is the first to grab a life preserver hanging on the side of the ferry's railing, but it's Ryan who is stripping, discarding his expensive coat, and kicking off his polished business shoes.

"Do you see her?" he asks me.

I'm not sure if he means the creature or the woman who is now in the sea. The water is strangely still now, and even the waves have flattened. But at long last, a head bobs up and I point, shouting, "There she is!"

Someone on the deck is screaming, and there is an emergency horn blaring. The crew is getting ready to lower the lifeboat. Ryan strips his pants off and then pulls his shirt over his head, discarding them on the wet deck. Being October, his skin reacts to the cold with a rash of goosebumps.

He climbs to sit on the rail as Duncan hands him the life preserver. I grab my brother's arm to stop him. "No! You can't risk it. Toss the preserver out to her."

But even as I say this, we see the woman's head go back under the cold, dark water and I taste salt on my tongue as if it is I who is drowning.

My brother shakes me off. "It's my fault. You told me not to take the ferry, and look what we attracted. Duncan, keep hold of the rope in case you have to haul us both in."

Without another word, my brother stands up and dives. His body makes a perfect arc of white as it flashes briefly against the somber gray sky.

Twenty-Four

Duncan uses a cleat on the side of the ferry railing to tie down the end of the life preserver's rope. Others rush forward to help, but they do not jump into the cold October sea to save someone.

Others lean over the railing, and their cries are like seagulls, high, raucous, and to no point. "Where are they?! Do you see them?"

At that moment, I hate them all.

Why must Underhills save them?

Despite our squabbles about how we view things differently, Ryan is my brother. I'm leaning so hard against it that the rail is cutting into my ribs. Spray and tears are making my face wet.

"Ryan has done nothing wrong. You *can't* take him. Give him back!"

Out among the waves, the life preserver marks Ryan's passage. He is dragging it behind him as he swims, and the rope lengthens as the coil feeds it out.

Ryan stops and I see his head turning side-to-side, trying to find her. The ferry passengers are shouting, pointing in the direction where the woman is flailing, but the waves are playing hide and seek with her, concealing and revealing her in turns. He strikes out again, bobbing like a buoy as the waves bring him up and down, while the current moves him yards away from the ferry and safety.

Someone grabs me around my waist, and it is the only thing that stops me from pitching into the sea. But it does not stop me from whispering, making promises, cajoling and pleading in turns to whatever powers that will intervene to save him, be it sky, sea, or wind.

"Ryan wants to set it right. Nolan and Owen can't, but *he* will. Give him back. We can't do what you want if we're dead."

Ryan is about ten feet away from the woman when he tosses the preserver forward. The soaked rope makes it hard for the life preserver to get to where it needs to be, and it falls short. People on deck are all shouting encouragement as if she is a racehorse they are betting on. "Grab it! Grab the preserver!"

I mutter, coaching my brother, who has no way of hearing me. "Don't touch her, Ryan. She'll take you down. Throw her the life preserver again."

We've learned from the same teacher, Grandfather, how to handle ourselves in the water. How many times has he told us you don't close in on a drowning person? Not unless you wish to be taken down with them.

As I fear, as Ryan comes closer, the panicked woman grabs his arm. They both go under as the sea swallows them. The surface is nothing but the movement of the waves. The breathings of the moon.

Let her go, Ryan. Surface. Save yourself, you idiot. I put forth all my will, trying to bring him to the surface, but still he doesn't. *Any moment. Now, come up. You will come up.*

The inflatable orange lifeboat from the ferry is making its way towards where the life preserver still floats, rocking back and forth on the surface. I am not sure how long they've been under, but he needs to breathe, and soon.

"Ryan, Ryan, Ryan," I utter his name three times like an incantation. "Come up, you asshole. What will I tell Jennifer?" Straining against Duncan's arm, I shout at the sea, putting everything I have into it. "We'll fix things. I swear."

There is a sudden pop in my ears and suddenly I hear Duncan saying, "They have him, Zoe!"

The life-raft crew is pulling my brother over the rim of the boat while two other men are wrestling the woman aboard. I collapse against Duncan's chest, and he pats my back and smooths my hair with his hand. "He's talking with the crew. He's okay, Zoe."

The crew on the boat play out like a pantomime from some viral news clip. They hand my brother a blanket and he ties it like a toga, a drape around his waist with the tail thrown over his shoulder with a flourish. The group on the ferry break out in a cheer and Ryan gives them a bow before he is forced down by the sudden rocking of the life raft.

I am calmer by the time he arrives back on the ferry. He struts, barefooted, across the deck to where we wait. His bare chest and wet black hair make him look like some conquering warrior. As he gives a lopsided grin at me, I race forward and embrace him. "Ryan!"

His wet arm slides across my shoulders, and he gives me a squeeze. "I'm okay, Zoe. And that woman will be fine after she vomits up all the seawater she drank."

Around us I hear the other ferry passengers gossiping.

"Underhill?" someone asks.

Someone else, "Nolan's grandson."

"Bancroft's boy."

"Robert Bancroft's son."

"Nolan Underhill is his grandfather."

"One of the founding families."

"Abraham's family."

As his identity becomes known, the crowd presses forward to shake his hand or to give him a manly pat on the back. They also shake mine and Duncan's. It seems we are all to be congratulated, even though Duncan and I had little to do with Ryan's dramatic rescue.

"Biggest humpback I've ever seen."

"That tail swept her right overboard."

"She's lucky to be alive!"

"She wouldn't be except for the Underhill boy."

"Abraham's descendant."

During all of this chatter, the ferry restarts and the loudspeaker advises passengers to return to their cars to prepare for disembarking. The intermittent rain has stopped and the stormy clouds from earlier are blowing away, with rays of early evening sunlight breaking through the punched-out holes of gray.

Everyone rushes off to their cars.

"You're quite a swimmer," Duncan tells my brother.

"The old man taught us." It is the first time I hear my brother say anything that might be praise of our grandfather. The two walk back to the car and I gather up Ryan's discarded clothes and shoes before trotting after them.

In the car, Ryan collapses in the front passenger seat. "Adrenalin kept me going, but it's catching up. My legs feel like jelly. You better drive, Duncan."

I climb into the back seat and fish out the car keys from Ryan's pants pocket and hand them over. When Duncan starts the car, I tell him, "Turn up the heater full-blast, Ryan looks half-frozen."

Before we can leave, one of the crew members waves us to pull over. Duncan puts the window down and the crewman with hands on his thighs bends over to peer in, his gaze taking us in one-by-one until it rests on Ryan.

"We've put a call in for the Kingstowe ambulance and the paramedics should be here soon to look after the lady. She looks all right, but you can never be sure. Are you positive you don't want to be seen, Mr. Underhill?"

Ryan hitches his blanket up where it is falling off his shoulder. "What I really need is a glass of whiskey. For medicinal purposes, of course."

The man chuckles. "Of course. We don't keep spirits aboard, though. Against regs."

I lean over the seat and ask him, "Can we have another blanket? We're trying to get him warm."

"Don't fuss, Zoe."

But the crew member goes off and gets one. When he returns, he is followed by two other men and a woman who also wants to congratulate my brother.

"Next time, though, leave it to the professionals," cautions the most senior of the crew.

"I certainly shall! One dunking in a lifetime is enough for me."

They step back from the car and wave as we start off. I reach over the back seat and wrap both arms around my brother's chest.

"You're strangling me, Zoe!"

He gives my hands an awkward pat, but he doesn't tell me to let him go.

When we get home, Jennifer hustles Ryan inside, calling for pillows, blankets, his bathrobe, and socks. She gets him wrapped up like a burrito, with blankets and heating pads on the sofa in the trophy room.

She even snaps at Grandfather to get out of her way when she is trying to adjust one of the three pillows that she is putting behind Ryan's back. Because Grandfather doesn't chastise her, I know he's also upset about Ryan's rescue effort.

"My boy, that was too dangerous. Even I wouldn't risk going

into the drink to pull out someone who was drowning. Best to leave it to the ferry crew."

Sally brings in a hot toddy, but before she can hand it to him, Jennifer sweeps it away and takes it to Ryan herself while cautioning him, "It's hot. Be careful not to burn your tongue."

She curls up next to him, watching his every sip like a hawk.

Aunt Belle enters the room with one of her arms in a temporary sling, and I draw back. We haven't talked since our fight over my mother's things, and this wasn't the time or place to renew hostilities. She will want to fuss over Ryan.

I fade back, getting ready to leave, but Duncan stops me before I can go upstairs. "Are you sure you don't want a hot toddy yourself?"

I give him a faint smile. "I'm okay. Just tired from worry and fear. Adrenalin."

"Let's go to the kitchen and get something to eat. We both missed lunch."

Listlessly, I trail after him. Sally is back in the kitchen and she's warming up chicken soup. It smells heavenly. Suddenly, I realize how bone weary I am. Just this morning I had been planning to run away to a new life and now I was back here, right after watching my brother almost drown.

Sally bustles around the kitchen. "I've got plenty to go around. Also, some fresh bread."

Duncan gets out bowls and silverware as if he lives here and sets it on the island's counter where I perch on a stool.

Sally says, "I was about to go. Do you think everyone will be alright if I do? You see, one of my boys has a game tonight, and I promised I'd be there."

"Go ahead," Duncan tells her. "I think Mrs. Bancroft will manage things if anything more is needed." My mind is moving so slowly that I take a moment to realize he's talking about Ryan's wife. Mrs. Jennifer Bancroft, not Marion, Ryan's stepmom.

In a few minutes, Sally has packed her tote bag and is out the door, giving us a wave. "Just set the dishes in the sink. I'll take care of them in the morning."

We are alone with a lot of topics to avoid: the water, what was in the water, me running away, and funerals. I brace myself for the questions I expect he'll ask me but instead, Duncan starts to talk about his college days and some of the funny anecdotes he had with his professors.

TWENTY-FIVE

At the nursing home, my last name opens doors, as it seems everyone knows who is paying Mr. Matthew's bill: Nolan Underhill. Before the attendant takes us to him, she warns me he may not know much.

"Alzheimer's. He doesn't even recognize his own son most of the time."

Knowing how rotten his son is, that could be a blessing.

"That's okay. I was told about his condition. Maybe we can just spend some time with him today?"

"He's in the public room with the others, waiting for the pet therapist to arrive."

The room is a bit chaotic, with some residents moving around, asking constant questions from the attendants, and one in the corner looking blankly into space. We find Matthews slumped in a chair near the window so he can see the gardens. When we are introduced, his gaze becomes panicked.

I'm quick to reassure him, "You won't remember me. It's been over ten years since we last saw each other."

His voice holds a shy tremor. "Are you the pet lady? We were told Sweetie would come today."

The attendant who is hovering explains Sweetie is the collie that the pet therapist brings. "Sweetie will be here soon," she reassures him, and leaves us to him.

I pull some magazines out of my tote bag. All of them deal with gardening, and I spread them across the table. His hand comes out to tentatively touch one and I open it so he can see the photographs inside.

As we turn the pages, I touch his fingers fleetingly. I understand, more than most, how memories can become damaged or fade because of illness or age. I've touched many who needed my help.

Too bad I don't have someone to help me.

His memory is a haunted house with Escher stairs that go nowhere, and doors that open to yawning voids. His ideas of people and time are mixed and things that happened long ago seem like they occurred today, while people he once loved are wiped away from his recollections.

There is one thing that he does remember: the Majestic. That towering oak that might be over five hundred years old, which dominates the front lawn of the Big House.

"That big tree. She's a beauty," he tells me.

"Indeed, she is."

Using the Majestic as an anchor, I go down the maze of his mind, finding images of him mowing the lawn and weeding flower beds. The repetitive motion of doing chores seem to be his strongest memories. People's faces? Not so much.

Over the magazine spread featuring the gardens of our nation's White House, I place a photo of Brynn, taken close to the time she disappeared. Her hair is long, and her nose freckled from the sun. She is grinning while shading her eyes with one hand.

"Do you remember?" Laying my hand over the top of his with its parchment skin, blue veins, and brown spots, I try to nudge his mind by providing it with a moving picture of Brynn smiling in her summer dress as she walks across the front lawn.

"The missing girl."

"Yes. That day she left; you were working near the Majestic. Do you remember?" This was a guess that I hoped would pay off, but nothing surfaces in the floodwaters of his mind.

Matthew's hands point at photos of tulips. "Damn squirrels. They always eat the tulip bulbs."

Around us, there is a murmur of excitement as a golden-brown collie enters on a leash held by a woman wearing a pullover and jeans. It is the therapy dog and Sweetie is greeted enthusiastically by the residents who are pressing forward, eager to touch her.

I stand up, defeated, but before I can leave, Matthews grips my wrist. I look down and his eyes are intelligent, and he speaks in a voice that is not his own. "You're running out of time to save Zoe."

It is her. I demanded, "Was I with Brynn that day?"

The eyes hold a cunning glee, and the Gale taunts me with Grandfather's catchphrase, "Don't you remember?"

"Where did Mother go that day?"

"Lunacy."

"What?" But whatever was there is now gone. Matthew's vacant gaze lands on Sweetie, and it lights up with happiness. Seeing his interest, the therapist brings her pet over and he starts to softly stroke the dog's head, saying in a pleased childlike voice, "Doggy."

Outside, as we walk to his car, Duncan says, "I've been thinking of your mother's box and its contents. Why don't you scan the letters and put them in the Cloud? That way, you can still read them whenever you want? We could stop by the museum and do that now if you like."

"Okay." I brace myself mentally when we enter the museum, but thankfully no ghost appears. Besides we go straight to the office area where Duncan sets me up with a computer and its scanner, showing me the process.

I'm very aware of his body as he reaches over to guide my hand on top of the computer's mouse, and his hand is warm as his masculine fingers cover mine. Duncan's cheek is so close that I can smell his aftershave, that rich deep blend of cardamom, cypress, and caramel coffee.

Since I've returned after running away, he's been careful about giving me space. I'm starting to find it irritating being treated like I'm breakable, but I'm uncertain about how to bring it all up. Perhaps he is re-thinking about wanting to be with me now that he knows more of my true nature?

He pulls away to sit at a desk across from mine and says, "Take your time. I've got some notes I need to write up."

Going through Mother's old box, I scan the letters and the envelopes. I number the filenames with the dates they were mailed according to the post office stamp.

The light of the scanner finishes reading the document on its glass, and I flip it over to do the reverse side. As I wait for it to finish, I watch Duncan's face, which is fixed on his monitor screen as he types. He's a smart one. An intellectual. *Professor*. Perhaps it is his aloofness that attracts me, for I have too many aggressive men in my life who shout and shove for attention. But it is this remoteness that I find hard to breach.

How do I ask if he still wants me?

He must sense my attention, for he looks up and asks, "Would you let me interview you about Abraham and your family's story about him?"

Startled, my thoughts about kissing vanish as I retreat quickly, like a hermit crab in its shell. "Surely Owen and Grandfather have told you all about it?"

"I always like to hear different perspectives about the same story. It gives additional insight."

"About the story or the person?" How still and watchful his face becomes at my question. "Anyway, Abraham's son, Seaborn, was Grandfather's father, so Nolan probably knows the best version."

"But they are men. I'd like the female perspective."

Where is Sarah? Duncan was right. Where are the women in the story?

"Is there any way we could find out more about Sarah's life?"

"I've mostly been focused on the events around 1898, and those dealing with Abraham, but you could search the newspaper archives. I remember seeing her name mentioned in the society columns in the *Beacon*. That can all be done from the computer now."

He shows me how to do that and for the next several hours I'm digging into articles about Mrs. Abraham Underhill. Just like Nolan and Kitty, Sarah is busy with the community. Visiting friends, hosting visitors, attending ice cream socials, or helping to plan the Fourth of July parades.

As I print out articles and jot down notes, a pattern emerges. Prior to 1898, Sarah was one society woman among many. She's usually listed in groups hosting dinners or musicals.

But by 1900, her name was listed more in a leadership role. She's not just helping to raise funds for the hospital but spearheading the campaign. She's president of this club, or secretary of another. When her son, Levi, leaves for Europe in 1917, she is the one who makes sure all those leaving get a proper send-off with a brass band playing at the train station as they leave.

In 1918, she welcomed a new baby, John, the same year she learned Levi died in northern France. After the war, it is Mrs. Abraham Underhill who funds the memorial that lists all who died. I've seen this brass plaque. It's in the courthouse and while it has Levi Underhill's name on it, the names are listed in alphabetical order, the names are all engraved at the same size with no preference given to an Underhill name. She was fair in her mourning.

For the next twenty years, she is attending picnics, organizing clothing drives for the poor, and planning a benefit for a widow whose husband died on his boat while fishing. Occasionally, her sons are mentioned: Seaborn, born three months after the Gale in 1899; Matthew, born in 1901, who later goes to college and moves to Boston; and sometimes John.

Sarah is not found the year World War II starts and there is no mention of her mourning the loss of her youngest son. John, born during World War I and who dies as a sailor on board the USS California when Pearl Harbor was attacked in 1941.

I flip back through the records, checking the dates of the news columns I've printed off. It is as I thought. The last time Sarah is mentioned in the newspaper is in August when she attends a picnic for Widows of the Sea. This is a month before the Long Island Express Hurricane passes Kingstowe in September.

And she's never mentioned again.

A year later, Abraham dies.

The door lock beeps and opens to reveal Owen. This is the third time we've bumped into each other here, but this time he seems relieved that Duncan and I aren't giving each other deep kisses. Well, at least someone in the room is happy about that.

Since the destruction of the conservatory, I've seen little of him. Whenever he enters a room, everyone grows quiet, as if they are in the presence of someone who has suffered a great loss, but no one wants to discuss it.

He shuffles in and gives us both a greeting. While he's making himself comfortable at his desk, his chair gives an irritating squeaking. "Did you two hear about Ryan's adventure on the ferry? They're talking about it all over town."

I dread to know but ask anyway, "What are they saying?"

"I was having breakfast down at the Egg's Nest with the Five —." Owen meant the five founding families, of which we are one. Every Thursday morning there is a regular meet up at the town's breakfast diner, where the town elders gather to pontificate. The purpose is to discuss how the town should be run, but really, it was just an excuse to share gossip, talk about fishing and boating, and brag about their grandkids.

"And they were saying a humpback came too close. Ryan saved a woman who fell in while she was taking photos of it. They showed me some photos on their phones. They say he's a hero."

"A humpback, huh? Do they migrate through here?" Duncan's comment is exactly the right thing to say as Owen brightens as he tells him all about the different varieties of whales and dolphins that we see around Kingstowe. "The harbor is deep enough they sometimes travel through, but they don't stay long. I wish I'd been there to see it."

"We were there and yes, it was exciting, but also very scary. Be glad you missed it," I say.

Owen tells us with some smugness, "The whole incident seems to have restored some faith in the town about the family."

This irritates me. "Ryan could have died. I'm sure that would have been very entertaining to talk about over your eggs and bacon!"

Owen is taken aback by the intensity of my anger. He's more used to the Zoe who hides in closets, runs away to funerals, and tries to blend in with the wallpaper. But I was getting a little tired of that version of Zoe who let things happen to her.

"Well, of course, I didn't mean— I'm glad Ryan is okay—" Owen stumbles, flailing, and looks as helpless as a turtle on its back. His helplessness makes me even more angry and for a moment, I really want to kick him while he's down, but I resist it.

I shut down my screen, and putting all of Mother's letters back into her box, I tell Duncan I'm ready to go if he is.

"Sure." He turns off his computer. "It's all yours, Owen."

TWENTY-SIX

We visit the church to make sure everything is set up for Mother's memorial a week before Halloween.

Ryan is in charge. He told the older generation to stay home and that he, with his wife, and myself would set up the tables and flowers. Of course, I brought Duncan.

I work on the memorial table arranging the photographs that we've chosen. There is a baby picture with Grandmother Kitty holding her where Brynn is trying to wiggle out of her lap; one of her fishing as a young teen with Grandfather; her high school portrait; and another studio-quality family portrait of her with Ryan and I, taken when I was still a baby.

Around these I place the more casual photos that Sabrina gave me that I had framed: Sabrina and Mother on the sailboat, and the Dead Poet's Society group photo as I had found the original one in a family photo album.

Jennifer is coordinating the flower deliveries coming to the church's service entrance. Not only is there the massive delivery that Grandfather ordered but also many more coming in from towns people. She is carefully jotting down the names on the cards in a notebook she has brought so thank you letters can be sent later by Aunt Belle.

I take one of Grandfather's arrangements and set it with the photographs. Done with the table, I go looking for Duncan. Duncan and Ryan are setting up the technical side of things in the reception room. Ryan has produced a short movie with music, photos, and slides quoting some of her poetry I had selected.

For several days, I've been wondering how to approach him, and there is never an opportunity. Either we are with others, or we are discussing the memorial. After today, everyone will start working on the Gale Anniversary celebration in November, and I am feeling like time is slipping away.

Duncan is reserved and is not as outwardly emotional as the men in my family. While I find that restful and he demands nothing from me, it also means things can be left unresolved.

In the past, I've always been the passive one, letting the man decide the flow of our relationship. But those relationships never worked out. When we were intimate, I'd have to block out their memories of other kisses and bodies. Eventually, they would sense my remoteness, and drift away, complaining that I was a cold fish, indifferent to their passion.

But the moment Duncan and I kissed, he had thought only of me. It was a powerful aphrodisiac, and it left me greedy for more. Especially today, when getting lost in physical sensations would wash away the tired sadness I was experiencing.

I find him in the basement, checking the breakers, as the sound system is giving them trouble. It is a dark area at the end of the corridor illuminated by only one bare lightbulb that swings overhead.

Seeing me coming down the stairs, he says, "We'll need to use a different outlet. I think the one we've been using needs a new breaker."

I clear my throat and dive in. "I've been thinking about what you said."

Our bodies are just a hand apart, and when he looks down to avoid my gaze, it gives him a close-up view of my breasts. He quickly returns his eyes to meet mine, his cheeks starting to blush in embarrassment.

Men don't blush if they don't like a woman, do they?

"What about?"

"Don't you know that princesses need to be kissed? That's what breaks the spell. That's what wakes them up."

His voice is soft and rumbles, like a rough purr. "In retrospect, those tales seem more like the guy commits a sexual assault. They're feminist scholars who think—"

While he's talking, I gently take his glasses off, folding them, and placing them out of the way on top of the electrical box. Reaching over his shoulder means we are even closer, and my chest is touching his.

"What if the girl kisses him first? Is she still a princess?"

He's wearing a long-sleeved dark blue turtleneck with a cable-knit sweater over it in cream. I slide my palm up under the bottom of his sweater, feeling the softness of his shirt.

As I touch him, he gives me the memory of us kissing in the museum office, and I know without a doubt that he wants me. *Desperately.*

He begins to say, "You don't realize—."

"What?" I whisper, tilting my chin up to stare at him.

"How tempting you are."

When our lips meet, he gives a low groan under his breath, and his hand slides around to my lower back and he brings me closer. My professor isn't remembering any past loves now, for he is too lost to the sensation of touching me. His hand slides down to grip the roundness of my bottom, and he lifts me ever so slightly so I am on my tiptoes, leaning into him to stay upright.

"I'm afraid I'm the one under the spell," he murmurs.

"I don't think princesses cast spells. That's witches."

"Maybe I've wandered into another fairytale."

He rotates me around so my back presses into the wall and he kisses me hard, our mouths urgent, all caution gone. It is what we both want, this excitement of exploring each other, learning more about each other than we ever could with words.

A voice at the top of the stairs calls his name. "Duncan! That circuit still isn't working."

We break apart, breathing hard, and his eyes are locked on mine as he shouts back to my brother, "You'll have to switch outlets. That one is dead."

"Okay. I'll try another one." The retreating footsteps tell us that Ryan is leaving.

I am shaking, trembling against him, both thrilled yet afraid of being discovered, of kissing him again, wondering when we can be alone, and how soon.

I whisper, "What if we're caught?"

The back of Duncan's knuckles is stroking the soft skin of my breasts above my shell-pink bra. "You're a witch. Make them toads."

My mouth opens to speak again, or perhaps giggle but he gives me no chance to do either. Intoxicated by the taste of him, I relax into his arms, yielding, wanting to give and take in equal measure.

"It's working now!" Hearing the footsteps starting down the stairs, we hastily break apart. Duncan moves so he is between me and my brother, and with my back to them, I quickly re-button my shirt, my heart pounding from elation.

Nothing will stop me from having this man for my own.

By the time Ryan reaches the bottom of the stairs, we are standing there with innocent faces. After they talk about the computer system, we all tromp back upstairs. Ryan and Duncan go off to complete their work as there is still the sound system at the pulpit to check.

After they leave, my sister-in-law raises an eyebrow and tells me, "Your shirt is mis-buttoned."

I retreat to the bathroom and fix it, but in the mirror, I see that my eyes give it all away.

On the drive home, Duncan and I sit side-by-side in the back seat. I can't believe my brother and his wife can't hear our thoughts. Our desire for each other. It's magnetic.

Dinner is torture. I do not want to talk about my mother's memorial, and so I retreat under a cloak of silence, letting Ryan answer Grandfather. I don't look at Duncan but under the table his hand comes over mine and the message that is passed between us in that contact makes me blush anyway.

He replays our kiss, the feel of the scratchy lace under his fingers before it slides over the soft skin of my breasts, my back relaxing into his embrace as I yield to his demanding caresses of my mouth.

It is dizzying, euphoric, and I almost stumble when I get up from the table, my thoughts, his thoughts.

After dinner, we all have to adjourn and speculate about what will happen tomorrow. Duncan and I are sitting side-by-side on the love seat again. While we don't touch, our thoughts are only of the bedrooms above our heads.

Eventually, we escape. He follows me up the stairs and when we get to our rooms, I stop him from reaching for my doorknob. His room has a lock and no history.

"Your room."

Duncan opens his door, and I pass him, my fingers become entwined with his and I pull him into the room.

*

"Sleeping beauty stayed."

At his comment, I opened my eyes to find him staring at me. It is sometime in the morning for early morning light is struggling to get in the window. My mouth is deliciously bruised and swollen.

For the first time in a long time, I'm pleasantly tired, limp, drained of worry.

His arm wraps around the curve of my waist, and his grip is strong as he pulls me closer.

"When I'm done here will you come visit me in Richmond? See what you think of the place."

I speak cautiously, not wanting to discourage him, but needing to let him know my commitments. "I've made some promises here that I need to keep first. I realize that now. There's no running away until I take care of a few things."

I made a promise on the ferry. Acorn promises. *To Mother. To Sarah. To the Gale.*

"When you're free, will you come?"

"Yes."

Without being really aware of it our feet have been caressing each other. Our bodies are still new to each other, and they crave to know the other's skin. We have hours before we must say goodbye to Brynn, and for now, I want to feel nothing but him. Trace the moles and freckles. Find the scars and kiss them.

TWENTY-SEVEN

The day of my mother's memorial service is sunny and clear. Perfect weather. *The tides is our blood, our words make lightning, and storms play in our heads. We are the weather.*

Grandfather arranges cars for the family. Nolan, Owen, and Annabelle are in the first limousine. In the second are Ryan and Jennifer, and I insist Duncan comes with us. Ryan offers no protest, for his mind is already on the service.

"Are you sure?" asks the man who I had made love to last night and this morning.

"Yes. Were you just kidding that I should come to Richmond?"

"I wasn't joking, but this seems very personal. It's your family."

I tug on his hand and bring him to the car. "I need you."

He stops protesting and gets into the limo.

When our cars drive through town, they elicit some curious stares from those on Main Street. I can almost feel their whispers, and I close my eyes briefly. *I'm here for Mother.*

The cars climb up the hill to the church where the service will be held. The First Episcopalian is one of the highest spots in Kingstowe and it is why some sought shelter here when the waters rose in 1898. One side of the building is covered with a tarp and has scaffolding alongside it that I don't remember seeing last night, but when we left, my mind was on other things.

Even though we arrive early to the church, there are already cars in the parking lot. It is going to be a full house.

Those who die young have a good turnout.

The limos park and when we exit, it is Grandfather with Aunt Belle on his arm, who leads the procession towards the entrance. Before we can mount the steps, a group of white-haired men all wearing black suits and white shirts approach Grandfather. They are part of the Five: the seniors of the founding families, their faces distinctive to their bloodlines even though they all now have white hair and stooping shoulders because of age.

Aunt Belle, with her black pill-box hat from the 1950s, has enough veil that it shadows her eyes. She stands stoically while holding the shiny patent leather black purse with its brass latch in front of her stomach with both hands. As the men talk, she is a soldier standing at attention, for she knows her place is to be silent and supportive when men talk.

Owen isn't as patient and he shifts from foot to foot, casting his glance from the parked cars to the church entrance. He's like a toddler who wants the ice cream he was promised, but today is not his day and no one is in a mood to indulge him.

Grandfather listens to the men with the attitude of an aging monarch. Occasionally, they glance towards Ryan and me as if we are part of the topic. Some of their conversation floats back to us where we stand a discreet distance away.

"— grateful to your grandson—"

"—Ryan Bancroft—"

"Of course, we wouldn't expect any less of an Underhill."

"She would have drowned otherwise."

They are talking about Ryan and the incident on the ferry.

"Of course, I'm proud of Brynn's son," says Grandfather loudly, as he waves Ryan closer. My brother brings Jennifer with him, and I tug Duncan over because I want to hear what they have to say.

Nolan introduces Ryan to the men. No wives. *Where are the women?*

"Us old sea dogs know it was foolish of him to jump in after a drowning person," says Grandfather. The other men nod, their speculative eyes weigh Ryan's worth as Grandfather speaks of him.

"The person you saved was my granddaughter," Mr. Fletcher says.

"Mr. Fletcher's oldest granddaughter—" repeats another.

A third in the Greek chorus gives more details. "She was coming home from work when it happened."

"Never a good swimmer," says the fourth, shaking his head. "Get's seasick on a dinghy."

"I'm thankful I could help," says Ryan, in an attempt at modesty, but the tips of his ears are growing red from what we all know is rather fulsome praise from these elders. Their admiration is unusual and not to be taken for granted. "I hope she's okay after her dunking?"

"Fine. Fine," says Mr. Fletcher. "Though shocked, of course. I don't think she'll go whale watching anytime soon."

I do not correct their misapprehension on the matter that it was a whale, for I've browsed social media and there are no photos of the incident featuring an unusual sea creature, only photos of a humpback whale. Listening to them talk, I wonder if all of it was a test: to see if an Underhill would protect someone from Kingstowe.

If Ryan had failed to honor his gift, then what would have happened? I'm glad we won't know.

Time is moving on and Ryan suggests, "We are about to go in for the memorial. Would you men like to join us?"

They agree and the men escort us like the Secret Service for the president, two on either side of our group, black-garbed and watchful. As the other visitors file in to shake our hands, they stand behind us in the receiving line like crows, examining who approaches us and making sure that no one overstays their welcome.

With each hand I shake, I receive a memory of my mother, some good, and some not so good. But they are all part of her, so I take them in, treating them as precious. I don't give any comfort today. I'll be lucky to hold it together for myself, let alone others.

Still, there are no memories of anyone murdering Brynn, and for that, I'm grateful.

Sabrina gives us a hug, and she takes a seat in the pew designated for family. The first two rows are for us and any who will speak today. The Bancrofts sit in the second pew next to Sabrina.

Robert Bancroft appears very subdued while his wife, Marion, looks triumphant. At Sabrina's urging, Grandfather is allowing Robert time to speak, but he required a preview of what Robert was going to say, and my mother's ex-husband was told to keep it under five minutes.

The turnout fills the church and some are standing along the back wall and in the entrance. *Everyone wants to attend a tragic funeral.* There is a reporter from the local newspaper, *The Beacon,* but he is being discreet and sticking to the periphery. I imagine tomorrow's headline will be about the unsolved disappearance of Brynn Underhill, a daughter of one of Kingstowe's founding families. It will not be a story that I will cut out, though I suspect it will go into Owen's scrapbook about the family.

It is time for us to take our seats, and with Duncan beside me, we walk down the aisle as if we are married. The town folk murmur as I go by, and their greedy interest pricks me like pins. Duncan lets me know he is here with a squeeze of his hand and a solemn, close-lipped smile. I let my shoulders drop. *I'm not alone.*

During the service, of course, I cry. That is why I crammed almost a full box of tissues into my purse. But it is subdued and none of us scream our grief aloud, even though we may be doing it in our minds. Ryan especially has a stony look on his face, his eyes unseeing.

Sabrina and Duncan were right to have someone else introduce the speakers; Grandfather wouldn't have had the emotional strength to get through the day if he had done it. Grandfather has buried a wife and now will say goodbye to his only child.

As it is, he is the first speaker and by the time he is finished reciting *Crossing the Bar* by Tennyson, his voice is hoarse from emotion. From the heavy silence all around us, I know the words are a sucker punch to those attending, for this is a community tied to the sea.

The flood may bear me far,
I hope to see my Pilot face to face
When I have crost the bar.

Grandfather 's voice cracks on the last line. The room is silent as he leaves the podium, and he shakes off the hand of the current minister of the Episcopalian church to help him descend the steps. He comes back to his seat standing upright, with a stiff back, and alone.

Robert speaks after Grandfather, and that is probably a deliberate choice for after his powerful reading, Robert's anecdotes about Mother come across as weak which I'm sure is what Grandfather intended.

Robert speaks of when he first noticed Brynn and gives a physical description of her beauty. But everything he says brings it back to himself. How Brynn made *him* feel, how *he* had made her happy, and the child *they* created. Thankfully, his eulogy is short.

Ryan is next, and he relates some stories I've never heard about our mother. These memories must be so private that he keeps them safeguarded even from his sister, the Memory Keeper.

When Mom took his side with a teacher who said he cheated on a paper because it was written too well. How she liked to visit

Nelson's ice cream parlor and always let him pick the flavor she would have that day. Playing on the piano and how she had given each of her children a separate lullaby that they would consider their own.

My fingers are squeezing wet tissues that are starting to fray in my hands.

Sabrina talks about her friendship with mother from middle school to beyond. Some of her anecdotes get nods from the audience, and even one gets a slight laugh from the crowd. She speaks in a good, clear voice, and her love for Brynn shines through.

I'm really glad she isn't a suspect.

The English teacher, Mrs. Lockwood, reads three of my mother's poems that Ryan and I chose from her journals. A harpist plays an arrangement while she speaks. The service ends with a prayer from the minister.

At the sound of the piano, our family stands to file out to the private rooms. When we get there, everyone takes turns embracing Grandfather and Ryan. Sabrina kisses my cheek, and Owen gives me a "hang in there, kiddo," comment, along with a clumsy pat on my back.

Aunt Belle doesn't spend long with us, for she is eager to meet the public and tell them about her grief. Owen glances at us, hesitant, but in the end follows her out the door. Ryan and I hug, and then we end up hugging Nolan together.

"It went well," says Grandfather.

"It was lovely," I assure him.

Jennifer hands Grandfather a glass of water and he drinks it down.

"It was good," he says again, nodding, as if trying to convince himself.

Ryan makes a suggestion. "Do you want to sit down for a moment before we go out there?"

"Only for a moment," Grandfather agrees. "We can't keep them waiting for long."

To Duncan, I murmur, "I'm going to the bathroom. I need a breather. I'll catch up with you at the reception."

There is a set of bathrooms for the staff at the back of the church and I head down the hall towards them, only to stop when I hear a pair of voices speaking: Robert and Marion. I had a vague memory of them passing by us in the private rooms. They are around the corner, so they can't see me when I stop to eavesdrop.

"Stop being so pathetic and pull yourself together." Marion's voice is low and drips with scorn.

"Brynn *was* my wife, Marion."

"Was being the operative word." He does something to her, for I hear her gasp in pain; it isn't a slap, or I would have heard the sound. An arm twist?

His voice is iron. "You don't understand how I feel about her. She was the love of my life."

"What nonsense," Marion hisses.

"I'm dead without her. A shell of a man."

Who knew Robert was so romantic?

Sentiment doesn't influence Marion, and she is as scornful as ever. "She was a toy you had to have. How *convenient* that she became pregnant that senior year and you got what you wanted, after all, even when she told you no."

"The pregnancy was an accident."

Marion's voice sneers. "How careful you were! Always with a condom in your pocket at every party. Every football game. Strange how the only girl you got pregnant was Brynn Underhill."

"We were meant to be together. Fate. Kismet."

His wife gives an angry laugh. "Together? You think she loved you? She couldn't wait to file divorce papers on you! Is that why you killed her?"

This time there is a slap. "Keep your mouth shut, Marion, or I'll shut it for you."

Marion can't help herself and pushes again. "Or you'll do me like you did to Brynn?"

"I didn't kill my wife."

"*Ex*-wife," Marion reminds him again. "You were gone that day and didn't tell me where you went."

"Because it's none of your business where I was or what I was doing."

Someone bumps into me, and it is Sabrina. Before I can silence her, she asks, "Are you okay? Nolan sent me after you."

The two around the corner become silent. I won't learn anything more now, so I reply, "Thanks for finding Mom's old teacher. She did justice to Mom's poetry."

Marion and Robert come around the corner. They give us a nod of greeting but push past, saying nothing. I should grab their arms and steal their memories, but the opportunity is lost.

I tell Sabrina, "Let me splash some cold water on my face and I'll come back."

"I'll go with you. I need some powder and fresh lipstick."

We are both facing the mirror, and I'm splashing my face when she tells me why the church has a tarp concealing its exterior wall.

"Someone spray-painted graffiti about your mother on it. The deacons saw it when they arrived this morning and they got it covered. They'll clean it later when they have time."

Looking into the mirror, I can see that she is deeply embarrassed. Of course, I want to know. "What did it say?"

"Nothing truthful. Just filth."

"Either tell me what it says, or I'll rip that tarp down myself."

She bites her lip, destroying the good she did with her lipstick tube. "It said they are glad she's dead."

It was obvious there was more. "And?"

"That she was a whore."

I roll my eyes. Nothing I hadn't heard throughout my school years after she disappeared.

Sabrina tries to reassure me. "The deacons got it covered first thing, so I'm sure no one saw it."

After turning off the taps, I pat my face with the paper towels.

I am wearing very little makeup, and my face is pale and drawn, my eyes red. It was a memorial service, so I think my looks can be excused.

"Marion and Robert were talking before you arrived. Marion accused him of the same thing you did. Making sure mom was pregnant so they would stay together."

"I'm really sorry, Zoe. I wish I had kept my mouth shut."

"No. I'm glad you told me. It helps me understand her, but I still haven't told Ryan and I don't intend to. If my mother was alive, it would have been her choice to tell him and since she never did, I'm not going against her decision. It's not my secret; it was hers. So please don't mention it to him."

TWENTY-EIGHT

When I return to the reception area, I approach Grandfather and the person he is talking with fades away to let me take my place beside him. Grandfather looks exhausted. His face is pale, and the craggy lines on his face deeper; worse, he looks his age of eighty-two. My hand slips down to take his in mine.

My touch is tentative at first since using this skill feels intrusive when applied to my family members. Still, I go ahead. Gathering up all the memories about my mother, I stitch them together in a quilt; my thread is love and my needle kindness. He has so many memories of her that pulling together his thoughts about Brynn makes me a little dizzy, and I lean lightly against his arm. Thankfully, none of them are about murdering her.

"It's okay, pumpkin." He reaches around my shoulders and gives me a quick hug as I throw my memory quilt over him, tucking it around his shoulders to comfort him. "She'll always be in our hearts."

Grandfather knows I can read memories but is unaware of this talent that I've developed from attending so many funerals. I break away, my hand sliding out of his.

I remark, "It's a good-sized crowd."

"It is. A nice showing of respect for the Underhills." Grandfather says this without any trace of sarcasm. He must not know what words the tarp is covering, and I don't enlighten him.

Across the room are Ryan and Jennifer, who are talking to a group of three. It looks to be Mr. Fletcher, and the woman Ryan had saved from drowning. "Ryan is popular."

Grandfather gives a closed-mouthed smile. "He's reminded them of our place in this community. Why they need us. Ryan has won their hearts, which is something I could never do," admits Grandfather.

Thinking of my family's history, and what happened in the museum, I ask, "You never met Sarah, did you?"

"No, they were both gone by the time I was born. My father didn't marry until he was in his forties." Grandfather's attention is focused more on the room than my questions, so when a couple shows up to give their condolences, I draw away.

I wander around, looking for Duncan, only to find Owen watching the memorial movie. Coming up to him, I ask, "You didn't know my mother very well, did you?"

He startles and almost spills his drink, and when I reach out and steady him, my hand on his arm, I take his memories.

An adult Brynn playing cards with him; a quick image of her yelling at Nolan; a glimpse of her in a broad sun hat holding my hand as we walk towards him wearing our swimsuits.

But like every time I've tried to read Owen, the recollections sink into a soggy melancholy that covers his mind like a blanket.

The long screams that become moans of pain when Natalie runs out of the energy to fight pancreatic cancer. She begs him for an overdose so she can die. The stillness of her body under the hospital sheet is an alien skeleton and not his beloved wife.

Owen stares at me blankly as if he doesn't fully recognize who I am. He tries to shake himself out of his dream and makes excuses for his distraction. "Funerals. I have a hard time with them. Too many memories. First, Natalie. Then Kitty. Now Brynn."

For a moment, I wonder why he clings to a woman's memory, dead over thirty years. Could love really survive that long? If she had Charmed him, maybe. Still, there was something about her he could never let go.

"How long were you two married?" I ask a question I already know the answer too but it gives him time to recover himself.

"Thirty years. Sometimes you have flash points in your life where everything changes in a heartbeat. We met on a blind date, and I knew it was forever. She was the love of my life. Did you know we married four years before Nolan did?"

His eyes go back to the screen flashing photos of child Brynn being swung up in the air by Nolan, the high school Brynn with her Poet club friends, and Brynn with Sabrina on Nolan's sailboat, both of them hiding behind their sunglasses.

Owen steps away from me abruptly, and in his hasty movement, he bumps into Robert. After an apology, I hear Robert ask him about the museum and the two start to talk.

Behind me, someone says, "You look just like her."

Turning, I discover a man who seems familiar. An older version of Duncan. "Are you by chance, Mr. Crane? Duncan's father?"

"Yes. Was it the nose that gave it away?" As we shake hands, I gather up some stray memories of my mother.

Brynn reading in the college library, her face serious. In a classroom with her hand raised and after she speaks, the room laughs at her joke. Her sitting on a motorcycle behind my father, Michael Gardner. All of them are tinged with nostalgia and a trace of sadness.

"Duncan told me how you knew my mother, but I haven't shared that yet with my family. If you wouldn't mind, I'd like to tell them in my own good time?"

"I completely understand. It's a delicate matter."

I brush against him lightly as I say, "Duncan told me you met Nolan when you tried to convince my mother to return to college." The emotional power of the memory almost makes me stagger back.

"Who are you again?" A Nolan, twenty years younger, in his sixties, is standing at the door of the Big House facing Mr. Crane. He fills the door frame and there is a terrifying energy that comes off of the man in waves. The memory holds this emotion strongly.

"I sponsored your daughter, Brynn, so she could enter college."

"I don't believe you."

"Did she not tell you? If only I could speak to her—?"

"No." The door closes. It is over. The ogre won. The beautiful princess would stay locked up forever in the tower. If he'd only been allowed to speak to her!

He leaves frightened and discouraged.

Mr. Crane won't be sharing any information with Grandfather about Brynn's past. Before I can speak, Duncan arrives with a woman about the same age as his father and my assumption that she is his mother is correct when he introduces her, "My mother, Olivia, and my father, Phillip Crane."

They are a cute couple and are clearly in tune with each other. He has salt-and-pepper hair, the older face of Duncan, and she is an inch or two taller, with thick shoulder-length brown hair starting to fade with age. Her eyes are curious and kind. Both are intelligent people, but Olivia is the more analytical of the two. When I touch her, she has no memories of my mother.

Normal parents, and people I might have met when I was still Ashley Maxwell, an elementary school teacher in New Mexico. They would be at the school to cheer on a grandchild at some recital or play. A loving family filled with warmth.

I might be part of this family one day.

"Dad really wanted to come. I hope you don't mind?" says Duncan.

I have to stop myself from touching him, holding his hand, or any other affection, which might show his parents we are lovers. Things are all still too fresh and I'm unsure what Duncan would want his family to know about us.

"I'm glad you both came. It means a lot to have those who cared for my mother be here today."

The couple exchange knowing looks and Mr. Crane says, "Duncan has told you everything about your mother. How I know her?"

"Yes, he has. I've always wondered — my family didn't know about Michael, you see. That she had fallen in love with someone at college. I wonder how the Gardner family would react if I contacted them?"

Mr. Crane says, "Regretfully, we haven't kept in touch except with Christmas cards, but I do think anyone who lost a son would be pleased to meet their son's child."

I wasn't sure about that. It sounded like a happy thought that people without hang-ups would have. Was Michael's family pleasant, normal people? Or were they twisted and bitter? Did they have a shrine to Michael in his bedroom?

Mr. Crane tells me more about my mother, some of which I knew from Duncan. But his father has personal knowledge, and his words give intensity to the images I get when I lightly touch his arm as if to comfort him. These memories show Brynn happy and free and will be treasured the most of the ones I've collected today.

My thoughts are interrupted by Mr. Crane saying, "Maybe Duncan can bring you to visit us? I have a few old photos I'd like to share with you, and we can talk more about your mother?"

I nod my head. "Certainly. I'd love to. Maybe when things quiet down here?"

Mrs. Crane touches her husband's arm to get his attention, and Duncan explains why his parents can't stay. "I'd like to take my family over to the museum before they have to start back home."

He's asking my permission to leave; he's thought about how I would feel if he left me alone at my mother's memorial. His courtesy touches me, and I almost begin to cry.

"Of course! You must see the exhibit. It's impressive. Don't worry about me, Duncan. Grandfather is going to be exhausted, and we'll probably have a quiet evening at home. Take your time."

Mr. Crane lingers despite his wife leaning away to leave. "I saw from the program that the poems Mrs. Lockwood read were hers. Your mother was a talented young lady, and she was very special to me."

"Yes, we found it among her papers. If you have time when you are at the museum, let Duncan show you her journals and letters. I think you deserve to see them."

"Are you sure they aren't too personal?" Mr. Crane asks. "I'd understand if you want to keep those private."

I shake my head. "No. I'd like for you to see them. I think they will give you a better perspective of Michael and my mother's relationship. While she might have disappointed you with her choices, they did love each other."

He gives me a sad smile. "With the advantages of age, I understand it better now."

Suddenly, I am caught in a hasty embrace, which is followed by a more sedate hug with cheek kisses from Mrs. Crane. Before they leave, Duncan asks me again, "Are you sure you don't want to come with us?"

Oh yes, I'd love to come with you. But I know my obligation. The Underhills must leave together and show a united front.

"I'll be fine. Enjoy showing the museum to your parents."

Another round of goodbyes and the three Cranes leave. When they are gone, Aunt Belle slithers up to me, and it is the first time since our fight she has paid me any attention. Is she ready to do battle again? Not knowing that funerals and memorials are my playground, does she think to find me vulnerable at my mother's memorial?

Her tone is sly. "Are you sure you can spare him for one night?"

"Listening at doors again, Aunt? Or just disappointed that I'm staying in a room with a lock?"

Before we can make a melodramatic scene, Grandfather beckons at me from across the room where he is standing with Ryan and Jennifer. People have been leaving, and the room is down to just about a dozen. It is time to think about going also.

Grandfather issues commands. "I want my grandchildren in the car with me. Belle, you can ride with Jennifer and Owen in the other. Where is my brother?"

Jennifer is the only one who knows. "I saw him go outside with Robert." We start to leave, and Jennifer wavers. "Shouldn't we stay and clean up? What about the flowers? The photos?"

Aunt Belle tells her in a superior tone, which reminds everyone in the group that Jennifer is not an Underhill, and thus is ignorant of how things are done in Kingstowe. "The Ladies Auxiliary will pack it away for us. They'll use some flowers to decorate the grave-yard, and the others will be taken to the hospital and retirement homes for people to enjoy."

Outside, while we wait for the limos to be brought around, I see Robert and Owen standing in the graveyard. They are examining one grave in particular, and it must be someone Robert knows, for he reaches out to touch the headstone, leaning on it with his head down.

"Belle, go collect Owen and make sure he goes in the car with you and Jennifer." The chauffeur is holding the door open, and Grandfather gets in. Behind him, Ryan mouths silently to me, *what is this?* I reply with a shrug and palms up.

Ryan and I sit with our backs to the driver, with Grandfather across from us. He's wearing black, and his tie is a dark gray. The tie-tack I recognize as one Grandmother gifted him long ago.

On the intercom, he tells the driver to take the long way home, up through the National, and to roll up the glass divider. He makes sure the intercom is off before he gives a deep sigh and begins talking.

TWENTY-NINE

"I had hoped to put off telling you two this, but Ryan has forced my hand by going to the harbormaster and getting my sale records." At my brother's surprised look, Grandfather says sharply, "Did you think Mr. Fletcher wouldn't call me? There are some who still owe loyalty to me as the head of this family, even if my own flesh and blood do not."

This statement makes Ryan bristle because he never wants to be accused of being wrong. He opens his mouth, but Grandfather holds out a hand to stop him. "We have much to discuss, and if you spend your time arguing with me, it will take the entire night. We don't have that. I want to talk with you two without Belle or Owen hanging about, listening around corners."

Giving Ryan a warning look, I ask Grandfather, "What do you need to tell us? Is it about our mother?"

"Not exactly. This is something about myself. There's no way to tell you two kids, but the straight way. I'm dying." It is a dramatic statement, but Grandfather says it quietly and the tired lines in his face and the sunken skin around his eyes prevent me from accusing him of lying. After all, he is over eighty and so this news shouldn't surprise me but it does. Like the Majestic, we thought Grandfather would be here forever.

When we don't respond, he clarifies his statement. "I had a heart attack about four years ago."

"That's not a death sentence," Ryan jumps in to contradict him, which only causes Grandfather to spit back, "It's my body and I think I know what's what!" He pounds a fist on his knee to emphasize his words.

I try a more diplomatic approach, playing peacekeeper, "Is that what your doctors say?"

Grandfather grunts. "Close enough. My days are numbered. Anyway, I'll soon be crossing the bar myself, even if you two don't believe me." This finally makes Ryan be quiet. "That's why I sold the sailboats. Tidying things up for you two, but I just couldn't sell the *Kitty*. Will you take her, Ryan?"

The seriousness of the situation is finally penetrating my brother's thick head. "Yes."

"Good. I'm glad to see the community taking a genuine interest in you today, grandson. It comforts me to know I'll be leaving Kingstowe in excellent hands."

None of us mention that he could pass the baton to his brother. No one in the car thinks Owen is competent to feed a goldfish over the weekend, let alone manage the complexity of the Five families. Besides, there was still that land deal Robert was planning, and Ryan would need to make sure that didn't happen.

Grandfather says, "All I ask is you don't go work for your father. He doesn't have the best interests of the town in mind."

"I promise you I will never work for him." The harsh certainty in Ryan's voice forces Grandfather to nod, acknowledging his words.

"The reason I wanted you both alone was to break this news to you, and to discuss my will." Neither of us protest that it is too soon. We are far too practical and there is a lot of money involved.

An estate this size just isn't handed over at the funeral with a 'wish you luck' pat on the back.

"There will be a legacy for Millie so she can enjoy her retirement, and Sally will get a year's salary. I've set up an educational fund for both of her boys; you and your wife are the trustees on that. Jennifer's taken an interest in those boys and Sally likes her."

"Right now, I'm paying for Mack Matthew's care at his nursing home, and that will continue until his death. With his poor health, I don't expect he will last long after I'm gone, and he might even go before me, but he never saved a dollar, so let's help him go out without worries."

I'd never thought Grandfather stingy, and his plans show that he's given considerable thought to those that have remained loyal to him all these years. He lists a few other charitable causes that he has supported and a brief rundown of how much they will receive. Notably absent is the museum and I am sure they will bitterly regret not naming that wing after grandmother when they find out how much Grandfather is giving to the hospital and Widows of the Sea fund.

"I know Aunt Belle hasn't been the most comfortable person to live with, especially for you, Zoe. I'm not blind, no matter what my brother thinks. But Kitty made me promise to give her a home as long as she lived and so I have, but I don't expect the two of you to keep paying on my debt. Personally, it's best that it ends with me. I've set aside a considerable fund for her, with Zoe as the trustee."

Surprised, I protested, "She'll hate that!"

Grandfather chuckles, seeing the expression on my face. "Maybe she should have thought twice before treating my granddaughter like dirt! But if I leave it to Ryan, he'll indulge her silly. This way, I know she'll get what I've put aside for her and no more. Ryan is welcome to give her more out of his inheritance."

Ryan looks down at his hands resting on his knees, so I can't see his expression.

"I've put the vacation cottage in Belle's name. She can use it or sell it to buy a house in Kingstowe. I got that property appraised recently and it will give her quite the nest egg if she sells it. Either way, she will be out of the Big House in six months after my death or she loses the money."

"That seems extreme when we have this vast house," Ryan protests.

Grandfather's eyes give him a measuring look. "If you think a household with your wife and Belle together will work for your marriage, I'll take back my estimation of your intelligence. Belle's possessiveness about you I've tolerated, but I doubt Jennifer will be pleased, especially when you two have children."

Ryan didn't like that remark about his wife, so before he could argue, I asked, "And Owen? You're not going to leave him out in the cold, are you?"

"Owen is a problem that I haven't quite figured out. What are your thoughts about it?"

Were we allowed thoughts? Most times I didn't think we were, and it is this question to us that convinces me he must really be ill.

Ryan says, "He's an Underhill and we should give him a home for as long as he wants."

I add, "You should give him money that he can use how he wants. Natalie died a long time ago, and it wasn't his fault that her illness ran up the bills."

Grandfather sighs and his fingers do a drumbeat on his knee while he looks out the window, thinking. "Owen and I never got along. I was always too impatient with him and didn't want to listen to his feelings being hurt over this and that. He's soft. Truth be told, I still find him as irritating as hell."

"A home in town," I say firmly. "Ryan can invite him over for dinner each week, but he needs his independence."

I don't add that if Grandfather had helped him earlier, perhaps Owen wouldn't be the mess he is today. Thankfully, Ryan at least agrees with me on this. "I'll keep a room at the house and let him decide, but yes, if he'd prefer something in town, I think we should help with that."

Grandfather nods. "I won't be around to argue with him, so if you two think that course is best, I'll agree to it. But don't come to my grave and weep that he's run through his inheritance and needs more. Money drains through his hands like water."

He finally relaxes and sinks into the back of the seat. "Now it's time to discuss you two. As my direct heirs you'll get the bulk of my fortune, but Zoe, I'm doing a 70-30 split, and I don't want you to throw a fit about it."

"That's fine," I say immediately.

"Why?" asks Ryan bluntly.

"Because you'll have the Big House to maintain. During Zoe's lifetime, I want you to provide a home for your sister whenever she needs it. That's in the trust, so you have no choice."

Ryan doesn't enjoy being made to do anything and becomes a little disgruntled at being ordered. "I would have done that without you forcing me."

"Perhaps, but this gives you an out with your wife. When she complains about Zoe, you can tell her it's part of the trust. If you break the trust, you lose the house and the inheritance. She might gripe, but she'll go along with it."

The trees of the National are going by, and some are almost devoid of leaves, so the blood-red sunset behind them makes them black skeletons. Ryan was right, things were ending.

"Zoe. The money is yours. No trustee. I hope you don't prove to be like Owen and go through it in a few years, but I can't bring myself to put you under restraints. We've tried to cage you, and you always escape. This time, I'm leaving the door open, and you can do what you want. That's the best I can do."

That night I'm awake when Duncan comes in. As he undresses, I roll over and ask in the dark, "What did your parents think?"

He pulls the blanket up over my shoulders, tucking it around me.

"Dad cried over Brynn's letters."

"He struck me as a bit of a softy." *Like you.*

"I'm glad you met them."

I don't ask why for it is obvious Duncan is making plans but for now, I'm waiting for my own promises to be resolved and can't spare much worry for the future.

His hand slips behind my neck, under my long hair, and its gentle grip brings me up as he bends over to kiss me. I do not admit out loud that I missed him, that even at Brynn's memorial when he spoke to me afterward, I wasn't thinking of my grief but of life. How much I wanted to touch and be touched, to remember only myself.

Perhaps he guesses it, for he slips under the covers and our limbs come together in knots that only eager lovers know.

In the morning, I wake him for another round of lovemaking. He's eager to speak, but I cover his mouth, stopping him. I want only our bodies to talk because they can be uncomplicated in their language.

Afterwards, we shower together, and later, wrapped in a towel and lying on the bed, I watch Duncan dress. The way he pulls on his pants and the buttoning of his shirt keeps me spellbound. I am drunk on him and ignore worrying about what the hangover will feel like later when I wake from this dream.

When he finishes, he says, "I'll escort you to your room so you can get some fresh clothes."

"No need."

"I'm not letting you go out there defenseless. When I came in last night, I got a telling-off from your aunt, who apparently thinks you're still sixteen. So, consider me your guard dog. I won't let you be subjected to any unpleasantness because of me."

My heart sinks. I imagine all the things she could have told him about me being 'crazy,' my running away, and a few minor troubles with the law. He comes over and, grabbing my wrist, pulls me up from the bed. "Don't worry. Nothing she says will influence me. She obviously has an ax to grind and can't be trusted."

I open my mouth and this time it is he who puts a finger over my lips to shush me. "I already knew that you're unique. Different. A girl from the land of fairy, bringing the magic of another world with you. What she says isn't going to stop me."

Stop him from what? I want to ask but don't. Don't spoil things by promising to be his forever and a day. Let him learn how cruel a girl from fairyland can be. Or that there are wicked witches along with good.

Thankfully, in the hall, we meet no one. In my room, it is turnabout is fair play, for the intense way he watches me dress, makes me blush like I am sixteen again. I hastily pull my sweater over my head.

"Did your parents like the new museum exhibit?"

"They did. But my mother asked where the women were? They seemed to be forgotten."

Smart lady.

THIRTY

THREE WEEKS LATER

The next three weeks seem normal, which actually makes me uneasy. November 25th, 1898, also began sunny and clear, and in forty-eight hours ships were sunk, people died, and the land was reshaped from the Nor'easter.

I felt calm before the storm, but it seemed I was the only one feeling pessimistic.

Since the ferry incident, Ryan is more relaxed, and I've actually heard him and Jennifer laughing. He no longer fights Grandfather or if he does, it seems to be good-natured squabbling, with both of them acknowledging the other one's viewpoint.

Since the revelation of his illness, he acts as if nothing has changed. But while he might pretend, we don't. I make sure I spend some time with Grandfather every day, preferably without Owen or Aunt Belle present. After I told Duncan what Grandfather said, he put aside his dislike of him and encouraged him to talk about his childhood and his father, Seaborn. I listen, hoping to get more information about Sarah, but it is all about the men and their accomplishments.

Duncan spends the days researching and writing. I help when I can by scanning through documents, sorting papers, and looking through microfiche files for any nuggets.

One evening, I peek into the conservatory and find it swept bare of everything. The wreckage of the bonsai trees and damaged glass is gone, with window frames covered with plywood. Sally told me they've ordered the replacement glass, but it won't be here in time for the anniversary party.

Owen acts like he never had that hobby. Instead, he is pouring all of his energy into his other obsession: documenting the family. I always knew he was proud of being an Underhill; perhaps it is because, without money or a job, our last name gives him status without lifting a finger. Or maybe it just gives him a sense of belonging to something grand?

He checks in every day with Duncan asking him questions about what he is working on and sharing his own findings such as the scrapbooks he's assembled on certain family members. There is one for his father, Seaborn, and his wife, Daphne. Since Seaborn married in his mid-forties, he and his wife had passed when Brynn was a child.

All we know of them are the family stories Owen and Nolan have shared. My uncle records this oral history on scrawling hand-written pages that he glues down on a scrapbook page. Owen also has a book for Abraham and for each of my great uncles: Levi, Matthew, and John.

"I've even started one for Sarah's little girls who died."

This is a white binder that looks almost like a wedding album and in it is the information Duncan discovered, along with a photograph of their gravestone. It is one stone which shares both of the girls' names: Catherine and Elizabeth.

"I visited Portland last week and took the picture. The statue on top is a lamb, which you find at children's graves. And the flower between their names is a Lily of the Valley which represents their virtue and innocence."

Mother hated lilies.

I almost ask about the gravestone he and Robert were looking at on the day of mother's memorial but don't for Robert is a sore point with everyone in the family. Not only does it look like the land deal will go through, but he's been calling to speak with Ryan every day, and sometimes even twice or three times. It's gotten so bad that my brother is turning off his phone. So far, Robert hasn't dared to show up at the house, but I imagine that will happen soon if Ryan keeps avoiding him.

Aunt Belle and I have nothing to say to each other, which makes my life much easier. I might have thought her reticence was because of our fight, but it is more than likely because of Duncan's presence. Whenever she starts to address me in a snide tone, he gives her such a penetrating silent stare that the words wilt on her tongue.

What I find especially delicious is I know she wants to attack me for having moved into Duncan's bedroom. She wants to tell the family I am a slut, and revel in embarrassing me, but they all know who I am spending my nights with as I have already told them.

None of them care. Ryan is pleased because he thinks Duncan will keep me here. Grandfather is more concerned about the Gale party than my sleeping arrangements; and Owen is proud about it, because he was the first one who saw us kiss, so he acts like he is a matchmaker who set us up together.

Every day, I read my mother's journals until I know most of them by heart. I've learned so much about my mother since being back home these last six weeks, but I still don't know who killed her and why. Since no one has shared the memory of doing the deed, I am beginning to think it is a stranger. *I hope it is.*

I'm still digesting Duncan's revelation of who my father is, and sometimes I scroll through the Internet trying to find out information about him. There is little about him, but I do find his sister and her family, as well as his parents. I do not friend them, but I save the website page so I can go back and stalk their social media, none of which is private.

How would I approach them? What would I say? Or tell them about myself that wouldn't sound weird? *Freak.*

Halloween comes and goes. Nothing odd at the house happens other than the usual strange knocking, doors slamming, and no one being able to find their car keys. Abraham seems to have calmed down after destroying the conservatory.

Early in November, the museum opens their new exhibit. Despite being shut out of it being named after Grandmother Kitty, all the Underhills go like good little community members.

While the Bancrofts won naming rights, you'd think they would be the center of attention, but Grandfather strides in like King Arthur. He still has some Charm, or perhaps it is the young prince that draws everyone to their orbit? They are soon surrounded, and Grandfather takes his time to introduce Ryan and Jennifer to all the Important People.

I'm on my own, for Owen is Duncan's twin. My uncle wants to share in the accolades of Duncan's research, so he follows the historian-in-residence around, nodding and parroting whatever Duncan says like an echo.

Duncan lets Owen share the stage. It would have driven me mad, but he has no prestige to maintain here in Kingstowe, so it doesn't bother him that Owen shines in his reflected glory.

Robert and Marion are there, arm-in-arm. Robert looks like hell. He has shadows under his eyes and hollow cheeks, as if he is not eating or sleeping. If you had asked me which of the two, Grandfather or Robert, was closest to death, I would have said Ryan's father.

My worry that Sarah will make an appearance is unfounded. She is either shy or uninterested in this noisy evening of congratulations and celebration. Instead of her absence relieving me, it puts me on edge. Sarah isn't gone; she's waiting. For what? *For me to remember.*

When the evening festivities for the museum opening wraps up, I give a mental sigh of relief. One more hurdle to go, and all of this would be over.

◆

The Great Gale 130th anniversary is a momentous historical occasion, as I'm constantly reminded by Grandfather and Owen. All the Underhills are expected to put on a show and be exhibited like the calves at the county fair.

It is the day before and Grandfather is going over his battle plans for tomorrow at the breakfast table. The state of the November weather is the topic that is making everyone nervous as the morning clouds can't decide if they want to storm or not. If it rains, there are tents, but most likely turnout would be low for the special day.

"But will the weather hold?" frets Aunt Belle.

"Of course it will," Grandfather assures her.

Grandfather has hired an event manager to coordinate it all, but Owen is her shadow, making sure that everything is double-checked. No detail is too small for him to micro-manage and he is driving everyone around him bonkers with his constant questions about matters already long resolved.

Owen is working himself into a maniacal frenzy. Even more than the museum opening of the Gale, the 130th anniversary celebration taking place on Underhill land, under the boughs of the Majestic, provides the validation he craves that he is an important cog of something greater.

Hence, why all must be perfect.

At the breakfast table, he has a notebook and is going over the checklist out loud once again. "The tents were set up last night, along with the Port-a-potties."

"Those are disgusting," interjects Aunt Belle.

"We cannot have hundreds of visitors using the bathrooms in

the house," Grandfather explains. "At least Owen has located them discreetly around the corner, out of the direct line of sight."

Owen is so busy reviewing his list that he doesn't even process this faint praise from his brother. Since the conservatory incident, Grandfather is trying to be more tolerant of his brother, and though he fails most of the time, I give him an A plus for effort.

However, there is no way Grandfather would have let his brother be the boss of this sandbox and hence the event manager. It's one of those undermining gestures that Grandfather is so good at doing; giving Owen the semblance of power, but never the ability to do anything.

She's out on our front lawn making sure the work crews are setting up the tents properly. Owen keeps looking out the window, yearning to join her, but Grandfather keeps us at the table.

Aunt Belle voices another worry and one that, like all the others, has already been discussed and decided. "I'm worried that the parking will destroy the grass. Especially if it rains. Why can't everyone park at the McAvoys?"

Ryan is toying with his knife, and I think for a moment he thinks of slinging it into her, before he tells her between gritted teeth, "The vendors need to be close to the house for electricity and access to water. As it is, we're lucky that Mr. and Mrs. McAvoy would let us use their barn lot for visitor parking."

The McAvoys are our closest neighbors, and they have just torn down an old barn and intend to build a guest house on the empty lot, but in the meantime, they've agreed to let us use the area for tomorrow. A shuttle will take people back and forth from their property to ours.

Aunt Belle complains again. "I don't know why we need to offer food trucks. Imagine the trash that will be produced."

Not for the first time, Ryan explains, "If we want a good crowd, they need to be fed and entertained. Especially children. No one under the age of forty is here to listen to speeches and admire a monster of a tree, no matter how old it is. Sorry, Owen."

This is the reason we are becoming a miniature fun-fair tomorrow with a face-painting tent, petting zoo, balloon animal artist, and even a magician who will be making the rounds of the crowd. There are also over two dozen stalls, which will showcase the local non-profits, such as the museum, the Fletcher Harbor Club, the Sea Widows Fund, and the state's weather service.

Grandfather had wanted a display of boats, but he was talked out of it. There wasn't enough room and *think of the grass!*

Owen continues to drone on about all our jobs and what he expects us to do. We each will have a radio headset, and we are to immediately contact him if anything goes wrong so he can get it fixed. What he really means is so he can relay the message to the event manager, who will then call us to fix it.

Ryan is in charge of the sound stage and food trucks. Jennifer is going to manage the entertainment. Aunt Belle is going to shepherd the dignitaries, and the invited speakers, around in a golf cart.

I'm given the job as Girl Friday, to run errands, so no one leaves their station. This doesn't disappoint me. It sounds like the ideal way to slip away when all of this mayhem becomes too much. Probably about thirty minutes into this crazy carnival.

Being a guest, no job is given to Duncan, but he says he'll be happy to help. Under the table, he squeezes my hand, and I squeeze back.

Thirty-One

The event is from ten to three and it doesn't take me long to discover that being a Girl Friday means I'm everyone's whipping boy.

"Zoe, I need an extension cord I left in the house," Ryan tells me via headset.

Aunt Belle criticizes everything and by bossing me around, it allows her to spew some long pent-up venom. "These water bottles aren't cold enough. Get more ice from the kitchen."

"Why aren't there any garbage bags at the petting zoo? Who forgot about those? I need them now!" Jennifer snaps on my headset.

If it hadn't been for Duncan, I probably would have thrown my headset into the trash and caught a bus for Montana, but he has a sense of calm humor about it all and answers each demand with an "as you wish" attitude.

As he tells Aunt Belle that he will get more ice, behind her back I mime placing a hangman's noose around my neck and being hanged. He stops himself from laughing just in time and ends up covering his smirk with his hand.

My plan to stick together and grab a quick make-out session in a quiet corner of the house isn't possible. Duncan and I end up splitting up because there are too many demands, and snatch a less-than-satisfactory kiss whenever we pass each other.

"Did you fix that breaker that was flipped?" I ask him, my arms carrying a large box filled with carrots, a head of cabbage, and boxes of gingerbread cookies.

"Yes. What's that for?"

"I scrounged all of this from the kitchen for the petting zoo. Jennifer says they're running out of treats for the animals."

We kiss and it is soft and delicious, making me think again of escaping to a private corner, but Jennifer's voice sounds in my ears. "When are you bringing those treats? The kids want to feed the animals!"

Ugh. Reluctantly we break away.

"Look, no pressure. But Christmas? Come visit my family." He drops this so quickly that I can tell he's been wanting to ask me for some time.

"Christmas? That seems very next level."

"Dad really wants to get to know you. Without Nolan about."

The light on Duncan's headset switches from red to green, and I hear Owen's frantic voice. "Duncan, did you find that fire extinguisher? The city inspector is about to shut us down and everyone in the food lines are growing angry."

"You better go," I tell him.

"Christmas."

"I'll think about it."

Duncan is about to run with the two fire extinguishers he's holding when I call out, "Stop!" He swirls at my command, and I blow him a kiss, which makes him grin before he dashes out the door.

Aunt Belle is playing the gracious lady of the manor, greeting anyone who is somebody. She buzzes them around in her golf cart, barely giving other visitors enough time to jump out of her way. If she doesn't hit someone before the end of the day, it will be a miracle.

At the petting zoo, Jennifer takes the cardboard box from me without even a thank you, for her attention is still on the kids. "Wash those hands!" she commands one before he can reach over the gate and pet a goat.

She has it all under control. Whenever an animal drops some poo, she claps her hands and a teen helper sweeps it away before it barely hits the ground, making me wish I had a few teen helpers myself.

Village elders keep interrupting Ryan at his work of running electrical cords and doing sound checks. They are the same group of white-haired men from the founding families who were at Brynn's memorial.

"Is that extension cord rated for that voltage?"

"I'm not hearing anything from that speaker."

"Check your hearing aid, Angus. That's your problem."

"You should tape that extension cord down. Someone is going to trip over it."

Before he can explode, I make sure that Aunt Belle knows he's under siege. She floors her golf cart and weaves through the row of tents. The couple in the back seat pitch first to the left and then to the right; their death grip on the cart's roof strut is the only thing that saves them.

I find Owen on his radio headset talking with the event manager, who tells him that the wind is causing some issues with the tent and all the stakes and rope need to be double-checked.

I look up at the darkening sky, and ask what everyone has been thinking, "Do you think the weather will hold?"

Holding his clipboard, Owen squints upward. "Hopefully, we can get the speeches done before we get a downpour. Lightning could be dangerous."

We are standing off to the side of the Majestic. The tree is roped off with some tape, but still, Owen has had to chase kids away. Some have collected acorns and are putting them down their friend's back, which makes me think of Ryan and our childhood pranks.

Someone calls for my help and I'm off again with no time to chat or sit down. Lunch is a turkey drumstick from a food truck that I eat standing up before Grandfather calls me.

I trash it and the lemonade cup and find Grandfather sitting alone in the main tent, looking very pale. Ever since the memorial, I can't stop thinking about how age is catching up with him. "How are you feeling?"

"Stop asking me that," he barks. I pull back, but he grabs my wrist and brings me down to his level. "Sorry, Zoe. Now, girl, there's a bottle of pills in my bathroom. I forgot to bring them down with me. Go get them for me and don't make a fuss about doing it."

"Okay, Alibaba." I use the old nickname because I know it will make him smile and it does.

"You're a good kid. Now run along."

When I start back to the house, something makes me turn to look up at the Majestic, whose limbs are creaking from the wind. Being a live oak, it will hold on to many of its leaves, and while the crown is now bare, there are some orange ones left along with the brown. If this wind keeps up, there may not be any by tomorrow, but if they are quick people could get some pretty pictures today before they are all dead.

I head back to the house, weaving my way through the masses who have shown up despite the chilly, overcast day. The only unlocked door is the kitchen one to stop the crowd from exploring inside. There is a limit to Grandfather's hospitality. I find Sally and the security guard eating cookies. *That's an easy job!*

I run up the stairs and down the wing that houses Grandfather, Owen, and Aunt Belle's suites. His door isn't locked and in the bathroom, I find several medications; the man is a walking pharmacy. He didn't tell me which he needed, so I stuff them all into my coat pockets and zip them closed so they won't fall out.

Heading back down the hall to where the staircase divides the wings, I hear a noise, like a person crying? Or laughing? Did someone get past the guard and are prowling around up here? Probably the guard was too busy eating Sally's baking to do his job properly!

Locating the sound, I realize it is coming from my mother's bedroom. *Some morbid snoop up here trying to grab a souvenir.* I am so angry at this thought that I throw open the door only to find Robert sitting on the edge of my mother's bed.

He is sobbing into one of my mother's dresses and it is a harsh guttural sound, almost animalistic, and a sign of deep pain. Perhaps I should be gentle as he is Charmed, and grieving, but I can't find the grace.

"Robert! You need to leave. This isn't the time or place for this."

He doesn't reply to my question but continues to weep.

Giving a sigh of exasperation, I sit down beside him. "Listen, I know it's hard, but we need to go out there and pretend everything is alright. Brynn would want that."

He ignores my words as he chokes out, "Your mother was the most beautiful woman I've ever known. It's so hard, that-she's-gone." He gulps between the last three words, trying, but not succeeding, to regain control of himself.

The whole situation strikes me as bizarre. The confident, arrogant Robert brought down to acting almost like a human being. It seems very out of character, and I wonder what sparked this episode. But like Grandfather had told me; Robert is scarred by the loss of the woman who had Charmed him.

Outside, the wind howls, rattling against the windowpane, and it reminds me of my errand to bring Grandfather his medicine.

Standing up, I put my hand on Robert's shoulder to shake

him, but that is my mistake, for the memory on the surface of his mind stabs me in the gut. "You killed my mother!"

THIRTY-TWO

My hand falls away as I stand up, staring with wide eyes at his bowed head. He moans, "I didn't mean to." But he doesn't have to explain what happened, for the memory is now in my mind.

Every awful moment of it.

"Why can't you leave me alone?"

"I love you."

"I'm done with you. Get out of my life."

His hands are my hands, and they are around her neck as he shakes her, squeezing harder and harder. Brynn's hands come up, fighting him, but she can't dislodge his grip, for he is too strong. A former high school football player who has continued his weight training into adulthood, she stands no chance.

"I love you; don't you understand?"

But she can't. Her eyes are bulging, and her skin becomes pale, shading to blue.

While I am frozen with horror, he reaches out for me, trying to grab my hand. "You understand, Zoe? I loved her. It was only love."

I back away. Realizing I'm in the room with my mother's murderer, I run for the doorway and race toward the stairs.

Zoe.

A sigh rattles the house, and there is a groan as if from a giant and the hallway tilts under me, becoming a funhouse floor. At the top of the stairs, I grab the banister, and my attention is caught by the view out the foyer window. It is the window that frames the Majestic like a painting.

A series of doors slam one-by-one down the hallway. There is a squeaking, like you hear on a ship, and in my nostrils the smell of the sea. In my ear, I hear an old lesson from Grandfather.

Without its mast, a ship cannot sail.

I watch in disbelief as the Majestic starts to split at the top, a cracking line slowly going down the center of its trunk.

The Majestic is a foot short of eighty-feet tall and its trunk is twenty-two feet in circumference. Elementary school facts. Facts about a legend too great ever to fall.

It is like the giant falling down from the beanstalk, but the giant and the beanstalk are one and the same. And so are we, as I feel a stabbing pain in my chest, but I am young and can keep my feet. Grandfather is not.

Grandfather, the family's patriarch. Our trunk from which we are all just branches.

My mind is screaming as I race down the stairs. When I burst into the kitchen, Sally is peeling carrots, unaware of the disaster happening outside. "Call 911," I yell at her, hurtling through the door, letting the screen door slam behind me.

Hold that door, child, Happy's words from long ago echo in my mind's memory, but I ignore it. I have tunnel vision, and every-thing in my periphery is dark. The only thing I see is the tree. The trunk is shearing from the crown to the base into two parallel pieces. Its massive weight from 500 years of growth pulls the split-ting half away from the other.

It is creaking and shuddering as it halves start to descend slowly. People are running away from it, screaming.

I am now at the main tent, where I had seen Grandfather last. I'm shoving people out of the way because everyone seems so slow, like statues. When I push through, I see that Grandfather is on his back, spread out on the grass, with a paramedic bending over him. Beside him are the emergency paddles that are used to restart the heart.

The paramedic is talking to Ryan, but in my panicked state, I only hear "hospital— heart attack."

Grandfather is alive, for now.

In the distance is the roo-roo-roo of an emergency vehicle as the Majestic finally hits the ground. The earth moans from the impact, and I almost fall to the ground, but Duncan is at my side and catches me.

Things move quickly and slowly at the same time. Grandfather is loaded into the ambulance while the rest of us are piling into cars. Ryan, Jennifer, and Aunt Belle in one car; Duncan, myself, and Owen in the other.

As our car follows the ambulance, visitors line up to watch the procession go by. They are blurs like an impressionistic painting, and I realize the downpour we had been waiting for all day is here.

It's raining. Aunt Belle won't be pleased.

The only thing that is real is the roo-roo-roo and the flashing red light in front of us.

My hand rests on the front dash of the car as if I can make us go faster with my urging. They've called ahead, so the ferry is ready to meet us. When we get there, our car flies over the ramp, and the bounce throws us all upward, so the top of my head brushes the interior of the car's roof.

But the ferry can only go so fast, and we are forced to sit in our cars and wait. The ambulance doors remain closed. My jacket pockets are empty of pill bottles because I gave all of them to the paramedics, who placed them in a plastic bag to go with Grandfather. Unfortunately, I couldn't tell them what he had taken that morning. *I'm useless.*

Duncan reaches over and laces his fingers in mine.

"We have an escort," he nods out to the water where there is a pod of dolphins leaping through the water. Dolphins, the friend of sailors everywhere.

The hospital is not a big one, and feeling removed about it all, I wonder distantly if they will decide to transport him to another. We enter the emergency room as a pack: Ryan leading, Jennifer beside him, myself and Duncan side-by-side, Owen, and trailing behind us all, Aunt Belle.

We get a glimpse of Grandfather as he is rushed back. A nurse shows us to a private waiting room for families. The brass plate on the door reads, "In memory of Catherine 'Kitty' Underhill."

Grandmother is here for him as she always was.

The room is dimly lit, and a Bible sits on the table with a cross on the wall. A place to pray for a miracle, or where you can howl your grief without shocking the other residents.

Ryan looks shell-shocked. Jennifer is at his side, rubbing his back, but even she, who is not grandfather's biggest fan, is pale with red eyes.

Aunt Belle ignores us all, thumbing through a magazine. She is the most composed amongst us and starts to talk about the season ender of some television show she favors.

Owen is seated next to her, his arms crossed, and his chin sagging to his chest. He doesn't respond to Aunt Belle's complaints about the predictability of the plot.

In a low voice, Duncan tells me what happened. It seems that soon after I left to get his medicine, Grandfather just slid out of his chair to the ground, unconscious. His heart had stopped, but the paramedic that the event manager had insisted on having was thankfully nearby, and he began CPR immediately.

My voice doesn't sound like mine when I ask, "What about the tree? The Majestic?"

Staring at his shoes, elbows on knees, Ryan answers me. "Lucky for us, we put a rope barrier around the tree to keep visitors back from it because I didn't want to discover that some idiot had carved his initials into it by the end of the day. We were getting ready for the speakers in the tent, and Grandfather was with me because he was going to give a speech about Abraham. The wind's been causing problems all day. Some were joking it could be a second gale, 130 years later. Of course, it wasn't, but, yeah, the tree limbs were creaking, but I just didn't know—"

"None of us did," I told him quickly.

We waited for an hour. Then two, before there is a tap at the door, and it is the doctor. He enters, standing in a white coat, while we all hold our breath. He reassures us that Grandfather is alive and aware. "Very weak after experiencing such an event, but for now, he's stable."

It doesn't escape my notice that the only one to look disappointed that Grandfather is alive is Aunt Belle. A strong hate rises in me, and I taste bile in my mouth.

The doctor continues explaining. "The electrocardiogram shows that he experienced a myocardial infarction."

"A heart attack," Ryan interjects quickly.

"Yes. That's a catch-all term. More technically, it was a ST-elevation myocardial infarction or STEMI. We'll be keeping him for observation until his situation improves, and he's out of danger. It's alright if you want to visit him but make it only two at a time and only family. Limit how long you stay. He's still very weak and needs the rest."

Ryan shakes hands with him and after he leaves, my brother lets us know he is going first with his wife to see Grandfather. He and Jennifer leave hand-in-hand.

I wet my lips and, turning my back to Owen and Belle, I say in a low voice to Duncan, "We need to talk. Privately."

Neither my uncle nor aunt seem to notice us leaving. We end up finding a place at the end of the hallway, near the stairwell. Not the best place for this discussion, but it is a small hospital and I'm not willing to be too far away in case Grandfather's condition changes abruptly.

I tell him bluntly, "Grandfather sent me into the house to get his medication. When I was leaving, I found Robert in my mother's bedroom. He told me he murdered my mother."

Duncan doesn't seem surprised, but he is not a man who would reveal it if he did. Unlike the Underhills he is a master at controlling his emotions and it is something I very much like about him. Instead, he asks, "Do you think he was telling you the truth?"

Feeling like he is calling me a liar, I snap, "Why would he lie about such a thing?"

Duncan counters, "Why would he confess?"

"He was pretty distraught. I don't know if he really realized what he was saying." I close my eyes and the memory that I don't want to see of him strangling my mother stabs my mind like an icepick. "He killed Brynn because he was in a rage, she wouldn't return to him."

"Where?"

"What?"

"Where did he do it? How did he get rid of her body? Where were you?"

I frown. The memory doesn't have a background, only my mother's face, her bulging eyes. Even closing my eyes and concentrating doesn't bring up more depth to the memory I had seen in Robert's mind. It is like a scene in front of a black curtain.

"I don't know. He didn't say."

"Did he say anything about you being there that day?"

Water laps-laps-laps, the wind against my cheek, the snapping of a sail. The sun is too bright.

"Zoe!" I come back to awareness with Duncan, holding my shoulders to keep me upright. "Do I need to get a nurse? You went white."

"No. No." I shake my head, but that makes me feel lightheaded and dizzy. My hand grips Duncan's upper arm so I can stay upright.

The snap of the white sail with the blue stripe.

"Let's sit in the stairwell." He guides me through the door and helps me sit down. Duncan is standing on the lower step, facing me, concern on his face. "You sure you don't need some water? A nurse? Your grandfather's heart attack and Robert's confession have to be shocking."

"No. I just— What Robert said—"

"It's a lot to deal with. Just take your time," Duncan reassures me.

I pound the heel of my fists against my forehead, angry with myself. "There's something in here I can't unlock. Where was I on the day my mother disappeared? Why can't I remember Robert killing her? It all doesn't seem right."

"Shock," Duncan tells me gently. "Don't force it."

Part of me is standing outside of my body. This Zoe crosses her arms and demands; *You know. Say it. Say it out loud.*

"I saw her die, didn't I?" My voice doesn't sound like mine.

Duncan sits down and, being lower he must look up, as his hands hold mine. "I'm afraid, my dear, you probably did." He reaches to wipe away my tears. "I had a long talk with your brother about you. And another talk with Happy."

I don't want to think about this. Grace, help me!

"Happy?" my voice sounds childlike.

"After we met Millie, I called her a few days later, because I had some questions about you, and she seemed the best person to go to. She told me that after your mother disappeared, you stopped talking that summer. They took you out of school for a year and when you went back, that's when you started pretending to be other people."

I protest. "That's not connected to my mother. That's my gift."

He is kind but firm. "Think, Zoe. The day your mother vanishes, no one knows where you are. You return, but Brynn does not. What happened during that time?" His hands cup my jaw, and his thumbs wipe my cheeks. "Do you remember going with Robert and your mother that day?"

Water laps-laps-laps, the wind against my cheek, the snapping of a sail, the smell of the sea. The sun is too bright.

I cover my ears. "Make it stop!"

"What, Zoe? Tell me, what do I need to stop?"

"The sound of the waves. I don't want to hear it anymore. It's always there. In my dreams. In my head. It's worse when I'm near the ocean."

He moves and sits beside me now, taking me into his embrace, my head under his chin. "Ryan told me you used to go out on Grandfather's sailboat and loved to swim. But when you were a kid you developed a fear of the water. Do you know when that happened? Your brother couldn't remember."

I'm starting to ugly cry, my throat choking as I shake my head. Duncan continues, speaking gently, "Happy thinks it was when you were in elementary school. Anytime Nolan would talk about taking you out on the water, you'd hide. One time he forced you to go with him and your screams made a woman at the marina report him to the security guard."

I mutter frantically. "I don't remember. I don't remember."

You know. All you have to do is remember.

"It's okay. It's okay."

Calm down. Stop crying. You were never here. This never happened. Remember that.

A shiver goes up my arms, raising the fine hairs.

"Duncan, I'm afraid. I was there. I know I was there."

"Shush, it's okay. We'll get it worked out."

"I was on a sailboat. Someone is telling me to calm down."

"Who is telling you?"

"I don't know."

"Man or woman?"

"I don't KNOW!" I shout, pushing him away. The need to run fills me. The personality of Vanessa Dickenson starts to surface, someone familiar with hospitals. I could slip away, forget everything. She knows how to get out of here without being seen. Her personality comes around me like a cloak. *I'm here now. I'll protect you from feeling anything.*

I stand up and wipe my nose with my sleeve, abnormally calm. "Let's drop it for now. I've got to get back. See Grandfather."

"All right."

We both return to the private room, where there is an argument happening between Ryan and Aunt Belle. I interrupt them. "Can I see Grandfather now?"

"He's waiting to see you," Ryan tells me.

"I'm going to take Duncan with me," I tell my brother.

"Slut," mutters Aunt Belle. Before I even think about it, I slap her. *Hard.*

"That's payment in kind for all the times you've hit me. Now, keep your mouth shut about me," I say coldly. "I can't stand you, but when Grandfather dies, I'll deal with you fairly if you behave."

Aunt Belle's face is filled with cruelty as she tells me haughtily, "Deal with me? What are you talking about, you silly child? When your grandfather dies, I'll finally be free of him and have my own money. Oh, yes, I know about it! Owen told me about his will and what's in it."

My laughter, and Ryan's embarrassment, makes her eyes go wide. Next to her, Owen has some decency to look embarrassed as I say, "Uncle Owen didn't tell you everything. Explain it to her, Ryan. I don't have the patience."

Thirty-Three

Seeing Grandfather in the hospital bed, the white sheets pulled up to mid-chest, and the blinking screen monitoring him, gives me a flashback to one of Owen's memories of his wife, Natalie. If my great-uncle had a hard time with funerals, he must be going through hell right now.

The ward is quiet, and the lights are dim. Duncan gets me a seat and I sit down by Grandfather's bedside, taking the hand that doesn't have an IV into mine. It is a man's hand with calluses and rough skin; and it is cool in my warm one.

I'm sitting there for at least ten minutes before he wakes; and even then, he's barely conscious. I reassure him, "I just want you to know we are all here."

"Good," he croaks. He tries to lift his other hand with the IV and it clunks against the metal sidebar of his bed before falling back weakly to the white sheets where his skin is almost as pale. "Water."

Duncan gets him some in a hospital mug with a lid and straw. We help him raise the bed and I hold the mug handle while he takes a few sips. When he's done, he gives me a limp stare. "Do you know yet?"

"What, Alibaba?"

"Who killed my daughter? That's why you're back, isn't it? You'd never have come back for me." I'm stunned speechless, and he pats my hand. "You can't fool an old sea dog. But I want to know before I die. Figure it out for me, Zoe."

"Are you giving me permission?" He nods and I touch his wrist lightly. "Where were you the day she disappeared?" And for the first time, he shares that memory, tinged with shame. He looks away, to face the wall and says, "Tell Owen and Belle I'm going to nap for a while. They can see me later."

We put the chairs back into the corner, and before I go, I bend over and give him a kiss on his cheek. "I'm glad you didn't kill her."

He gives me a weak smile. "It doesn't ease my guilt. If we hadn't fought the night before, or if I hadn't been away from home. What if I had involved the police earlier and Charmed them to look for her? Maybe she would have been found alive."

"I don't think any of those things would have changed the outcome. Now, just get some rest. We need you."

When Duncan and I are in the hall, he asks, "Where was he?"

"With a woman. Just some woman he Charmed into his bed. She's so unimportant, he doesn't even remember her name."

Ryan is in charge.

"Zoe and I will take the first shift. Owen and Aunt Belle? I've talked to the event manager, and it looks like things are under control, but I'd feel better if you two reviewed everything. Make sure everyone is safely off the grounds; that the tents are removed. All that stuff."

Ryan sends Jennifer with them so she can pick up some fresh clothes for him. With siblings sometimes you know things without speech, and I can tell Ryan wants to talk with me alone.

I suggest to Duncan that he go with them. "There are some things I'd like, if you wouldn't mind picking them up? And perhaps grabbing us both some dinner? I'd rather not eat vending machine food."

We all go down to the hospital lobby and are surprised to see the Kingstowe elders sitting there. They approach us and ask.

"We wanted to check in—"

"See if there is anything we can do?"

"How is he doing?"

Ryan, with Jennifer beside him, deals with them. My brother is stepping into his place as Grandfather's heir, for his inheritance is not only money, but responsibility.

It is a good opportunity to talk with Duncan privately before he goes. "At home, there is a blue journal with stars on it. There's some loose paper tucked inside of it, and I'll want that. Also, a pile of photographs in an envelope with them."

"Are you sure you'll be okay staying here?"

We are standing so close to each other we might as well be wearing each other's skin. My hand touches the soft cotton of his shirt, feeling the texture of the fabric, his vitality. "Ryan wants to talk to me. I'll be fine but do come back."

His hand trails down my spine, which responds with a pleasant shiver. "Of course. Anything else you need?"

"Just pack a bag with a pair of clean jeans, a couple of shirts, and clean underwear. My toiletry bag is in my bathroom. I don't need to wash my hair but would like to wash my face and brush my teeth if we are here long. And a pillow. I expect both Ryan and I will be sleeping here tonight."

It looks like Ryan's conference is done, so we all say goodbye. When they are gone, Ryan and I head back up in the elevator. There are other people in it, so he says nothing until we are back in the waiting room.

He sits down heavily, blowing out a deep breath. "What a crazy day."

"Yes." On top of Grandfather's health scare, I'm exhausted thinking about what Robert shared with me, and worried about what I can't remember. Until I get more clarity, I'm not going to share any of it, especially not with Ryan.

"Nolan's heart attack is part of it all." I say nothing because Ryan has something to share, and he is clearly uncomfortable telling me. "Kitty's stroke. The Majestic. I told you the family is cursed."

"Come on. That's a heavy word to use."

He says abruptly, "Jenn would be furious to know I told you, so don't tell her I shared this, but she's had a couple of miscarriages. Nothing medically seems wrong, but we just can't seem to have a child."

This is what Ryan wants fixed.

"Last Christmas when Jenn and I visited, we hoped to tell Nolan the good news, but that's when we lost the last one. I should never have brought her. The Big House is nothing but poison."

"I'm really sorry."

"Yeah, that's why I didn't want her doing the petting zoo, but Aunt Belle insisted. She doesn't know about us not being able to have a child, so I don't think it was a dig."

Knowing Aunt Belle, I wouldn't put it past her knowing and doing it out of spite, but no need to tell Ryan that. I ask something I've always wondered. "Did you Charm her?"

"Jennifer? You may not believe me, but no. You and Nolan showed me when I was a kid what happens when you Charm someone into loving you. I can't say I wasn't pretty tempted, though. That's the danger of being able to have anything you want. You just take it without thinking."

Ryan reaches his hand out to me, palm up. "Can we be friends?"

I say rather carefully, "Isn't being siblings enough?"

He gives a wry smile. "No. Because I need a friend more than a sibling. Family judges, friends support."

I put my hand on top of his, palm down, and squeezed it hard. When we let go, something has healed between us.

He sighs, and stretches back, putting his long legs in front of him, crossing them at the ankle. "When Nolan goes, everything is going to get complicated fast. There's a lot of real estate to be turned over, accounts to manage, the goods in the house and its contents. Charity commitments. All the tangled allegiances to the Kingstowe families to juggle. They can be touchy as hell. And of course, Owen and Aunt Belle."

Owen and Belle. Those were the two biggest problems. "Neither of them will fight you about the will. I'm sure they'll agree to whatever you want."

"Will they?" he speculates, cocking his head. "Large amounts of money twists people."

"Well, if you need to, apply a little Charm."

"That will work on Aunt Belle, but did you know I've never been able to Charm Owen? I asked Nolan why, and he said he couldn't either. He thinks it's the Underhill blood that protects him, but back when we were kids, I Charmed you, so I don't know if I buy that explanation."

"You've never liked him. Why?"

"Honestly, probably because a lot of what Nolan says about him is true. He's weak and clingy."

"Isn't Aunt Belle the same?"

Ryan gives me an exasperated snort and roll of his eyes.

"Obviously you don't like her, and I get it. She gave you a rough time, and personally, I'm tired of arguing with you about her. You can get your own back when Nolan dies, and her money is in your hands. But Aunt Belle does help. She manages Sally, so Nolan doesn't have to; takes care of the household bills; and keeps up with Nolan's social calendar, which, let me tell you, is far more extensive than you can imagine. Owen? He sponges. He's a lay-about."

Oddly, I leap to his defense. "Owen does social stuff, too. Like his museum work. Maybe if Grandfather hadn't made him dependent on him for money, Owen would be a different man."

Ryan shrugs. "You asked why I don't like him, and I'm just calling it as I see it. Sorry, but Aunt Belle pays in kind for her room and board; Owen does not."

There's more than he's telling, and I press. "You've disliked him since I can remember, and I remember a lot."

All except for why I keep hearing the sea and wind. Why did someone tell me to never remember being on a sailboat on a sunny day?

"Is it really important for you to know this right now?" I nod. "He's underhanded. Sneaky. I've seen him in action when he thought no one was looking. He's sly and spiteful."

I challenge him. "Specifics, Ryan."

"When Kitty was still with us, I saw him deliberately pretend he didn't know Nolan was screwing a certain woman. He brought her to the house for lunch during one of Kitty's social gatherings. Humiliated Grandmother in front of her friends."

"Maybe he didn't know about it?"

He raises his eyebrows dismissively. "Even I knew, and I was only about what? About ten or eleven? But he pretended throughout lunch he didn't and asked the woman questions, all designed to push a knife into Kitty. I'll never forget the look on his face when she couldn't hide her flush of embarrassment. He was gleeful. He enjoyed torturing her."

I didn't know what to say. Grandmother Kitty was gracious and welcoming to everyone. Notorious for her kindness, her patience was often described as saintly. There would be no reason to hurt her.

"He must have done it to hurt Grandfather."

"Probably, but he certainly didn't care about the collateral damage. Also, he's always snooping. Back in high school, I was reading in that big wingback chair in the library, and he didn't see me, but I saw him snooping through Nolan's desk, looking through his checkbook, nosing around in his private affairs. And he hates Robert with a passion. Not sure why? But if he had a gun in his hand and knew he could get away with it, he'd top my dad in a heartbeat."

"I saw them talking after Mother's memorial. They seemed friendly enough."

"Ha. If Owen was nice to my dad, then you can bet there was an alternative motive to it. He wouldn't spit on Robert if the man was on fire."

I stop myself from sharing Robert's memory. The whole thing didn't sit right with me, and I needed more time to review it before sharing that damning information with my brother, who was not known to be a careful man. Hesitantly, I say, "About Duncan."

"Hm. Are you two engaged?"

This time I'm the one surprised and rush to say, "No! Nothing like that."

He gives a genuine laugh. "Well, he's going to propose, so you best decide on what you're going to say. The man is a goner. When you took off, he was like a lost little puppy, worried we wouldn't find you. That you'd flown the coop for good."

I blush all the way to my ear tips, which makes Ryan laugh even harder. "If you could see your face!"

"Ryan! I have something serious to say." When he finally settles down, I say primly, "Duncan told me who my father was."

That stops him in his tracks. "Really? How does he know?"

I tell him about the connection between Brynn and Duncan's father and Mother's romance with Michael Gardner, his teaching assistant.

"You think he's telling the truth?"

"I do." Before I can say more, he reaches over and pulls me into a bear hug. "That's great news. I'm really happy, you know."

"You are?"

"Of course! But when are you going to tell the rest of them?"

"I wanted to talk with you first, then Grandfather. But with Grandfather getting sick, I'm not sure—?"

"Maybe not tonight, but I think he'd want to know, before, you know, it happens."

Before he dies.

"Alright. I agree. I'll tell him in the next few days if he's feeling better."

Jennifer calls Ryan and updates him on what they discovered when they returned home. It seems between the Kingstowe elders and the event manager, the mayhem after Grandfather's collapse was quickly contained.

No one was hurt by the Majestic falling and the grounds were cleaned up with the removal of the food trucks, the petting zoo, the tents, port-a-potties, and trash barrels. She was going to stay at the house to make sure it all got done, as Aunt Belle really needed a rest.

Should she get a tree removal guy in?

"Absolutely not!"

"Is that Zoe? Am I on speakerphone?"

Ryan says sheepishly, "Sorry, Jenn. Yes, you are. You're doing great, but don't touch the tree. We'll get a specialist out to see what can be done."

"Owen says he knows some people—"

"Don't let him mow you over. If he wants to give us some names, text them to me so I can look and review them, but I want to be there when they are examining it. If there's anything that can be done to save the Majestic, we have to do it. And I want to know why it fell in the first place."

"Okay. I understand. Your dad is here. He seems very upset but won't say why."

"Is Marion with him?" Ryan asks.

"No. I hate to say this, honey, but he seems drunk. Utterly

plastered. He doesn't look good. I'm not sure how much he's been drinking, but he's practically incoherent."

Under his breath, my brother mutters, "I cannot deal with this now."

Jennifer asks, "What? I didn't hear that?"

"Get him a guest room at the house. Let him know I'll see him tomorrow at lunch if I can. Call Marion and tell her he's there. If she doesn't answer, just leave a message. She turns her cell off all the time, especially if the two of them have had some sort of row, and they love to row."

"Okay, honey. I think I better go now. The clean-up guys are here, and they want to ask me something. Any more news about your grandfather?"

"No, and no news is good news at this point. Go ahead and deal with them and we'll talk later. Thanks, Jenn."

When he finishes, Duncan walks in, carrying a satchel and a pillow tucked under his arm. Behind him is Owen, with his hands full of paper sacks holding food.

THIRTY-FOUR

After we eat, we break into separate camps. Ryan goes to check again on Grandfather. Owen opens a book to read, Duncan gets on his laptop, and I work through the journal that Ryan had given me about two months ago after he found me teaching in New Mexico as Ashley.

I draw a line through Grandfather's name. He said he didn't do it, and he provided me with his alibi. Maybe he's fooling me, but I don't think at this stage in his life he would. There is something about facing death that makes people honest. Besides, why use the alibi of having yet another affair? It didn't reflect well on him.

Aunt Belle. I could see her doing it. But wouldn't poison in a teacup be more her style? A voice counters: *how would I know it wasn't done that way?* Brynn was only skeletal remains.

I sketch out a fantasy in my mind. Aunt Belle invites Brynn to a conciliatory drink after their fight. Something to put her asleep or that kills her? Would she have the strength to take Brynn's body and put it in a car, drive her to the National, and dump her into a well? Unlikely.

And that didn't explain where I was that day, and why I'm haunted by the sound of waves and wind.

Pulling out my phone, I text Ryan: *Can you show me with a map pin where they found Mother?*

He sends it to me. Yes, it's the National, but what Ryan didn't tell me earlier was the location is Blackberry Island, a place you can see from the top floor of the Big House if you look east on a clear day. She had been that close.

What is more important is that the only way to get there would be by boat.

The heavy smell of the sea. Water laps-laps-laps against the side of the boat. The sail with the blue stripe snaps in the wind.

Although I've never seen her on a boat, I know from photos of the youthful Belle that she and Kitty were often on Nolan's sailboats. Would she be able to take out one of Nolan's on her own and manhandle Brynn's body? I couldn't imagine her having the strength to do it on her own, so if she was involved, she had a partner in murdering my mother.

Who would help her?

Boats.

I pull out Sabrina's photos from the envelope and flip through them to find the one of Mother on the sailboat with Sabrina. She's wearing huge sunglasses, grinning at the camera, and behind her flies a white sail with a blue stripe.

What is the name of this boat?

In the dim light, I can't make it out. I leave for the nurse's station and ask if they have a magnifying glass. Owen follows me out and goes down to the end of the hall where there is a coffee station for family.

First, I look at the reflection in her sunglasses. The person taking the photograph is a man, but that is all I can tell at this magnification. I move the lens to see the boat's name. I suck in my breath, biting my lip.

At the nursing home, Matthews had tried to tell me. Lunacy. *Luna Sea*.

Stunned, I hand the nurse back the magnification loupe and return to the waiting room. When I enter, Duncan gives me a questioning glance, but I just give him a small shake of my head. Not yet. Let me think.

Putting aside the photo from the photo envelope, I pull out and unfold Ryan's list of sailboats that Nolan has sold. There is no *Luna Sea* listed. I text my brother again. *Can you use the name of a boat to know the owner?*

Yes. But better to have boat registration numbers.

I do a quick Internet search and find where to enter the information to pull up the *Luna Sea's* record. The last owner was Owen, but it shows it is now out of commission. Salvaged.

My heart is hammering, and I can barely breathe. What to do? What if I go to the police with my suspicions? There is no physical evidence, and the only eyewitness is a girl who can't remember exactly what happened. The one who runs away from home playing make-believe. Who believes she is other people. Who was institutionalized. The weirdo.

Owen returns and settles in the chair across from me. As he drinks his coffee, our gazes lock and it is as if a lightning bolt of communication flashes between us.

You bastard, you killed my mother.

And you can never prove it.

His smug smile is evil.

"Zoe?" Ryan is standing in the doorway. "If you want to see Nolan for a little while, now would be best."

Automatically, I get up and say, "I'd like to see him." Handing my journal and photos to Duncan, I ask him, "Would you take care of this for me?"

"Of course."

At the door, Ryan stops me with his hand on my arm. "Are you okay? You have a funny expression on your face."

For a moment I want to tell him, but he would explode and probably murder our uncle right here in the hospital. "Just a lot on my mind."

Naturally, Grandfather, with his status and wealth, is in a private room. When I enter, a nurse in scrubs has her back to me as she checks his IV. I take the chair at his bedside and sit down, deep in thought.

Grandfather's eyes are closed, and he looks to be asleep in the darkness; the only light is the glow of the monitor recording his vitals by his bedside.

With her back to the light, and her face in shadow, the nurse addresses me.

"Will you let the lies destroy us all?" Sarah stands there in ordinary blue scrubs, her hands clasped in front of her, as she looks down at me. Her voice has an odd timbre to it, as if it is larger than the body that speaks. "Sarah gave Seaborn to the Gale so Kingstowe could live. In return, the babe resting between her hips, waiting to be born, was given two gifts: Charm and Memory."

"Sarah did it again in 1938, didn't she? To protect us?"

"She came back to us."

My mouth opens, but nothing comes out for I'm too stunned to speak. There is too much to think about, and too much to fear from what the Gale wants from me.

"Now Seaborn's descendant has fouled the bloodline with parricide. Gifts given to protect all, and to remember the family's truth, have been used to deceive my own. The Memory Keeper denigrates us when they lie. When the heartwood rots, you all suffer for you are joined, root and branch."

Kitty's death. Nolan's loss of influence. Jennifer's miscarriages. The splitting of the Majestic.

As if she is reading my thoughts, she adds to my list of disasters, "You."

I dismissed her statement. "I'm fine."

A hand falls heavily on my hunched shoulder. "Child, you are nothing but cobbled together pieces of make-believe! Your personalities are defenses against the horror you saw. You are my Memory Keeper, you must remember and align yourself with truth again."

I am barely holding myself together. "Why can't you do it?"

"Human cause; human cure. I am but the spirit of water and wind."

"I can't—" is my immediate reaction, but under her stare, my protest becomes a weak mumble. "I don't know what I can do."

She comes around my grandfather's bed and I look away, not wanting to meet her eyes. Her hand latches onto my wrist, and it is a cool shackle. "When will you tell the truth, Memory Keeper?"

I swallow and lick my dry lips before addressing her. "I have to remember the truth first before I can speak it."

Sarah is implacable. "Your memories are still there, wrapped up, tucked away. It's behind the wall you created to deal with what you saw."

My personalities. Those I had taken from other's minds and that I had crafted into new people who let me forget that I am Zoe Underhill. Grace. Ashley. Vanessa. They were my wall.

Finally, I dare to look up into eyes as vast as the night skies. "I want to remember, but I don't know how to let them go. Or if I even want to?"

Her hand pulls at me, tugging me up, and as she embraces me, she whispers into my ear, her breath warm, "I will help you remember, my child. My daughter of my daughter's daughter."

I am standing on a sandy beach, and behind me are the dunes covered with clumps of native grass. The sky is overcast and there is a lightning storm happening out over the water. To the left are the cliffs, which mark the land that Robert Bancroft is buying.

I'm familiar with this area, but it is all wrong. The profile of the buildings that should be there are not. Neither is the boardwalk down to the sea, and there are no ships out on the water. Nowhere is there a bird, and the only sound is of the waves as they roll onto the beach.

It is not a natural place, but a space created in the mind.

"Zoe Underhill. My daughter of my daughter's daughter."

Standing there is a tall woman with thick auburn hair. She has a broad, weathered face, with a spattering of freckles over the cheeks. Her chin is square, and her mouth is wide. A strong, serious face that has survived hardships: the death of twin girls to disease; and her oldest and youngest boys to two separate wars.

"Give me your hand." I do as she commands, and as we touch, I am given the gift of her life and all of her memories. It is a lot to take in, and my mind reels from under the weight of it.

Her mouth gives a compressed smile. "That is a gift for you to consider later. As a Memory Keeper, you are to remove the lies. Abraham was too ashamed to admit Sarah's role, but he was always an arrogant, weak man. Seaborn only repeated what his father told him and discounted the worth of his mother.

Owen has widened the wound with the memory-fantasies he put into other people's minds. He is the reason why no one in the household remembers where you were that day or when you came back. Why Robert Bancroft thinks he murdered the woman he loved. He has used our gift to keep the secret of murdering his niece."

She starts to walk to the sea, and I follow her even as fear rises in me as my bare toes touch the lapping waves.

The breathings of the sea. The waves created by the gravity of the moon.

The sea recedes and leaves the outpourings in their original state of purity.

As the water swirls around my ankles, I follow her like a child being led by her mother, trustingly. The water is as warm as blood.

When it is chest high, the strength of the waves hit me so hard that I sway backward; the force lifts me and the soles of my feet, and I can no longer feel the sand. Frightened, I look towards the deserted shore.

"You must let go of your fear, if you wish to remember the truth," Sarah chides me.

"I do want to remember!" My voice trembles.

Sarah's red hair is wet now across the forehead and her long braid floats and wiggles in the water like a rope. She raises her other hand to the sky and summons one of my earliest personalities.

"Rosalinda McGuire!"

I hadn't thought of Rosalinda in years— my dog-training self who worked at a pet shop in Omaha, Nebraska. Rosalinda was a girl I knew in college before she decided to return home to California.

"With you at her side, Zoe didn't have to face things all alone in college. You took care of all the difficult things. She thanks you for it, but she's strong enough now to stand on her own. She is ready to let you go."

"Really? Are you sure she doesn't need me anymore?" My accent is that of Rosalinda, breezy and warm as the California sun.

Sarah encourages me. "Let her go."

Rosalinda, as me, is facing me. She is treading water, adept in the sea. She asks me, "Are you sure? Really sure?"

"I love you, but yes. Thank you for helping me when I needed it."

She is like a feathery dandelion disintegrating in the breeze and in a moment she is gone upon the wind. I expect to feel grief over the loss, but I just feel lighter. It's like releasing a weight I didn't know I was carrying.

"Do you remember helping Carolyn Morton care for her terminally ill mother? Until the worry of it drove her into her own early grave?"

Carolyn's funeral was one of the saddest I have ever attended. It happened within a year after her mother's death. The woman never had a chance to really live, and I took her on to give that memory joy.

She cries, holding me tightly, cheek-to-cheek. I stroke her hair and tell her, "It's okay. Your mother doesn't need you any longer. You can let me go. Let us both be free."

I'm holding nothing. She is gone, and with her the responsibility of caring for her, and her responsibility caring for me.

Sasha Whitmore worked as a librarian in Phoenix, and we became friends because I would often stay at the library for a few hours when Carolyn and I needed a break from each other. She was generous with her time and her memories.

"I loved working in that library in Nashville," I told Sasha.

"Books can always be there for you. That doesn't need me," Sasha reminds me for she was a practical, no-nonsense woman without much sentimentality. But while she leaves with a smile, I am crying as she vanishes.

There are many more to say goodbye to. Some are just brief memories of someone from middle or high school; a couple of people who I never had time to shape into a full identity, but still memories I had used to embroider into a larger personality.

Goodbye to the dream life of a dead girl named Ashley Maxwell, who had died in a car accident in Indiana. As she goes, I promise to send her classroom a gift to remember her by.

Goodbye to Vanessa Dickenson, the girl I was when Ryan and Duncan found me in the café. Vanessa doesn't have enough substance to be a ghost, and she flies quickly away from my fingertips like a sparrow.

I feel odd, free of weight I didn't know I had been carrying. Like I've awoken with still the shadow of a dream that I can't remember in my thoughts.

Sarah summons the last and the first. "Grace, come forth."

It is my childhood friend, that invisible companion who is my youngest protector and the oldest personality. The water is so deep that Sarah must hold her on her hip, as if she is Grace's mother.

I'm sobbing. "I can't let Grace go! Not her!"

Grace speaks up in her high-pitched child's voice. "You're strong enough now, Mommy. You don't need me to play hide-and-seek anymore."

She leans away from Sarah's arm, wrapping her arms around my neck, and I take her fully into my embrace. As I stroke her sea-wet hair, she tells me earnestly, "Don't cry, Mommy! I've got to go so you can feel better, don't you see?"

I nod because my throat is too clogged with tears to speak.

She tells me "Just remember to love horses forever and ever!"

I blink and she is gone. So is Sarah. I'm alone and treading water so far out that I can't see land.

Riptides, Zoe. Always be aware of them. They'll sweep you out to sea and you'll be lost forever. Grandfather's advice.

"Time to remember." Sarah's voice rings in my head as a wave washes over me. Something grabs my ankle and pulls me down into the darkest memory I have.

Thirty-Five

Remember everything.

Mother tugs me along, and it is hard for my short legs to keep up. In the end, she picks me up, holding me against her side, my sand bucket knocking against her stomach.

We are crossing the lawn of the Big House, and as we enter the garage, we find Uncle Owen. He is about to pull his SUV out of its parking space. Seeing us, he stops and calls through his open window, "Brynn. You look in a right fury."

My mother approaches him. She is fuming. "It's Aunt Belle. *Again.*"

After all this time, to hear her voice makes me feel strangely disoriented. She sounds young! So terribly heartbreakingly young.

"Tell you what, I'm about to go sailing. Do you and Zoe want to come along? On the way to the harbor, we can grab some sandwiches and make a picnic out on one of the islands?"

She doesn't hesitate. Brynn wants to be as far away as possible from this suffocating life, where she is always being told what to do and how to behave. "Sounds great!"

My car seat is transferred from her car to his and when she buckles me in, she gives me a quick kiss on my cheek. Her eyes sparkle as she tells me, "Let's have some fun today." The tote bag filled with beach towels and sunscreen is tossed into the back car seat beside my sand bucket.

Owen says mischievously, "Let's sneak out of here and not tell anyone where we're going. Make them worry a bit. That'll show her."

Brynn agrees. She's sick of Aunt Belle's interference in her life and the idea of making them fret when they realize they won't know where she's gone pleases her.

At the harbor, no one sees us arrive because it's mid-week during lunchtime and the place is mostly deserted. Sneaking around becomes a game as we make our way to Owen's sailboat, the *Luna Sea*.

Brynn, unlike Grandfather, insists that I wear a life jacket. "Smells funny," I complain.

"If you don't wear it, I'll take you right back home and you can watch your brother play video games all day."

I don't want to do that. Besides, it's useless to cry anymore because when Mother uses that tone of voice, she never changes her mind. On Owen's sailboat, she settles me down on a towel and pulls out the bag of toys we had grabbed before leaving the house. My toy horses, a stuffed teddy, and a book where you thread laces in and out of holes to make patterns. She's trying to teach me how to tie my shoes.

Brynn puts my sun hat on before helping Owen maneuver us out of the harbor.

Water laps-laps-laps against the side of the boat while the sail with the blue stripe snaps in the wind over our heads. We see a pod of dolphins but no whales. Lunch is cold Lobster rolls, a bag of salt and vinegar chips, with soda.

Mother and Owen talk about the family, but I'm more interested in playing than hearing gossip. I lie on my tummy and gallop my horses around the zig-zag stripes of the beach towel. They are running free across the fields and having horsey adventures.

"Robert wants me to take him back. Can you imagine that? After all that he's done to me?"

"Well, he is Ryan's dad." Owen's voice is lazy, almost disinterested. He's lying on the deck, a hat over his face, with his hands laced over his flat stomach. Owen wears a wide striped rugby shirt of blue and white, khaki shorts, and brown leather deck shoes.

"I don't mind Ryan seeing his dad, but Robert needs to stop thinking we will ever be a couple again."

"Isn't he married now, anyway?"

"Yes, but Charm means I'll never be rid of him. I wish I could go back to my old high school self and warn me not to use it on him."

Owen grunts an acknowledgment.

Over the next hour, the conversation drifts, but it eventually returns to Brynn's complaints about Robert. Eventually, she brings up his parents, Vincent and Doris, her ex-in-laws. "They blame me for ruining their son's future, always forgetting their precious Robert helped make that pregnancy happen!"

Owen is getting bored with the topic, and says dismissively, "Well, with the divorce, they are out of your life now."

"You'd think! But they are determined to destroy me. And destroy the Underhills. It's why— I shouldn't tell you this, but—" Her pause seems significant, and Owen pulls the hat off his face, to glance sideways at her. "What?"

Brynn looks away, her hand shading her eyes as she gazes out over the sea's horizon, for the *Luna Sea* is well out on the ocean now. "It's about Natalie, your wife."

He sits up. His wife died nine years ago but to him, the Memory Keeper, the pain is as sharp as if it was yesterday. There is a tenseness in his body as his attention is suddenly laser-focused on Brynn. "What do Robert's parents have to do with my wife? She never knew them."

"I shouldn't have said anything." Brynn tries to get up, but Owen grabs her wrist, bringing her back down with a thump.

"Tell me!"

"You're hurting me, Owen. Please, stop."

But he doesn't. Instead, he wrenches her arm behind her back and holds it so she arcs her body in pain. "What do you know about my wife? *What do you remember?*"

Owen is a Memory Keeper, but he has kept that part of himself hidden away, a secret to gloat over in a family where he is seen as the least. In him, it's become a twisted gift.

"I know you think it was father who stopped Natalie from getting treatment in that medication trial, but he didn't. He wanted to help. It was Robert's dad, Vincent. His pharmaceutical company was doing the drug trial, and he told them to remove her from the list."

Owen's face is shocked, stunned by the revelation.

"I'm sorry, Owen. Really! They just wanted to get back at me because they blame me for Robert's missed dream."

"You're telling me that Natalie died because of you?" He has not let go of her and seeing my mother crying makes me whimper. *Why doesn't he let her go?*

He goes white and then red with rage. Owen's hand goes around Brynn's neck, even as she tries to fight him. Brynn can barely speak, as she chokes out, "Stop."

"Because you were a slut like your father and Charmed a boy, my Natalie had to die?!"

Brynn is slapping at Owen's arms, but she can't get him off of her. While he is older than she is, he has a man's strength, and the wiry toughness of all the Underhill men. He starts to shake her back and forth and her arms flail at him, beating at his chest and neck.

I'm frightened and begin to cry, but I'm ignored as my mother fights for her life. She lands a blow on Owen's ear, and when she tries to gouge his eyes, he goes wild and swings her around like a doll. When he slams the side of her head into the boom, there is a sickening crack, and Brynn fights no more.

Water laps-laps-laps, the wind against my cheek, the snapping of a sail. The sun is too bright.

There is a pool of dark blood on the deck, seeping from her head. He wraps her body up in one of the beach towels and I no longer see her staring eyes. Still, I'm screaming the frightened high shrill of a six-year-old who until this moment has known only love.

When he comes to me, even my child-self knows he is thinking of killing me. His hands that clutch my shoulders have my mother's blood on them, and his eyes hold the embers of madness.

"Forget," he commands me sternly. "Forget this. It never happened. If you can't forget, Zoe, you'll have to join with your mother."

I feel the pressure of his mind on mine as he tries to shape a false memory, but something inside me is stubborn. I take this true memory and begin to fold it, firmly creasing the edges, before folding it again and again until it is so small that everything about that day disappears like a magic trick. I tuck it inside a box, and lock it, hiding the key.

He pats me on the head, satisfied.

In a blink, in a sigh, I'm an adult standing on the deck of the *Luna Sea*, the sail over my head whipping hard from an angry wind. The sky is stormy; the lightning is overhead, and thunder is giving ear-splitting booms.

Brynn's body and the pool of blood are gone.

Owen is standing opposite of me with his legs spread wide as his body absorbs the pitch of the boat which is heaving from the waves. He is wearing the same clothes from the day he murdered my mother, and his face is of his younger self. His body is strong and full of vigor. Once again, I am struck by how similar he is in appearance to Grandfather. He appears in the form he sees himself: how he looked the year Natalie died, when he was fifty-one, and his life stopped.

He is not cowed in finding himself here. "Have you brought me into some dream of yours? I didn't know you had it in you, little Memory Keeper. You'll have to share the trick of it with me."

Despite my anger, I make my voice sound calm. "This is the Gale's doing. She's angry with what you did, Owen. For killing Brynn, her great-great-granddaughter. For being a Memory Keeper who lies."

He eyes me speculatively, unrepentant. "You remember it all now, do you? At the memorial, when I saw that photo of Brynn and Sabrina on my boat, I knew it was only a matter of time. In the waiting room, that's when it clicked, didn't it? I saw it in your eyes."

"Yes. That's when I realized you murdered my mother."

"It was an unfortunate accident."

"It was murder! And all of these years you've lied to us all. You even hid her body on Blackberry Island! Did you look out sometimes and gloat over where you had buried her?"

"I knew about the old house from way back. Nolan and I explored all the islands when we were teenagers."

He put Brynn in a place that Grandfather knew and then watched his brother tear himself apart, wondering where his daughter was? Sadistic bastard.

Owen is just as angry as I am. "She had to pay for what happened to my Natalie."

I cannot understand his lack of remorse. Does he feel no sorrow or regret for killing his niece in front of her child? I scream at him. "She didn't! It was the Bancrofts. And who knows if that experimental medicine would have helped her, anyway? She had stage four cancer!"

"Natalie would be alive if your slut mother hadn't Charmed a boy! She was as arrogant and careless as Nolan, always using their power to control others."

He needs a villain to focus his anger on, and Brynn is the scapegoat. It justifies his murder of her. *Memory Liar.*

There is icy rain now hitting my face like drops of stinging acid. The gale storm is growing. It will wreck this boat and kill us both if I cannot resolve this.

Cut away the dead wood.

Still, I hesitate. I cannot do this alone. Others have a say in this matter.

Sarah's descendants are all one piece. A tree with many branches, but one bloodline.

"Nolan Underhill! Come to me!" I shout my grandfather's name to the stormy sky. In a heartbeat, he steps out of the shadows to my right. Perhaps Grandfather thinks this is just another dream, for he seems unfazed by the appearance of his brother.

"I'm here, Granddaughter."

In this dreamworld, Nolan appears exactly as he does in life, making him strangely appear older than his brother when, in reality, they are only a few years apart.

Blood and Bone.

"I need you, Ryan Underhill!" Suddenly, my brother appears on my left. At first, he appears surprised and confused, but as I beckon him, he steps to my side and takes my other hand.

"Is this a dream?" he asks me, looking from me to Grandfather.

"More real than a dream. I know who killed our mother and I need your counsel. Remember this." I give them both what I had forgotten for twenty years: how Brynn met her death at the hands of Owen.

As the memory floods him, Nolan's grip tightens, and his expression deepens with grief. He bows his head even as Ryan's chin comes up. My brother raises his other hand and is about to let go of me to make his way to Owen when the sailboat pitches with a wave.

We three stagger, even while Owen remains upright. He rides the deck like he's on a bucking horse. Water slides over the deck, soaking our feet, before returning to the sea.

"Sarah saved us all in 1898 by inviting the Gale into what she held in her womb. And Seaborn carried the Gale, giving us all a part of the storm's gift: Charm and Memory. As a Memory Keeper, Owen's lies have broken a sacred trust. It is past time that we make it right."

I know that if justice is not done, Grandfather dies. Ryan will never have a child. Duncan and I have no future.

"Kill him," judges Ryan, furious.

My mind is floating outside of my body, like a balloon that threatens to become untethered. Nothing seems real. My mind is operating on another level, and I channel Sarah, "If we kill him, we commit his deed of parricide again and the poison spreads."

Beside me, Grandfather's spirit-self is as light as a feather. He is staring at his brother with a mix of horror and pain.

"How could you do it, Owen? How could you conceal for twenty years what you did to my daughter?"

Owen is non-repentant. "Help for Natalie was denied. We meant nothing to you! Our pain meant nothing, and I owe you nothing in return."

Sad regret from Grandfather comes through his hand to me, but Ryan is nothing but righteous fury. "You murdered our mother, you piece of filth!"

I ask them again, "What sentence can we give that is just and fitting?"

Grandfather's voice is low and faint. "The only cure is amputation."

"Let's start with his head!" snarls Ryan.

In my mind's eye, I see again the Majestic, splitting in half, part of it falling to the ground. I know what to do. "Exile. Expulsion from the family."

Ryan is not happy with that. "It's not enough! Eye for an Eye. He needs to be punished for what he did to her. What he's done to *us*. Twenty years, Zoe! *Twenty years*!"

I squeeze his hand, which makes him finally turn to me. "Ryan, trust me on this one, okay?"

He wavers but after a low growled curse, nods his head.

Grandfather is still staring at Owen, but when I nudge his hand, his chin lowers, his eyes are downcast. "I support whatever you decide, Zoe."

Owen is still defiant. He crosses his arms, a sneer on his lips, but it is bravado, for he senses that some decision has been made even if he cannot understand what I mean. "Like you three ever treated me as one of the family, anyway? I'll be fine without you all."

The sleet is changing to snow as the temperature drops.

If this is not done now, the Gale will come again, and we will all go down into the sea.

"The Gale takes back what was gifted. The Underhills take back their heritage. You are cast out. Exiled. Alone, without name or power." As I finish speaking, the sky cracks open with a streak of lightning that is so bright and close that it blinds us.

Wind and Water.

The tides move in our blood, our words make lightning, and the storms play in our heads. In our blood is the breathings of the moon, the tide which gives and leaves purity behind.

A whirlwind wraps around Owen. Inside the funnel, his piercing cry is shrill and metallic. The wind tunnel enlarges, forcing us back. Suddenly it spins away, leaving a trail of drifting snow behind.

Blood and Bone
Bind and Hold.

Owen lies lifeless on the deck, stunned like a bird who has struck a window.

It is done.

Thirty-Six

When I open my eyes, I'm sitting beside Grandfather's hospital bed, my hand covering his which lies on the mattress. Behind me stands Ryan with his hand on my shoulder.

I sigh. "It's done."

Ryan gives me a shoulder squeeze, but otherwise says nothing. This, like so many odd Underhill things, will never be discussed.

I rise and lean over the metal side frame of the hospital bed and kiss Grandfather's forehead. He mumbles something, but since he doesn't open his eyes; I pull back. When Ryan and I leave the room, we are surprised to see nurses rushing past us.

Duncan is standing outside in the hallway and is so focused on what is happening in the waiting room, he doesn't notice us immediately. I touch his arm and ask, "What's going on?"

"After your brother left to check on you, your uncle fainted. The doctor is working on him now."

I try to care but can't quite bring myself to do so. For the first time since he murdered my mother, I am not haunted by the wind and sea. I hear no waves; smell no salt. There are not dozens of personalities crowded into my head, waiting for their moment to be on stage.

Owen is paying a bill twenty years overdue.

Ryan cranes his head to get a look in to see what they are doing, but there are so many medical personnel that it's doubtful he sees anything. When he comes back, he whispers to me, "Did we kill him?"

"I don't know."

With my hands on their arms, I draw Ryan and Duncan down the hallway so we are out of the medical personnel's way and can't be overheard. Ryan crosses his arms as he stares back down the hallway.

Duncan asks me, "How is your grandfather? Ryan was worried about you being gone so long."

"I wanted some private time with him, but he slept through my visit. He'll be okay; I'm hopeful about his chances."

A nurse brings an emergency gurney down the hallway and into the room. A few minutes later, Owen comes out. He's moving his head back and forth, crying out in pain. They take him a few doors down to a patient room.

Seeing us, a nurse makes her way to where we are standing. She has a clipboard and a pen with her. "I'm wondering if you can give us any information about what happened?"

I tell her, "I'm sorry. We weren't there. We were with our grandfather."

Duncan says, "I was the only one in the room but don't really know. Ryan left to go join his sister in their grandfather's room, and maybe about ten minutes later, Owen started touching his head, saying he had a horrible headache. That was just before he collapsed. I called you immediately."

"Okay, thanks. Anything else? He wasn't complaining earlier about any pain? Feeling hot or cold? Dizziness? Fuzzy vision? Did he eat anything that would disagree with him? Was he taking any medication?"

With each question, Duncan gives a confused shrug. "I'm sorry. He said nothing like that when I was in the room."

Ryan interjects. "We had sandwiches, but that was at least four hours ago. He picked the food, so I don't think he'd choose anything that he'd be allergic to. As far as I know, he isn't taking any medication, prescribed or otherwise. He brags that he's healthy as a horse."

You can tell this is just routine information gathering. "Okay, I'll put that into his chart and let the doctor know."

In the morning, on the way back to the house, Ryan tells us he got a call from his dad, and he is deeding the land he bought to a conservation group. It will be made into a park named Brynn Underhill Bancroft, for she had not given up her maiden name at the time of her death.

It seems Ryan had suggested this solution to Robert at the Gale anniversary celebration about an hour before I found Robert in our mother's room crying over his belief he had murdered her. It seems guilt can make a man change, even one as hard and self-centered as Robert Bancroft.

I'll have to remove that falsely planted memory in Robert's mind that Owen had given him at my mother's memorial. It hadn't been a grave Robert knew that made him bend over that gravestone, but Owen changing his memory. But I'm not so kind that I'll do it before the land is legally tied down as a non-returnable gift.

Jennifer must have been looking out the window for us as she opens the door while the car drives up. She is glad to hear Grandfather is doing better, but gives a concerned frown when she hears about Owen. "A brain aneurysm? Will he be alright?"

Ryan says diplomatically. "We'll have to wait and see. They took him out on the Medi-flight to a bigger hospital. He'll need an operation."

In the end, Ryan uses a little Charm to convince Aunt Belle to go out via a hired car to Owen's hospital to represent the family. There is no way Ryan and I would do it, and she is pleased to do something for Ryan.

For me, I have other plans.

"I need to go over to Wellston by three o'clock today." I tell Duncan.

"Today?" He would take me, but I take pity on how exhausted he looks.

"Let's take a nap in a proper bed instead of a hospital couch for a couple of hours. It's not even nine now, so we have plenty of time."

We end up sleeping for about three hours. I wake first, and I'm brushing my teeth when he starts to stir. "Feeling better?"

He nods and cracks an enormous yawn. Rinsing my mouth out, I come over and sit on the side of the bed. His hands come around my waist and I bend over to kiss him.

He grins. "Minty fresh."

"C'mon, sleepy head. We've got to get going."

"Are you going to tell me what this is about?"

"It's a surprise. But one you'll like, I promise."

Outside, we find Ryan standing near the Majestic with a couple of men wearing hard hats. I change direction and join the group. They stop talking when I approach, and Ryan thanks them and shakes their hands, before dismissing them.

When they retreat to the other side of the Majestic, Ryan informs me they are tree specialists, "Arborists. They think some damage happened at the top of the trunk years ago. It probably made a hole that allowed water and insects in. It's rotted inside, all the way to the heartwood."

"What's her chance of making it?" I ask. He just shakes his head, gazing down at his feet, which are kicking acorns. I give him a pat on the back. "Well, I don't think you should give up on her yet. She might surprise you."

When we are on the ferry, Duncan and I get out of the car to take in the view. Although it is mid-afternoon, the air is still chilly from a storm that blew in the night before, around midnight. The weather is changing, moving into winter, the season of rest. There is a pure baby-blue sky with white cotton ball clouds racing high above us.

We are both wearing coats. Duncan has an evergreen green puffy one that makes him look broader than he really is. Mine is a navy blue peacoat from my closet, but the scarf wrapped around my neck and the hat with the pom-pom ball on top is from Mother's closet.

We are standing at the rail, looking out to the horizon of the open sea. "You said you'd share what happened at the hospital."

"It's not that I don't want to, but—" I shrug and say it bluntly, "Owen murdered my mother." I tell him what I pieced together using the clues of the sailboat and the memory I finally recalled.

He puts an arm around my shoulders and brings me to his side. "At least you know."

"Yeah." I let out a heavy sigh that drops the last of the tension from my shoulders. "I don't think he meant to kill her. It wasn't planned or anything. But he's always been obsessed with his wife and how she died. Owen's never been rational about losing Natalie."

Duncan throws me a lifeline. "He could have killed you that day, but he didn't."

"That was probably the only thing that will save him in the end. Maybe."

The ferry captain waves at us from the pilot's house, and I

wave back, my hand high over my head. Dropping it, I lean over the rail and look at the waves hitting the side of the boat. "I told Grandfather and Ryan about it last night."

Duncan isn't stupid, and he's been around the Underhills for a while now. "When I was with Owen? I see."

He probably did.

On the trip to Wellston, I ask him about Richmond. "Isn't Virginia horse country?"

He nods. "I know nothing about horses, but there are horse farms all over the place."

"Your mom is a therapist, right?"

"Technically, she's a professor, but yes, she has her own practice."

I've got it in my head what I want to do and continue peppering him with questions. "Isn't there some sort of therapy you do using horses?"

"Well, there's a physical therapy option or a mental therapy you can do with horses. But that isn't the type she does."

"Could she put me in touch with someone who does it? I'd like to do that. Especially if it helps kids."

As he drives, we talk about his job, his parents, and anything that has nothing to do with Kingstowe and the Underhills, until I cry out, "There! Slow down." We are on a two-lane state highway and cars are parked on the side of the road. "Someone's pulling out up there. Grab that space."

As Duncan parks, I look up the hill to the big white barn. It is just as Sarah's memory remembered it.

"An auction?" Duncan asks.

I don't answer him because I'm already out of the car and heading up the gravel driveway. I hear the beep-beep of him locking the car even as someone calls my name. I stop walking and realize the woman coming down the driveway is Mrs. McGuire, the old lady who had taken me to Vanessa's home after the funeral.

"My. My. Are you visiting this part of the world again?"

"I'm just here for the auction. A friend told me about it. Is it a good one?"

She holds up her arm, which is draped with several quilts. "It is! The family's been here for at least a hundred years and the barn is stuffed with things the current descendants don't want." She brings the blankets closer to me and points at their colorful circles. "These are handstitched. Not a sewing machine in sight! What are you looking for?"

"My friend here is into old books." I introduce Duncan, who has reached my side. "He works for the Smithsonian."

Duncan shakes the hand that emerges from the pile of quilts like a turtle's head from its shell. Playing along with what I said, he tells her, "You can often find some interesting things at these country auctions. Books, journals, diaries, and ephemera."

"Ephemera?" Mrs. McGuire asks, unfamiliar with the word.

"It's stuff like cards, advertisements, catalogs, ticket stubs."

Duncan would probably have gone on explaining, but I pull him away. "We don't want to miss anything!"

"I won't keep you two," she tells me, and waves goodbye.

Duncan asks, "What *are* we looking for?"

"Just what you said. Papers and books."

Entering the cool darkness of the barn, I breathe in that musty smell of old hay. Duncan is handed a program listing what is for sale and a number sign. The auctioneer is calling out for the next bid as Duncan scans the list. "Looks like there's a family bible."

I lace my arm into his. "Oh definitely, let's bid on that."

"And a stack of cookbooks, farm registers, and miscellaneous papers."

"We need to get those, too."

Duncan stops reading and asks me, "Are you going to tell me what this is about?"

There is no more time to discuss it, as one of our lots is coming up for bidding. I nudge him, and he raises up his paddle.

In the end, it seems most people are here for the farm equipment and the furniture, so the boxes of miscellaneous paper goods go for almost nothing. We end up with about a dozen boxes, and I chortle with victory, like a dragon counting its hoard as I squat to leaf through some of their contents. "Look! Old photos too."

Duncan is opening the Bible, and his hand freezes on a page. He says accusingly, "You knew about this, didn't you?"

"What did I know about?"

He turns the Bible so I can see the page, but in the barn's dimness, the ornate script is hard to read. I squint while trying to figure it out, but he explains it to me. "This Bible has the name of Sarah's aunt in it. The family who owned this place is related to her, aren't they?"

"How interesting." Standing up, I wipe my hands on my jeans, trying to get the dust and cobwebs off of them. "I wonder if these boxes have anything about her?"

Duncan snorts. "I bet you do."

One of the auction staff lends us a pull-along wagon so we can trundle our loot down to Duncan's car. After we load up the boxes, he grabs me, pulling me into a tight embrace.

"Are you coming to my family for Christmas?"

"Of course, I'll come. It will give us time to talk about writing Sarah's story."

"Is that what's in the boxes?" he asks, even though he has already guessed it.

I nod. "After the Great Gale, Sarah came here for a while to recuperate while Abraham got their house repaired. She returned in time to give birth to Seaborn in Kingstowe, but she was here long enough to write down some of her experiences."

"In the end, the women have their say, after all?"

"It's about time they do, don't you think?"

GENEALOGY & TIMELINE

FOUNDERS

Abraham
b 1857
m 1891 (34)
d 1939 (82)

Sarah
b 1869
m 1891 (22)

- Twin girls (24)
- Levi (28)
- Seaborn (29)
- Matthew (37)
- John (49)

vanished 1938 (69)

Their children:

Twin girls
b 1893
d 1896 (3) due to Diptheria in Portland, Maine.

Levi
b 1897
d 1918 World War I, northern France (21) buried overseas.

Seaborn
b 1899
m 1946 (46) to Daphne (d 1982)
d 1988 (89)

Matthew
b 1901
d 1986 (85)

John
b 1918
d 1941 (23)
World War II, *USS California* at Pearl Harbor, body not recovered

CURRENT GENERATION

Nolan
b 1946
m 1979 (32) to Catherine (29) (d 2011)
current age 82

Owen
b 1948
m 1976 (28) to Natalie (24) (d 1999)
current age 80

Brynn
b 1980
d 2008 (28)

Ryan
B 1999
2008 (9)
current age 29

Zoe
B 2002
2008 (6)
current age 26

Significant historical years
1898 Nor'easter, Portland Gale (Great Gale)
1910 census destroyed by fire
1938 New England Hurricane (Great Long Island - New England Hurricane)
1952 Abraham and Sarah sculpture installed in the town square of Kingstowe
2028 130th anniversary year of the Great Gale

Join my newsletter at ByrdNash.com
to receive 10% off my books
and notifications of new book projects before they release

Acknowledgments

There were so many themes I wanted to explore in this one: memory and how we recall it (sometimes wrongly), a family where a girl grows up surrounded by dominating males, the impact of a childhood trauma, and a neurodivergent character with a condition similar to (but not) Dissociative Identity Disorder (Multiple Personality Disorder).

The title of the book comes from the Venerable Bede (Saint Bede), an Anglo-Saxon scholar, trying to explain tides without understanding it was linked to gravity.

*"But the most admirable thing of all is the union of the ocean with the orbit of the moon. At every rising and every setting of the moon the sea violently covers the coast far and wide, sending forth its surge — It is as though it is unwittingly drawn up by some **breathings of the moon**—"* (Opera de Temporibus, Section XXIX, the Venerable Bede, 703 AD)

This is a story that would never have made it except for the guidance of Mikaela Pedlow, my developmental editor. The entire front of the book was re-worked and after that the story took off.

Sincere thanks to my earliest alpha readers who read an early draft of the first five chapters and gave me feedback: Davida DLH, Cindy S., Lyric, Gloria W., Tanja G., Chad B., and Jennifer H. Some of you have been with me since the first book, and your trust in me is so very much appreciated.

And thank you, reader! By reading my books, and sharing your thoughts on them, you help me find new readers.

BYRD NASH